Prince of the Prism

Prologue

In the Prism world below Earth's surface, winter began its descent in the cold foothills of the high western mountains. The light in the evening sky changed from bright orange to brilliant hues of turquoise blue and emerald green.

Groups of travelers, seeking a new home, gathered near a roaring bonfire. Men, women, and children, mostly dressed in raggedy clothes, huddled for warmth against the cold night air. The youngest children nestled in the arms of their parents, while others, mostly orphans, brothers and sisters, and strangers, held one another tightly.

An old man, with long silvery gray hair and a long beard, which flowed onto his chest, began to unfold his story in a serious and soothing voice. His words seemed magical, and his eyes glowed in the firelight. As he began to speak, it became so quiet that one could hear a twig snap in the distance, and younger children were so entranced that they flinched when burning logs crackled and popped loudly in the flames.

The old man captured the attention of everyone as they moved closer to hear him better. Despite the cold, somehow his words, along with the burning embers, warmed them in ways that they had not known in a very long time.

His nearly hypnotic voice with its high and low tones heightened everyone's imagination. Everyone seemed to close their eyes from time to time as they pictured his words. Pictures from deep within themselves, from memories that they had only seen in dreams, merged into one dream, then slowly intermingled with the next.

They knew one story he told but had forgotten it. They knew it was somehow their own story. The old man yawned, stepped away from the firelight momentarily, and lit his pipe. He then blew large smoke rings, which almost magically appeared on the other side of the fire, as he continued the story.

Chapter One

From the exposed top platform of an ancient stone castle, which rose from the side of a snow-covered mountaintop several hundred feet into the Prism sky, a young man named Ammon, pulled and reeled a white string. It was attached to a very large and brightly colored long- tailed kite, soaring, rising, and dipping into the many hues of early evening. The Prism light slowly faded into shades of orange and pink amid a green and blue background, as layer upon layer of vaporous clouds slowly intermingled with a rainbow of colors.

The large flags of the king and the kingdom curled and ruffled in the wind above the platform, as Ammon pulled and ran at times to the very edge. Using the string skillfully to move and control the triangular kite as it darted and sped across the sky, it almost magically glimmered like a mirror, reflecting the last remnants of fading light. As he reeled the kite closer and closer to the edge of the castle platform, he nearly lost his balance which would have sent him hurdling hundreds of feet to his death.

At that precise moment, his father, King Hyperion, appeared from the castle doorway below, along with several torch-bearing attendants, and began to ascend the spiraling gray stone steps of the platform. Ammon regained his balance and peered over the edge to the ragged rocks several hundred feet below.

"Ammon," King Hyperion called out, "you need to be more careful. I've warned you about the dangers of this place. Walk with me back to the reception hall. I'd like your opinion on a matter of some importance." The king briefly walked to the edge and looked down, then shook his head and, taking Ammon by the shoulder, pulled him further away from the precipice.

One of the king's attendants approached Ammon and then smiled, as he took the string and carefully reeled in the very large and beautiful kite. Ammon walked beside the king, smiling broadly as they turned and descended the stone staircase, re-entering the castle at the head of the procession, illuminated in the orange glow of the burning torches.

After walking leisurely down the winding staircase, they entered a long corridor where the walls were covered with large hand-woven tapestries and open windows that allowed the soft orange and green glow of the fading light to enter. Attendants exchanged their torches with elegant silver candelabras, burning ivory candles. At last, reaching two massive oaken doors, the king and Ammon paused as the attendants unlocked and slowly pulled the heavy doors open. A great hall with its arched ceiling, carved with rough, chiseled stone, rose more than a hundred feet to its crest.

On the highly polished black granite floor stood an ornately carved wooden table running the length of the room in front of two forest green drapes that extended from floor to ceiling. More candles on the table illuminated the many elaborately hand-carved wooden chairs, cushioned in deep red velvet, the arms gleaming with inlaid platinum and gold, stationed around the table.

The king placed his arm on Ammon's shoulder, walking the entire length of the hall, and took his customary seat at the head of the table, urging Ammon to sit beside him. The king's chair, larger than any other, was encrusted with jewels and crystals which seemed to glow even brighter when he was seated.

"Is there news of my mother? Have you found her?" Ammon asked excitedly as he looked hopefully at the king.

"All we know is that she is being held somewhere and, at least for now, we believe she is safe." The king looked down and sadly shook his head.

"You've heard something, haven't you?" Ammon asked cautiously.

The king produced a neatly folded piece of parchment from inside his cloak and placed it on the table in front of Ammon.

"This was found beside the door of my sleeping chamber early this morning."

Ammon unfolded the parchment carefully and read the contents. "Isn't there anything we can do? Can't we find out who is responsible?

"It must be someone powerful, Ammon, powerful enough to go undetected, at least for a short while, until the magic turns on them. And I assure you, it will. Perhaps it already has."

"I wish there was something we could do," Ammon said faintly, almost hopelessly.

"Tomorrow morning, son, I want you to visit Master Deimos with me. People passing through the gate have told my counselors and guards troubling stories."

"Do you suspect..." Ammon started, but his father, the king, interrupted. "Guards!" he called out in a tone that immediately commanded respect and authority. "Seal the Grand Reception Hall doors!"

The guards followed the king's command without hesitation. They pulled the massive oaken doors closed and then stood at attention in the corridor outside.

❧ ❖ ☙

Down the long corridor, slightly illuminated by the burning torches, the guards could barely see a dark figure scurrying from one shadow to the next.

"Did you see something move down there?" the younger of the two guards asked.

"I saw nothing. Stay at attention!" the other guard responded.

Still, something shadowy moved again and this time, they both saw it. They also heard the swishing sound of a flag blowing in the wind or long robes brushing against stone floors, although it quickly became silent again. The guards looked at one another briefly and then returned to attention, as if not wanting to admit what they had heard. Hearing the swishing sound again, they both looked down the dimly lit corridor, catching a glimpse of movement in the shadows. Again they looked at one another curiously.

"Did you hear that? I heard something move," the taller and older of the two whispered intensely.

"What do you think it was?" the younger guard asked, leaning over to where he could better see down the corridor.

"I don't know, probably nothing. Maybe a mouse. Go investigate. I'll stay here and guard the king," the older one suggested confidently.

"Guard the king from what? A mouse? Let's both go; it's only fair. What if it's that ugly old woman? She gives me the creeps every time I see her!"

"You mean the witch?"

"Witch?" the younger guard responded, a surprised and fearful expression suddenly covering his face.

"That creepy old woman was once a witch. Everyone knows it. She's not allowed in this part of the palace. No need to worry. Like I said, it's probably just a mouse. Now go, and don't let your imagination run wild."

The older guard shook his head and smiled as the younger one presented his spear and cautiously proceeded down the corridor. As he turned back toward his companion, the hinges of a door squeaked from the shadows. He quickly turned around, prepared to stab whatever had made the noise.

"That was no mouse!" he whispered as loudly as possible.

The other guard joined him, and they both extended their spears as they proceeded down the torch-lit corridor, inspecting each shadow. Finding nothing, they gladly returned to the doors of the Grand Reception Hall and stood once again at attention.

"Nobody ever told me that old hag was a witch. What's to stop her from coming into this part of the palace?"

"Have you ever noticed the bright orange cloak she wears?" the older guard asked.

"Yeah, what about it?"

"It's so bright that if she were to show up, we or someone would notice her immediately and she'd be thrown back into the dungeon."

"So what's to stop her from wearing a different cloak?"

"She can't change it. The king and his wizards made sure of that a long, long time ago."

"If it was such a long time ago and she used to be a witch, don't you think she would have figured out a way to fool everyone, even the king?"

"I guess. It has been so long now that I never really gave it much thought. She stays to herself mostly. Besides, no one can fool King Hyperion. Everyone knows that!"

As the guards talked, behind a secret door in the shadows of the corridor, the witch had, in fact, fooled everyone and crept through the shadows to a long-forgotten closet within the corridor of Grand Reception Hall.

"Old woman, they call me, good for nothing hag, suited only to clean up after them and their little brat children. Well, King Hyperion and your little brat Ammon, now it's my turn." The old witch struck her fingernails against the stone wall and ignited one of them, which she then used to light two black candles, revealing a small chair and a small wooden table. The smell of the burning fingernail quickly traveled beyond the closet door and down the corridor.

The guards winced at the foul odor, each blaming the other until it passed. The witch slowly removed her black hood, revealing scraggly black and gray hair, which was matted and dirty from years without washing or combing it. Her skin was also gray with an almost greenish tint that became brighter on its edges, especially around her mouth and nose. She exposed her hands to the light and extended her long fingernails; curled, their tips, cracked and ragged, were packed underneath with thick and slimy dirt.

Two large black rats, almost the size of small dogs, scurried across the floor of the small room and climbed onto the table in front of the witch. They sat on their hind legs and made a slight squeaking sound as they rubbed their little pink and black paws together. She stroked their greasy fur, picked them up, and held them close to her face as she spoke. The rats licked her dirty fingers and squealed with delight at the sound of her voice.

"A task for you, my little darlings, a task for your beautiful friend Morgana; a task to give us all the power we need to be free again." The rats squealed again with delight as she whispered into their ears. When she had finished, the rats squealed again, revealing their sharp yellowed teeth, and then crawled onto her shoulders and licked her neck and cheek as she cooed with delight. "Now go, my little friends. Soon we'll be free, and I'll reward you. Go and do my bidding!"

The rats squealed and scampered to the small doorway, as the witch opened it just enough to allow them out into the corridor. They then scurried down the corridor, closer to the guards, who continued to talk about the old witch. The guards remained standing at attention beside the Grand

Reception Hall doors and hadn't noticed any further movement in the shadows.

As the rats approached them, one suddenly leapt onto the leg of the younger guard and sunk its razor sharp teeth into his leg. The biting and gnawing evoked a high-pitched scream from the guard, as he pried the rat loose, hurling the squealing rodent onto the floor. The other rat leapt onto the arm of the older guard and sunk its sharp teeth deeply into his skin. Both guards dropped their spears and fell to the floor, crying out in pain from their bleeding wounds. The rats then dashed away in the opposite direction of the witch's closet, as the guards tried to recover. Finally able to stand again, they grabbed their spears and ran awkwardly after the beasts.

From the shadows, which concealed the door to the small closet, the witch appeared in the corridor. Still using the shadows to help conceal her, she quickly arrived at the doors of the hall. Ever so quietly, she opened the heavy doors far enough to hear the conversation taking place between the king and Ammon.

॰❖॰

Unaware that the guards had been attacked and were no longer at their assigned posts, or that the witch was listening, the king and Ammon continued to speak without concern.

"I've suspected Master Deimos of using magic for some time now, but I had always hoped that he were wiser than to use it for his own benefit and greed," the king continued, looking at Ammon seriously.

"If what you say is true, won't it be dangerous to visit him?"

"He's not expecting me, Ammon. If you come with me, along with our guards, I believe he'll think that it's a mere coincidence, merely an introduction to my son, the prince. We'll be friendly and respectful but, depending on his behavior, I think we'll be able to see through his deceptions. Also, I've sent word to Orestros, asking him to discover what he can of Deimos and his possible involvement against us and the queen. I'll be depending on your help, Ammon. Do you think you're up to this challenge?"

"Yes, Father. Do you think he's responsible for Mother's disappearance?"

"Perhaps," replied the king. "Regardless, after the visit and report from our friend Orestros, I want you to take a journey to the Earth's surface. There are dangers there, but if what I believe is true, you'll be safer there than here in the Prism. I'll send those necessary to ensure your safety. If what I fear is true, I'll need your help before this is all over. You'll be of no use to me, your mother or yourself, if you're not safe on the Earth's surface until then."

"I've never been to Earth before, Father. I've never traveled beyond the Prism," Ammon said curiously, while maintaining a sense of caution.

"It will be safe if you listen to those I'm sending with you. Will you listen?"

"Of course, Father, but who will be going with me?" Ammon asked excitedly, still wondering and a little fearful of the possibilities that such an adventure might offer.

"We'll speak of that tomorrow. For now, I want you to rest. Tomorrow promises to be a long and perhaps dangerous day."

The king embraced Ammon for a moment and held him tightly, unable to hide his concern, before releasing him and reaching under the table to pull a secret lever. The lever rang a bell in the corridor, summoning the guards. The king waited a moment for a response and then pulled the lever again; he did not notice the witch, as she carefully closed the door and once again disappeared into the shadows and her secret closet. The king rang the bell again and at last the guards returned and opened the doors.

"Why did you delay in opening the doors?" the king demanded, as the guards entered the hall.

"I'm sorry, Your Majesty, but we were momentarily chasing two enormous rodents that attacked us. They were the largest rodents we've ever seen!"

"Escort us to our rooms and be sure that the creatures are disposed of tomorrow without fail."

"Yes, Your Majesty. Sorry for the delay."

The guards turned the keys on several locks to the hall doors and then escorted Ammon and the king to their sleeping chambers. Constantly looking for any sign of movement in the shadows, they concealed the growing pain of the rats' bites.

ॐ ❖ ॐ

In the witch's secret closet, she groomed and stroked the large rats as they returned. A big brown spider crawled across the small table, and she struck it with the palm of her hand. She then dangled its eight-legged body in front of her face for a moment, before she consumed it, crunching it between her dirty, cracked, and yellow teeth. She licked the palm of the hand that had crushed it and smiled. From the inside of her cheek, she felt something still moving and, opening her mouth, she plucked two long, wiggling spider legs and fed them to her rats.

"Tomorrow we'll be free, my fine little friends," she snarled, as they quickly devoured the spider legs, almost smiling as they did so. "Tomorrow we'll be free," the witch repeated, "and take the little brat with us. Oh, yes, my fine little friends, and take the brat with us. Perhaps a few others, to serve us, just for good measure."

She pulled a foul-smelling clay jug from beneath the table, uncorked it, and took a large drink. Its contents spilled from the corners of her mouth, as she gurgled and then hissed with delight. Small yellow sacks, twisting and squirming as if they contained something living, fell from her chin and onto the table. She stroked the rats, as they drank the spilled stinking liquid from the table and chewed the small yellow sacks, revealing tiny maggots that squirmed and wriggled from the corners of their mouths. Clutching her hands together and rubbing them briskly, her eyes began to glow a dark green. The rats squealed softly, as they lapped up more of the foul liquid from her ragged blouse, enjoying their nasty treat.

Chapter Two

The following morning, Ammon awakened from a restless sleep in which he dreamed of his mother. Master Deimos, whom he had never met, also appeared in the same dream. As he sat up in bed, he remembered that in the dream his mother, Queen Thalia, had tried to warn him to beware of Deimos.

After Ammon got out of bed, he went to the table across the room, cupped his hands in the basin, and splashed cold water on his face. He then gazed out his window, high among the castle's numerous towers, onto the village far below. His memory of the dream began to fade, as he looked up and saw not the blue skies he had heard of on Earth but the colors of the Prism sky as they cascaded in a spectrum of lights. He had heard of twinkling points of light, called 'stars,' but since he had never been on the surface of the Earth, he had never seen such strange lights.

As the Prism light, along with long ivory candles, continued to light his room, he marveled at the prospect of at last traveling beyond the Prism. 'It must be a wild place,' he thought, 'with very few, if any, people living there.' He wondered if animals still lived on Earth and what kinds there might be. He also wondered if stars could be seen at any time of day or only during the darker sleeping hours, when even the Prism seemed to darken into its deep blues and emerald greens.

As he dressed, he thought about the journey ahead of him to visit Deimos, who ruled a different part of the Prism, of which little was known, even by his father. He then considered the other part of the journey ahead, to Earth, of which he had only heard legends and myths. As he wondered, fragments of his dream returned to his mind, along with the image of his mother and with her warning. No matter how hard he tried, only bits and pieces of the dream came back to him.

He did not want to admit it but even the mention of Deimos's name made him feel uneasy. Perhaps today, he would at last find his mother who had been missing for several months. Perhaps Deimos would help him and his father find her, although he doubted that Deimos was someone to be trusted, especially after what his father had said.

The king suspected something was wrong; maybe even the use of magic should be discouraged because of its ill effects on whomever used it. He also wondered about Orestros, whom he had met only once, and what he would discover about the mysterious Deimos.

After descending the long spiral staircase from his tower, Ammon arrived at the Grand Reception Hall and found the door open, with several of the king's most honored Royal Guards and high counselors seated in their customary red-cushioned chairs at the long table. At their places were cobalt blue glasses, pitchers filled with fresh spring water, and pewter plates with small wedges of yellow cheese and thick slices of sweet, dark brown bread.

Upon seeing Ammon arrive, the king called for everyone's attention and then ordered the doors sealed. "Today, gentlemen, the prince and I, along with these select guards, plan to travel to the Prism kingdom of Master Deimos. Some of you may know that my father appointed him years ago, though I have not visited him since I was of the age the prince will reach this very year. We all know of the rumors circulating from the gates, telling stories of corruption and Deimos's use of magic. What I have not told you is that we have heard rumors that he may be responsible for the queen's disappearance.

"With the prince's help, as well as the report from Orestros, whose help we have already requested, we hope to find out if there is any truth to these stories. If our suspicions are confirmed, we plan to leave Deimos without alarming him and later return with our armies to bring justice to him and to the people he has misused. If our fears are indeed accurate, and before we begin an invasion of such magnitude, we will send the prince to the surface of the Earth for safety, and return him when the time is right. Now is the time for questions and suggestions from our trusted counselors and our trusted Royal Guards."

A gray-bearded and very dignified old man stood up. "Your Majesty, King Hyperion, no one has traveled to the Earth's surface in more years than I can count in a lifetime. We have no allies there and do not know what has become of the surface since we first escaped to the Prism. Are you certain it will be safe for Prince Ammon?"

"If the rumors I've heard about Deimos are true, there is nowhere in the Prism that will be safe for the prince," replied the king. "I will send allies with him to Earth, and we shall pray for his safe return."

Another older man, also very distinguished and gray-haired, clothed in a dark golden tunic and an elongated beret of brilliant silver, stood beside his chair and spoke earnestly. "Is Your Majesty aware that two of your personal guards were found unconscious with high fevers and near death after attending you and Prince Ammon last evening? Small, deep wounds were found on both men. The physician suspects they were bitten by some sort of poisonous animal."

The king appeared distressed as he looked at Ammon for a moment. "The guards were delayed in opening the Grand

Reception Hall doors after a conference and said they had been chased two large rodents."

The council members laughed momentarily at the thought that rodents, such as mice, might have caused such illness in two very capable Royal Guards but quickly regained their sober expressions as the physician stood and spoke, striking his staff on the stone floor. "I assure you, gentlemen, these men are near death and, as of late last night, have been unable to awaken or speak. The leg of one guard and arm of the other, filled with poison and infection, have swollen to twice their normal size. I've never seen the likes of it before."

The counselor with the long gray beard stood again. "Your Majesty, this may be a sign to postpone our plans until we discover what lies behind these attacks. If your personal guards are vulnerable, might you and Prince Ammon be next? Perhaps the attack was meant for you, not the guards. This could be a distraction for something yet to come."

Before he could continue, one of the select Royal Guards stood up and spoke, "Forgive my interruption, King Hyperion and counselor, but what if this attack was intended to cause a postponement in your journey to visit Master Deimos? Perhaps he has grown suspicious or used spies to uncover your plan, and needs more time to prepare a trap, or worse. I suggest that we act quickly and send not only double the number of Royal Guards but also several knights to insure your safety and, if necessary, your escape from any possible treason by Deimos." The guard smiled confidently, pleased with his suggestion. He sat again at the long table, taking a goblet, filling it with water, and then sipping from it.

King Hyperion arose, after a long moment of consideration, and struck the handle of his dagger onto the table, as the other counselors and guards were talking among themselves. Everyone immediately fell silent and listened to him.

"This is my decision!" he stated with authority. "We will delay only long enough to consider these matters and gather the knights and guards we need to ensure the safety of Prince Ammon and me. No harm must come to him under any circumstances. Attendants, bring food and drink to the Grand Reception Hall!"

Several attendants immediately left the hall, as the guards and counselors began discussing the problem. Prince Ammon turned to the king and whispered, "Father, may I go and see the injured guards? Perhaps I can learn more of what has happened. They have always been kind to me, and I'm worried about their condition."

"Do so at once. Take two guards with you and summon two of my knights to this hall without delay. Also, entreat Axel to report to the council as well."

"Axel rarely attends our conferences; of what value could he possibly be to us?"

"His father gave his life to save me many years ago," said the king. "He is much the same as his father, as you are in many ways the same as me. Shall I trust you?"

"I hope so, Father," Ammon replied modestly.

"Then also trust Axel. One day your life may depend upon him."

"As you wish, Father. I will welcome him to our council and listen to him without prejudice, if that is your command."

"It is! Ammon, we don't always know what's to come. Sometimes youth is stronger and more trustworthy than age and experience. Do you understand that?" The king smiled warmly and affectionately placed his arm around Ammon's shoulders.

"I'm not sure if I understand all of what you mean, Father, but I know that you are wise and you love me. I live only to obey you and the law."

"Trust Axel. Now, follow my sincere requests and be sure that everything possible is being done for the injured guards."

"Yes, Father." Ammon secured a small dagger on his belt and spoke briefly to two of the Royal Guards at the table. They rose and led Ammon toward the hall doors. The physician followed at a distance and then walked quickly out of the hall. Before reaching the doors, Ammon looked back at his father. As he did, he momentarily caught a glimpse of two small dark green lights, side by side, in the shadows near the green drapes far behind the king. He rubbed his eyes and blinked several times. When he looked up, the green lights were gone. He turned toward the doors and then turned back again, but the strange green lights were not there.

"Prince Ammon," one of the Royal Guards called from the doorway, "There is much to do. Are you ready?"

"Yes, of course," Ammon replied and followed them into the corridor, still wondering about what he had just seen.

Chapter Three

One of the elegantly dressed Royal Guards with a long sharp crystalline sword at his side was waiting in the corridor. "Where shall we go first, Prince Ammon?"

"To the infirmary," he said.

As they descended several stone staircases and walked along winding corridors, they came upon Axel perched on the edge a large open window, looking despondently onto the village below and holding a small book in his hand. His brown hair had grown to shoulder length since Ammon saw him last. Axel's bangs were still cut sharply across his forehead, and he wore a handsome and very sharp silver dagger on his belt. Ammon remembered it was the same dagger that Axel's father had once carried with great pride.

"Axel!" Ammon called out, but Axel looked up only briefly.

"Good morning, Prince Ammon," he offered half-heartedly, deeply unsettled by his own thoughts and distantly staring into the changing colors of the Prism sky.

"How is it with you today, friend?" The prince tried his best to be confident and friendly, remembering what his father's words about Axel and the importance of their friendship.

"Friend? No offense, My Prince, but I wasn't aware we were friends."

"I'm afraid that's my fault, Axel. I'd like to change that, if you'll reconsider all that's occurred. Our fathers were the best of friends once; perhaps we can find that friendship within ourselves as well."

"Prince Ammon, my father is dead; perhaps you've forgotten," Axel said, looking dryly at him before turning away and looking at the Prism sky as it continued to change colors and hues.

"I haven't forgotten. I don't see you very often. I'm sorry, Axel. I guess I could have sought you out. I've been busy these past few months," Ammon offered with a slight smile.

"What is it you really want, Prince Ammon? Suddenly you want to be friends? I find that a little hard to believe." Axel looked at the prince momentarily and then returned his gaze to the horizon.

"The king and I are preparing for a journey and would appreciate your counsel. The king asked that you attend him in the Grand Reception Hall immediately," Ammon finally said sternly. Then, turning to the Royal Guards, he shrugged his shoulders and started to walk away.

"Prince Ammon!" Axel called out, "I'm sorry about your mother, the queen. I hope she's all right. I'll be in the Grand Reception Hall in a few minutes, as requested." Axel smiled at the prince.

Ammon waved his arm in acknowledgement without turning or looking back. He continued on his way to the infirmary.

☙ ❖ ❧

As Ammon entered the infirmary, the Royal Guards briefly inspected the room and then took positions on both sides of the entryway. Ammon stood between the beds of the two injured guards and, taking the older guard's hand, leaned over and spoke softly, "I'm sorry, old friend. Are you feeling any better?"

The guard moaned in pain and turned his head violently from side to side, as if experiencing a nightmare.

"Easy old friend, try to rest," Ammon whispered, as the guard gripped his hand more tightly and muttered at times, almost shouting, "Evil black rats! Be careful, Prince Ammon! Tell the king! Evil black rats!"

"Is that what did this to you?" Ammon asked, as he grasped the old guard's hand and tried to stop him from sitting up.

The feverish guard began shouting, "The old woman! The old witch! Must tell the king!" He forced himself to sit up and opened his eyes momentarily, pointing to the far wall. "Green eyes! She's here! You've got to get away! You must save yourself! Prince Ammon, you must save the king!" He then closed his eyes and collapsed once again on the pillow. He gasped several times, struggling for each breath of air.

Upon hearing the disturbance, the physician appeared from the far end of the room and tried to comfort the old guard. After a few desperate minutes of struggle, the guard stopped breathing altogether. A peaceful calm seemed to momentarily cross his face, as if a great burden had been lifted and the appearance of sleep finally fell over him.

Ammon gently brushed the guard's hair away from his eyes but recoiled and quickly pulled his hand away. A strange green pallor rapidly covered the guard's face, and the already foul smell of drainage from his wound became so repugnant, it was almost more than Ammon could tolerate. He pulled a white handkerchief from his pocket and covered his nose and mouth. "What's happening?" he asked the physician fearfully.

"I'm sorry, Prince Ammon. There's nothing more I can do for him now." The physician pulled the sheet over the old guard's face. He bowed his head in a gesture of respect and then walked to the bedside of the younger guard in the bed beside him.

Ammon walked to the wall, which the guard had pointed to, but found nothing. There certainly were no green eyes.

Then, as he stood beside the younger guard's bed, he thought back to the small green lights he had seen in the Grand Reception Hall.

A slight green pallor was noticeable on the young guard's skin already, but his breathing was regular, and he seemed to be resting without distress. "Do you think he'll be all right?" Ammon asked.

"He's younger, Prince Ammon. Perhaps he's a little stronger for that, but I've never seen anything like this."

"What do you suppose he was talking about?" Ammon asked, nodding his head to the covered body a few feet away.

"It's hard to say with his fever as high as it was. Men see and say strange things when fever and infection are raging through their bodies."

"Were there any signs of rat bites?" Ammon asked in earnest.

"The same sort of wounds is present on both men. I've seen rat bites before, but I can't believe wounds this big could have been made by a small rodent."

The physician pulled back the young guard's wound dressing for a moment, revealing two large, deep tears in his skin, which oozed with the foul-smelling, green drainage. Ammon and the physician nearly gagged and covered their mouths and noses, as the physician covered the wound again.

"Can we speak outside?" Ammon asked, as he rushed away from the bedside, still covering his nose and mouth and coughing.

As the physician joined him in the corridor, Ammon tried to recover himself. "Please do everything you can for him," he finally managed.

He turned to the Royal Guards standing on either side of the door. "Find my father's knights and convey the king's command for them to attend him in the Grand Reception Hall at once."

The guards hesitated, "We need to be at your service, Prince Ammon. You may be in danger."

"As you say. One of you, stay with me, though out of sight, and the other, do as I've requested. We must not hesitate in this matter."

"As you command, Prince Ammon," the elder of the two responded. The younger guard immediately left to find the knights.

"I need a few moments to think," Ammon said to the guard left behind with him.

"I understand, I'll try not to get in your way," the guard responded, as Ammon walked cautiously down the long corridors, trying to grasp what had happened and why.

ଓ❖ଓ

As Ammon entered a courtyard, he smelled fresh apple blossoms and almost absentmindedly picked a beautiful white rose from one of the many bushes and smelled its sweet fragrance.

A young lady, dressed in a long, flowing, white gown and wearing a sparkling silver necklace, brushed against him momentarily, as if she had appeared from nowhere. "Excuse me, sir. I'm not accustomed to sharing the courtyard with anyone else."

Ammon looked up in surprise at the beautiful young lady, as she dropped a white lace handkerchief onto the stone floor. He immediately picked it up. "I'm Prince Ammon. I don't believe we've met," he said, offering his hand and the lace handkerchief.

"Oh, but we have met, Prince Ammon. You don't recall?" she asked, taking her handkerchief and his hand briefly, before releasing it. As she did, a young man approached and bowed slightly before speaking, "I'm sorry,

Princess Leda, but there's a message for you from your father."

"Just a moment," Princess Leda responded and, with a wave of her hand, dismissed the young messenger. She then returned her attention to the prince.

"I'm sorry, Princess Leda, my mind has been preoccupied."

"You need not be so formal, Prince Ammon. You may call me Leda. I'm sorry to hear about your mother's disappearance. My father and mother sent me to ask if there is anything we can do to help. I certainly understand why you didn't recognize me, as we were introduced only a short time ago. The people within my father's rule are concerned about your mother, the queen, and as always, we remain in the service of King Hyperion."

"I wish there were something to be done, Leda. Perhaps my father and I will accomplish something today," Ammon said, still envisioning the guard's death and fearing for the other's life, as well as his father's.

"Say no more but know that my best wishes are with you and the king, and of course, with your dear mother, Queen Thalia."

"Thank you, Leda. Perhaps after these things are resolved, we can meet again. Forgive, me, I must return to the reception hall." The prince kissed her hand delicately, handed her the white rose, and rushed out of the courtyard, only briefly looking back.

"Prince Ammon," Leda called after him, but he could not hear her. She called out again and then pursued him toward the hall, although to her dismay he was already out of sight. She held the white rose he had given her in one hand and her lace handkerchief in the other, looking at them as she walked determinedly toward the hall.

ာ❖ာ

Leda arrived there to find the doors open. Guards and knights, as well as counselors and special advisors with long gray beards and strangely colorful tunics, nearly filled the room, all discussing what appeared to be matters of great importance. Royal Guards stopped her at the threshold of the massive oaken doors. "I'm sorry, Princess Leda, but no one is allowed into the Grand Reception Hall today without direct orders from the king."

"I merely wanted to speak with Prince Ammon for a moment," Leda offered, looking among the many men crowded into the hall.

"I suppose it will be all right but only for a brief moment, Princess Leda. I think you'll find him near the king, toward the back of the hall."

The Royal Guards then allowed her to pass, and she made her way to the back of the long room, eventually arriving near the green drapes behind the king's chair. She curtsied to the king, but he was engaged in conversation with several advisors and did not notice her. The prince was nowhere to be seen but as she turned to walk away, she momentarily heard a strange sound from behind the drapes which seemed to rise from the dark shadows. Believing she had heard a whisper and seeing a glimpse of a small pair of green lights, she stepped into the shadows, hoping to find Prince Ammon.

Axel arrived at the Grand Reception Hall and was immediately recognized by the Royal Guards. As he entered the hall, he noticed Leda in her elegant white gown disappearing behind the rear drapes among shadows that lay beyond the light of the torches. He followed quickly hoping to have a word with her before the council began, knowing she would be asked to leave.

After reaching the back of the hall, Axel also disappeared into the same shadows. One of the guards noticed but thinking his eyes had deceived him, rubbed them and blinked several times, before returning to his conversation and forgetting the entire incident.

Ammon arrived a few minutes later, as did the two knights, wearing light armor and long crystalline swords that glowed like opals from their belts. They were tall, formidable men who immediately gained everyone's attention and respect. Without delay, they proceeded to the king and bowed slightly, before standing on either side of him.

The king spoke, "Clear the room of all those without specific purpose in the matter before the council, and seal the doors." Several guards politely escorted people from the hall until only the counselors, knights and Royal Guards remained. Prince Ammon **took** his seat near the king.

"I asked that Axel be present and yet I don't see him," King Hyperion said to his son, as he looked around the chamber.

Ammon stood and said, "I spoke with him, Father, and he assured me he would be here."

One of the guards interrupted, as the prince took his seat. The counselors around the table began to whisper among themselves about Axel's absence.

"Your Majesty, he was in this very hall only a short while ago. I believe he was about to speak with Princess Leda who was also here. I have not seen either of them since."

The king cleared his throat with a deep cough and spoke softly, "It's unlike Axel to defy a royal summons, even for Princess Leda. Nevertheless," his voice rose for everyone to hear, "let us continue." He left his seat and stood before the two large drapes that rose to the ceiling of the great hall. Raising his arms wide, he commanded, "Open the gates to the travel chamber."

Two guards walked briskly to either side of the drapes, and each slowly pulled a long, heavy cord that parted them. Metal iron bars also parted, and crystal glowing padlocks shattered and fell in streaming lights and sparks as they struck the stone floors.

While all of the fire and deep blue explosions occurred, the king was holding a glowing medallion high in the air above it all. As the iron bars finally withdrew behind the drapes, a dim blue light slowly revealed a large glass room with the emerging outline of a doorway.

"Gentlemen, behold the travel chamber!" King Hyperion said, as he spread his arms before the glowing blue spectacle.

From the outside, it appeared that the entire travel chamber was filled with a glowing, light-blue fluid, in which small and sometimes large bubbles rose regularly from the bottom edge. Tiny lights, like blue sapphires, sparkled almost like they were exploding from within the fluid, appearing, disappearing, and reappearing at random.

Everyone in the room gathered around the travel chamber, including Ammon, to gaze at the magical sight. The doorway to the chamber became more and more visible the longer it was uncovered. A large bright platinum handle gleamed in a silvery light, revealing gems of red rubies and diamonds, shining and twinkling.

The king stood on a pedestal in front of the chamber, with his knights on either side. The prince stood before him and, as the king turned, his words filled the grand hall. His wizard Xandros stood just out of sight and within the shadows, dressed in glimmering dark blue robes and observing the men in the room, as they watched in amazement the sight before them.

"Today, my friends and counselors, my son Ammon, and loyal subjects, all of whom I am bound to serve and protect, we are about to embark on a journey of great peril.

The chamber you see before you will transport us within the Prism and without, even onto the surface of the Earth."

As the king spoke, all the men and women sighed in disbelief and wonder, not only at his words but also at the brilliant spectacle of the travel chamber standing before them. In the center of it all, the king's medallion and the crystal within it gleamed with a miraculous light, which did not allow anyone to look at it for long without feeling a burning sensation in their eyes.

Chapter Four

The king and the prince planned to be the first to enter the chamber with specially selected Royal Guards and knights. As they approached the doorway to the chamber and the prince at last placed his hand on the jewel-encrusted handle, he could feel his heart racing. The king placed the medallion around the prince's neck and held his hand tightly. As the prince felt the medallion weigh heavily around his neck, he asked, "Are you sure we'll be safe, Father?" His hand trembled, as he held the chamber door handle and looked at his father.

"We'll be fine, Prince Ammon. We're visiting an old friend before we enter into the world of Deimos. The world, to which we are about to travel, is as safe as anywhere in the Prism. So safe, that I've decided to leave the guards and knights behind. They would only draw attention to us anyway. Without them, we may not be noticed at all," he said assuredly, as he patted Ammon on his back.

"It's all right, son, open the door and then enter the chamber quickly. I'll be right beside you with a firm grip on your hand. Once inside, just try to breathe easily and allow the fluid to cover us. It will not harm us; it is truly more beautiful on the inside than it is from out here."

The prince firmly pulled the chamber handle and, as he did, a high-pitched tone, unlike anything he had ever heard before, immediately issued from inside, as a light blue, glowing fluid parted enough for them to enter.

The king pulled the door closed. Once they were inside, the fluid began to envelop them, immediately covering their feet. As the fluid continued to rise, the high-pitched tone seemed to grow louder and louder. When the fluid reached Ammon's chest, he turned to his father fearfully.

"It's all right, Ammon. Just inhale normally." The king smiled with reassurance, as Ammon felt the fluid saturating his clothes. It was warm and soothing, though his heart raced, as it was about to cover his head. He instinctively thought he must try to hold his breath or be drowned. As he held his breath, the warm blue fluid covered his head, and he began to panic. He looked up to his father but could no longer see him through the glowing blue fluid, as tiny sparks of sapphire light gleamed and exploded all around him.

He clutched his father's hand and felt it firmly holding his own, as bubbles floated through the fluid and tickled his skin. He held his father's hand more tightly, as he quickly was losing the ability to hold his breath any longer. The high-pitched tone was still present but had changed somehow; it sounded more like a long uninterrupted note being played on a violin and was very soothing to hear.

Slowly releasing more air from his lungs, Ammon strangely began to feel relaxed; he thought he should panic and try to get out. He felt his father's hand on his shoulder and, to his surprise, heard his voice clearly as the lights and bubbles continued to surround him. "It's all right, son. You can breathe now. Don't worry; just take a deep breath."

Reluctantly, though for some unknown reason, Ammon was feeling calm and safe. He finally released the remaining air from his lungs and breathed in the glowing blue fluid that surrounded and submerged him. As he did so, he could at last see his father clearly and, through the glass, the wonder on the faces of the counselors, guards, and knights. He waved back at them, although the movements seemed to be ever so slow, as if he were moving effortlessly underwater, yet strangely able to breathe.

"It's like being a fish or something," he said to his father, as bubbles emerged from his mouth, somehow carrying his words inside of them.

"Be calm, Ammon, and hold onto my hand so we don't become separated during the passage of time. We're about to begin the first part of the journey." The king finished speaking and then pointed under their feet, where he and Ammon could see a swirling, bubbling area that grew larger and larger by the second. Within a minute, it had surrounded them. As they were caught in its swirling center, they realized that they were also spinning faster and faster. The once nearly agonizing high-pitched tone changed again from something resembling a pleasant violin note to a series of erratic notes played faster and faster, as if a hundred or more violins were playing different notes all at once.

Ammon felt his father's hand clasp his own more firmly, as the spinning somehow seemed to take the fluid away. In another moment, it felt as though they were in a wind-filled tunnel being forced against its outer walls. It had begun so drastically but gradually subsided and even before he could regain his balance, he was standing on a stone floor with his father still holding his hand. His clothes were completely dry, and his father was smiling and re-adjusting his shirt collar.

Just in front of Ammon was the beautiful platinum handle of the travel chamber, but it had somehow changed. The jewels of the handle were still stunning but different. The handle itself was attached to a delicately carved, arched wooden door, and the chamber was no longer glass. The door was now surrounded by a gray stone wall, covered in lush ivy which nearly concealed it. As he began to regain his senses and leaned with one arm against the door, he noticed that the image carved into the door looked almost identical to the one in the Grand Reception Hall, in which they had been standing only a few minutes earlier.

"What happened, Father?" Ammon asked, still confused at what he had just experienced.

"We have arrived," the king responded calmly, as if nothing out of the ordinary had happened.

Ammon patted his own chest and arms and then his legs and stamped his feet, as if to convince himself that he was really awake and alive and standing on firm ground. He took a deep breath and then exhaled. Everything seemed normal: the fluid was gone, and his clothes were dry. He felt his head and even his hair was dry. He felt around his neck and beneath his shirt, and touched the medallion. He then turned to his father again. "Where are we, Father?" he asked, noticing they were standing in a courtyard filled with odd-looking bushes, trees, and flowers. He had never seen such flowers and plant life in the palace courtyards. "This is not our palace, is it, Father?"

"No, son, we've traveled a very long way. I don't believe we've been noticed, but our friends will know that we have arrived before long, if everything is safe." The king looked cautiously around the courtyard, as he kept one hand firmly on Ammon's shoulder and his other hand on the hilt of his crystalline sword. As he did, a very pleasant voice came from the far side of the courtyard.

"Your Majesty!" the voice called out, and a strikingly beautiful woman walked gracefully towards Ammon and the king. Beside her walked an equally beautiful younger woman. The king removed his hand from his sword and opened his arms slightly, in a gesture of recognition and friendship.

The two women approached and bowed deeply, while smiling, their faces almost shining in the soft prism light of the early afternoon. The prince, although still shaken by his experience in the travel chamber, took a deep breath and exhaled, relieved at last, upon sensing that they were apparently safe.

"Arianne!" the king said with a smile, as he kissed her hand respectfully. "And this must be Aleah."

"Yes, sir, I am Aleah. Welcome," she said, smiling shyly.

"This is my son, Prince Ammon," the king said, drawing him closer to his side, as the prince bowed slightly.

"It's a pleasure to meet you both," he finally managed to say.

"If Your Majesty and Prince Ammon will follow us, we can retire to my home. It's not far from here," Arianne said, as she gestured toward the far end of the courtyard.

The king took her arm and walked casually beside her, as the prince and Aleah followed. "How did you know we'd arrived Arianne?" the king asked. She softly whispered her response to the king, though Ammon overheard her mention his mother's name.

"Excuse me, but do you have news of my mother? If so, I'd like to know without delay." Ammon's tone bordered on being impolite.

The king turned and glared at him. "Son, please hold your questions until we are in private. All will be answered in time." He then turned to Arianne. "Forgive him, My Lady; I assure you he was not raised to be impolite to our friends and hosts. Were you, Prince Ammon?" the king turned and asked him directly.

"No, sir. Please forgive my display of poor etiquette. It won't happen again. I become anxious whenever her name is mentioned. I apologize, Lady Arianne."

Arianne looked at the prince with her deep aqua-green eyes, revealing what seemed to be genuine sympathy. "You need not apologize," she said just above a whisper. "I think you'll find that we share the same concerns and fears at the mention of her name. It is a name very dear to me."

Arianne turned and continued to walk with the king until they reached the front gate of a very elegant but modest estate, on what appeared to be the outskirts of a much larger village. A neatly dressed young man, clothed in blue overalls and leather gloves, appeared in the yard. Laying down a gardening rake, he stepped quickly to the Iron Gate and opened it. Arianne whispered something to him and after she and her guests entered, he locked the gate behind them. He then picked up his rake and returned to the garden, though carefully observing everyone, as Lady Arianne led her guests into the house.

Once the door was closed, she affectionately but respectfully embraced the king. "Thank God, you're here," she said. "When I heard that someone was arriving in the chamber, I didn't know who to expect. Please, everyone, make yourselves at home. Aleah dear, would you prepare some refreshments for our guests?"

"Yes, Mother," she responded without hesitation.

"Ammon, please assist her. Then we can all share with one another what we've learned," the king requested.

"Of course, Father," Ammon answered. He and Aleah left the room, both looking silently at the other and wondering who the other might be.

When they returned with glasses and a pitcher of juice, Aleah explained that it was made of the queen's favorite wild fruit. The king and Lady Arianne were already deeply absorbed in conversation but readily raised their glasses and toasted Queen Thalia.

"Ammon," the king started in a serious tone, as Aleah and the prince took seats beside them, "Lady Arianne has just informed me that Master Deimos has found a way to travel through the boundaries of the Prism and was here two days ago."

Lady Arianne continued with what she had started telling the king, looking at times directly at the prince. "Deimos asked many questions about you and your father but answered few of my questions, if any." She then pulled her sleeve back and revealed a large and very unsightly bruise on her forearm. "I revealed nothing, but he threatened us and promised he would return soon to gather what information we might be hiding." As she finished speaking, Aleah pulled her nearly waist-long blonde hair aside and revealed the bruises on her shoulder and neck.

"I'm so sorry, Lady Arianne. I've acted like such a fool! Can you forgive me for my lack of courtesy and understanding?" the prince said.

"Of course," Lady Arianne continued. "We know how you feel. We both love your mother very much. She has been a dear friend for many years, though we've tried to keep our friendship a secret to protect one another in the event of trouble. Somehow, Master Deimos has reason to suspect my friendship with your dear mother and means to know everything. Because of things he said and fears he has grown to harbor, I'm certain that our beloved Queen Thalia, your mother, is still alive."

As she finished speaking, Lady Arianne placed her hand on Ammon's arm, "You have to have faith. If she were dead, I believe we would all somehow sense it. I'm certain she is alive and well for the time being."

"Thank you, Lady Arianne," Ammon said, as he placed his hand on hers briefly and then wiped a tear from his eye.

The king stood up and paced back and forth several times before facing the three of them. "There's no doubt in my mind that you, Arianne and Aleah, must travel with Ammon to the Earth's surface this very day. Master Deimos may return at any moment; it's obvious that it's no longer safe for either of you here. Go now, I pray you, and collect what personal items you need. Anything else will be provided at the palace upon our return. Quickly now, gather what you need, yet not so many things as to bring needless attention before we can reach the chamber."

Lady Arianne and Aleah quickly retired to their rooms. Ammon and his father looked impatiently onto the garden space beyond the sitting room. The gardener continued raking leaves in the distance, although Ammon watched him closely.

"What about him, Father?"

"We either take him with us or... ." As they looked at one another and briefly considered, then looked back, the gardener had disappeared.

"Help our friends. There's no time to spare," the king commanded.

Within a few minutes, the king, Ammon, Aleah, and Lady Arianne were approaching the courtyard where the wooden door with the jewel-encrusted handle was covered in dark green ivy. Strangely, just since their arrival, the ivy had grown over the handle, and they had to desperately search for it. Upon uncovering it, the door refused to open. The king instructed Ammon to hold his medallion into the air and pull to open the tightly closed door.

Despite numerous attempts, the door remained sealed. "What's wrong, Father?" Ammon asked.

The sound of horses accompanied the steady march of soldiers approaching; leaving no doubt that a large force of soldiers would arrive within minutes.

"Someone's coming with others! We must leave now!" Lady Arianne said, just above a whisper, desperately urging them closer to the doorway, while looking around the courtyard for another possible way to escape. "There's no other way out," she whispered urgently. As the approaching sounds became louder and more than frightening, terror could be seen in each of their faces except the king's. They heard the horses and soldiers arriving in a frightening commotion, closer and louder with each passing second.

'Present the medallion in front of the door. Think and believe in all that is important in life and then pull up on the handle with confidence,' said an assuring voice in Ammon's mind, although the noise of an approaching army was really all he could hear. He knew the voice within him was that of his father.

Ammon thought of his mother and the two guards in the infirmary. He remembered his encounter with Axel, and suddenly of Aleah, as well as his father and Lady Arianne. As he did, the blue crystal inside of the medallion began to emit a bright white light, and the door handle of the travel chamber glowed blue and red as the door slowly but steadily began to open.

"It's working, Father! It's working!" But, as the door was ajar enough for Aleah to go through, a huge silver axe, nearly half the size of Ammon, struck the middle of the door just beside his head with a thundering force so powerful; he had never imagined such a thing possible. A rain of sparks and wooden splinters showered around them, shaking the ground and forcing the door closed again. Ammon continued to pull the door open, when another huge axe struck the door, shaking them, as the concussion of the impact knocked them to their knees.

The king stood up and shouted, "Enough!" He then turned to face whatever was responsible for the attack. As he raised his crystal sword in the air, it shone forth like a blinding beacon. Ammon had never seen such brightness and covered his eyes, as did everyone else.

King Hyperion then turned for an instant to his son and spoke calmly and clearly in a voice which resounded through space, "Open the door now, boy, else we perish on this very spot at this very moment!"

Without hesitation, Ammon pulled with all his might and, surprising even himself, managed to open the door wide enough to allow Aleah and then Lady Arianne exit.

"Go, Ammon!" the king commanded, but Ammon braced himself like a wedge to maintain the opening. "You first, Sire," he insisted.

At that moment, yet another axe struck the door, shaking them both and leaving a deafeningly loud thunder in their ears. Despite the blow, Ammon remained wedged in the doorway.

Realizing he would not move, the king dropped his exquisite, gleaming sword and managed to slip through the small opening into the chamber, grabbing Ammon by his arm and pulling him through as he passed.

The king desperately reached through the small opening in an attempt to retrieve his sword, as another axe cut his arm completely off, and it fell onto the stone floor of the courtyard. He then withdrew the stump of his arm quickly, as yet another blow from the axe sealed the door shut behind them.

Almost immediately, fluid began to fill the chamber as it had before. Lady Arianne pulled a scarf from her neck and wrapped it tightly around the stump of King Hyperion's arm to stop the massive bleeding. They each looked at one another frightfully as yet another thundering boom shook the chamber, causing hundreds of bubbles to waft from the floor beneath them.

"Is it too late, Father? Your sword? Is it lost?" Ammon asked urgently.

"I hope not. It was said that only you could wield the sword," the king responded, as a series of thundering blows were heard, one after the other from just a few feet away. Ammon, Aleah, and Arianne grasped each other's hands, imagining the massive axes striking the door and hoping the door would hold. The king, a formidable man in size and strength, braced his body against the door and was jolted, almost collapsing, with each additional concussion of blows from the outside.

The blue, luminous fluid continued to fill the chamber, more slowly than it had before. As the liquid reached their chins, they looked down into the glowing pool. Just as before, small sparkling explosions of sapphires filled the watery fluid rising from below. Each held the other's hand tightly until they were all connected. Once again, the high-pitched tone sounded in the chamber, though it was interrupted by deep reverberating blows, sounding like thunder, just beyond the door a few feet away.

After a few moments the violin-like tone overcame everything, and the king was able to stand away from the door. Completely submerged, they all felt the warm fluid swirling around them and comforting their fears, though dark red blood continued to seep from King Hyperion's severed arm.

As the prince tried to see Aleah through the glowing, magical blue liquid, he felt a gentle kiss on his cheek and held her hand a little more tightly. Trusting in his father, Ammon knew that the palace, his home, must be getting closer, if only the door would hold a few minutes longer.

Distantly, even through the heavy, sparkling blue fluid, the crash of thundering blows again broke through the sounds of the chamber, as the swirling fluids and rushing currents pressed all of them against the shaking walls. With each blow, a massive rush of bubbles erupted below them, and the vibrations from the force of the blows coursed through their bodies.

The erratic sound of violins that Ammon had heard earlier grew in intensity as the strong currents began to transform the fluid into air. He was, at last, confident that the journey had been a success, when, from above his left shoulder, he noticed a return of water which seemed to slow the swirling motion and air replacement. Aleah, Lady Arianne, and the king coughed violently as they expelled the blue liquid from their lungs and tried to catch their breath. Ammon held his throat as he coughed and spat fluid from his own lungs.

The king looked up at the expanding water above them and dropped to his knees. "We must get out of here. The chamber has been damaged," he muttered desperately, once again collapsing into a long and prolonged cough.

Ammon reluctantly released Aleah's hand and, though unable to see through the glowing blue fluid lapping against his chest, he tried to find the door handle. Taking a deep breath, he submerged himself and, while beneath the surface, he could hear the distinct percussion of blows flowing through the heavy fluid. He rose to the surface and looked at the king.

"I can't find the handle, Father. Is there anything else that can be done?" he asked, swimming toward Aleah and supporting her as she kept coughed.

The king looked up to the expanding leak above them and shook his head. "I'm sorry, son. They have damaged the chamber. The door cannot be opened until the entire cycle has been completed. By then, I suspect we all will have drowned."

"Can we plug the leak?" Ammon asked desperately, before breaking into a prolonged cough.

"Perhaps," his father answered, "and then what? We remain here until we starve to death or even sooner when we run out of air?" As he finished speaking, the loud thundering blows began again. With each powerful blow, the leak of glowing blue fluid from above them increased, inch by inch raising the liquid above their chests and advancing toward their heads.

Lady Arianne had been quiet, except for coughing, until that very moment. "Perhaps our enemies have become our salvation," she said, as she quietly ran her fingers along the walls of the chamber, carefully following each crack on its surface. At times, she submerged into the fluid, before appearing at another point far beyond where she had disappeared.

"What do you mean, Lady Arianne?" Ammon asked but before she could answer, Aleah spoke, "They want in. We want out," Aleah added. "The question still remains: what they will do with us when we get out or what will we do with them when they get in?"

The king collected himself and managed to speak, "The fluid will continue to flood this room. I don't know what will become of us. Perhaps we'll drown or as the chamber recovers, we might complete our journey and return to the point from which we came, the Royal Palace."

Ammon whispered to his father, "Must we idly sit by and watch the worlds fall into evil? If Deimos wins, everyone will suffer all because he has found a way to use his dark magic."

"I'm sorry, son and my two dear friends, I underestimated Deimos. For my mistake, we are trapped between the borders of the Prism. A hundred years from now—perhaps a thousand—we will be freed, or at least our bodies discovered." Everyone turned their heads downward.

"Magic," Lady Arianne said softly as she rose to the surface. "Perhaps it's time that we also employ 'magic.'"

"Are you willing to pay the price, Arianne?" the king asked, looking most seriously at his old friend.

"Do we have any choice?" she responded.

Chapter Five

Near the high summit of snow-covered mountains overlooking the city of Deimongar, Orestros completed the hundred-foot descent of an icy precipice. The pine-covered ridges in the distance were submerged in the early morning mist of autumn. Spiraling oaks, towering maples, and fragrant pine trees shot from the forest floor toward the Prism sky, all competing for its orange light.

The final light of the Prism faded, as Orestros found an open spot and lit a small fire in a clearing of pine trees. He quickly constructed a shelter, using his blankets and some fallen limbs and branches to protect him from the freezing winter elements. Gray squirrels and meadowlarks danced in the trees, squeaked and chirped as they flew and leapt from branch to branch.

Wrapping himself in his heaviest blanket, Orestros sat by the fire and warmed his hands. He pulled a thick piece of dried beef jerky from his coat pocket and chewed it, as he looked down the mountainside to firelights of the city below. Tired after climbing since early morning, he sat on a cushion of pine needles as he watched his breath steam in the freezing mountain air, knowing it would be a cold night ahead.

After adding more wood to his fire, he leaned back and withdrew a tightly rolled scroll from his knapsack. Holding it closer to the firelight, he carefully read the message written on the parchment:

Orestros,

You are the only one who knows the secret mountain passages of the Prism, and the only one physically capable of making such a journey. We humbly ask you to make this journey to Deimongar and discover what Master Deimos is plotting. More importantly, we have reason to believe that Deimos may be responsible for abducting and imprisoning our beloved Queen Thalia. No matter what, should you find her and cannot free her, we ask that you tell her we will be coming for her and that she have faith in us. You are perhaps our last hope, before all-out war is waged against Deimos. Please, dear friend, do what you can and return yourself safely to the palace. —King Hyperion

Orestros looked at the royal seal, rolled the scroll again, and laid it on the flaming logs. The fire quickly consumed it, as Orestros leaned back against a log and closed his eyes, now growing heavy with sleep.

Freezing wind and snow blew against his blanket and soon extinguished the campfire, as he crawled into the small shelter.

✥

Morning light found Orestros covered in a blanket of fresh white snow. He roused slowly and began to move tentatively in the freezing wind.

Shredding strips of cloth from his shirt, while gathering twigs and splinters hewn with his silvery axe from fallen logs, he cupped his hands and struck a match, carefully lighting the kindling into a warming fire. He rubbed his cold, stiff hands against the flames and once again pulled a large piece of jerky from his knapsack. He heated fresh water from snow, splashed his face, and rubbed his eyes, looking out on the scant burning lights of the city below.

Orestros paused for a few minutes, deep in thought as he chewed the dried beef and sipped the hot water. He then loaded his knapsack and slung his climbing ropes over his shoulder. On the outside of his knapsack he secured his razor-sharp axe, and from his belt he hung his long knife. Eating a handful of fresh snow, he began the long journey down the mountainside.

The slopes became greener and warmer as he descended. He neither saw nor heard any birds, and he thought that was strange, as he paused occasionally and listened closely. A few flowers arose from the lush green grasses but nearly everything seemed to have been trampled under the heavy human feet. He saw no animal tracks which also seemed strange. The only pleasant sound was that of a small creek trickling downhill from the snow-capped mountains.

After continuing his descent into the lower valleys and pastures, Orestros began to see what had become of the land of Deimos. Smelling fire, he followed a small stream of smoke and came upon a farmhouse burned to the ground, with the remains of its former occupants littering the grounds around it. Long arrows protruded from the victims' bodies, and Orestros had to cover his mouth and nose from the foul odor of decay.

Hearing men shouting in the distance, he moved quickly into the woods. He covered himself with small branches and fern fronds, crouched down beside a fallen pine tree, and waited as the voices were not far away.

A large black raven flew by overhead and circled once before landing atop the remnants of the farmhouse chimney. Orestros kept low and covered but felt that, at times, the crow was looking directly at him. As it cawed loudly several times, it flew into the air, circled a few times a little closer to the trees where Orestros was hidden, and then flew away toward the village and the sound of the soldiers.

As he watched the road leading to the burned house where it emerged from the trees, he noticed two soldiers carefully darting from one tree to the next, with their bows partially drawn and long arrows mounted, ready to be released at a moment's notice. He knew they could not have seen him but felt increasingly uneasy. He then heard a twig snap behind him and as he looked back, two more soldiers appeared with their bows drawn. One of them released his arrow and it struck a few inches from Orestros's head. He quickly rolled over toward the soldiers as the other released his arrow which grazed Orestros's axe and lodged in his knapsack. Before either of the soldiers could draw more arrows from their quivers, Orestros came to his feet. The two soldiers fell backwards and tripped at the sight of him.

"Look at the size of him!" one gasped. "He must be ..."

"A bloody giant!" the other gasped as they both scooted backwards desperately on their elbows and reached for their swords.

Orestros stepped forward, reached down and, lifting them up by their necks and collars, slammed their heads together and released their limp bodies to the ground. He then gathered their bows, quivers of arrows, and swords and without further hesitation, he moved quickly into the cover of forest.

The other two soldiers arrived after a few minutes to find their comrades lying motionless. As one soldier tried to rouse them, the other one carefully surveyed the surroundings with his bow drawn and ready. "Are they alive?" he asked, not taking his eyes from the surrounding terrain.

"Both dead!" the other responded.

"Of what?" his colleague asked nervously.

"Looks like they hit their heads together! I don't see any other wounds," he answered, crouching low to the ground.

"What's the matter with you? Get up!"

"One more thing," the soldier said awkwardly, keeping low and looking in all directions, as he visibly began to shake with fear.

"What?" the other demanded.

"Their bows, arrows and swords are miss..."

Before he could finish, arrows struck them both with such force that they passed completely through them. They fell slowly to their knees with surprised looks on their faces.

After hiding the weapons of Deimos's soldiers, Orestros buried the bodies of the family that had lived in the house, as well as the soldiers, and hid all remnants of their presence.

Leaving the road, he followed it toward the village while remaining covered by the thick forest. As he traveled, he saw home after home either burned or deserted, or both. He saw Deimos's soldiers every few hundred feet and the same black raven alighting and squawking wherever large groups of soldiers congregated.

Linked together with long chains, men and women pulled carts packed with large bundles and sacks of food toward the village. Heavy iron collars were attached to their necks, as their chains were connected to the one in front or the one behind them.

Orestros witnessed from the cover of the trees many of the prisoners collapse. Soldiers whipped them until they could stand again and if they could not, children that followed them were whipped and commanded to help release them from their collars and were then left on the side of the road. The chains and collars were then reconnected to the next prisoner, and the procession continued without mercy. Those left behind with their children trying to help them were whipped and pushed and kicked into the nearby woods, by two and sometimes three soldiers. After a few minutes, only the soldiers emerged from the forest, using bits of torn clothing to wipe fresh blood from their swords and axes.

❧ ❖ ☙

After traveling for several hours, Orestros finally viewed the castle of Deimos, perched on a rocky outcropping that overlooked the village. It was made of a very rough-hewn stone, which appeared almost black in color.

The Prism sky overhead filled with rich orange and blue hues as light faded, and Orestros, weary and terribly sad from what he had seen, rested with his back against a giant oak tree. He tried not to remember the horrible sights he had seen since arriving in the Dominion of Deimos, but the images of suffering and dying women and children were more vivid than he could forget. He splashed a handful of cool water from his pouch onto his face to wipe away his tears. He remembered King Hyperion's message and considered what might be happening to Queen Thalia, if she were still alive. He closed his eyes and tried to plan an entrance into the castle.

As the Prism sky began to darken, Orestros climbed into a large oak with long limbs overhanging the road. As a heavily laden cart, drawn by men and women in chains, passed below him, he dropped from the tree limb onto the cart and quickly covered himself with sacks and other stolen treasures.

In the cart behind him, he noticed the prisoners' faces as they saw him drop. He crawled to the end of the cart and tried to gesture to them to remain silent. One of the men pulling the cart started to call out. Before he could speak, the man next to him struck him mercilessly in the throat, silencing him. The man grasped his throat and struggled for air.

Soldiers immediately rushed beside them and struck them both repeatedly until they fell to the ground. "What's the matter here?" one soldier asked the man who had hit his companion.

"Nothing, sir. He insulted my wife," the man said, rising to his feet and continuing to walk without hesitation.

"Is that the truth? Speak up, fool!" the soldier demanded of the other man.

The man nodded in agreement, as he clutched his throat in pain and looked in fear at his companion.

"Move along! There'll be plenty of time for your wife later. We're all looking forward to it!" The soldier laughed and then lashed both men with his whip before stopping to scratch his head and pluck a fat tick from behind his ear.

Orestros covered himself again as both carts continued on, until they finally passed through the outer gates of the village. Partially pulling a large sack to the side, he could see the entrance to the castle's prison. He heard the lashing of whips and commands coming from the soldiers pushing prisoners into the torch-lit descending corridors. He closed his eyes and tried to think of nothing at all. He carefully placed his hand on his knife and waited for whatever might happen next.

As men and women were lashed and forced into the lower levels of the dungeon, Orestros bowed his head and followed in the single line of prisoners, trying to disguise his height and size. As the staircase descended lower and lower, the steps became immersed in a dark, foul-smelling watery slime.

Orestros noticed men and women in front of him, wading into dark pools, while slapping their legs at small squiggly creatures circling around them. It wasn't long before he felt bites on his own legs and instinctively slapped and tried to catch whatever was biting him. As he pulled a slimy wet creature from his leg, blood filled the foul water around his leg. A rush of the squiggly creatures surrounded the slight flow of blood, yet he tried to quietly maintain a lower and smaller stature. Men and women in front and behind him sobbed as the creatures bit them. The soldiers laughed and lashed them with their whips, and pushed them down the water-covered staircase into pools of stagnant water, all the while standing on a ledge above them.

Despite his pain and his desire to help those around him, Orestros remained silent and continued toward the dungeon, where he hoped he might find Queen Thalia.

He looked up at the small ledges that extended along both sides of the slimy path. He could hear the sounds of rusted hinges, as doors slowly opened, then slammed shut with an echoing ferocity. The rustle and shuffling of chained feet resounded, as the guards began pushing up to a dozen people into each cell, men and woman alike. Parents called out for their children and received lashes for their complaints.

Before he could be locked in a cell, Orestros noticed that only one guard was present, and he reached up, taking him by his leg and pulling him down into the blackened water. Orestros held him there as the squirming creatures covered the guard's leg and slowly moved across his body, until he was left pale, white, and limp.

The prisoners around Orestros patted him on the back. "What now, friend? Do you know the way out, the way to find our families?" Orestros signaled them to be silent as he leaned over and pressed his ear against the stone wall.

From the depths of the dungeon, Orestros heard the faint cry of a woman. He held his breath and listened more closely. "If it's you, please help me!" the faint voice of a woman called out.

He looked to the man who had saved him on the cart. Reaching down, he pulled the guard out of the water, placed him beside a cell door, and removed his sword. He handed it to the man who had helped him.

"What shall I do? Show us the way and we'll follow you," the man pleaded, as all of the others looked to Orestros hopefully. He motioned to a guard advancing on the ledge in front of them.

The man, who had received the sword from Orestros, waited and then lunged and stabbed the guard on the ledge. He then pulled the key ring from his belt and threw the keys to Orestros.

He turned to the men and women gathered around him, some still holding children on their shoulders as they prepared to run. Orestros waved his hand and everyone knew to be silent. He listened for the queen, as he made his way down the small walkway to the bottom steps of the deepest level.

"Queen Thalia," he called as loudly as he could, and then stood still and listened. He heard the faint sound of the queen's voice again. The small ledge was slippery, and the black slimy water looked much deeper, as he looked to the other side where he thought he had heard the queen's voice.

"Queen Thalia, it is Orestros. Can you hear me?"

He listened, but there was no reply. "Queen Thalia. Here. I am here. Orestros. King Hyperion has sent me!" he called again. He felt his heart pounding, as he took a mighty leap, grabbing the cell door on the other side of the blackened waterway and grasping the black metal bars. He pulled himself up and looked into the dark, dank cell. At last, he could see Queen Thalia, lying on a scant layer of straw, cringing and terribly pale in one cold corner.

Struggling, Orestros pulled the bars apart and managed to force the door open. He picked her up and carried her most gently. With help from his fellow freed prisoners, he made his long way out of the dungeon and started toward the main gate.

Torches burned throughout the castle, making it impossible for them not to be seen. The guards caught sight of them almost immediately. The other prisoners began shouting and running in all directions, as the tower guards sounded their horns in alarm, bringing all the guards and soldiers towards the entrances to the castle and village.

Queen Thalia faintly looked around seeing the oncoming guards. "Go, Orestros! Leave me here and make safe your escape," she pleaded.

Orestros pulled his handmade knife from its sheath and, without hesitation, struck down two soldiers as they attacked. Several other soldiers approached and then turned away, realizing his formidable size and strength.

"Please, Orestros, return to the king and tell him I will survive as long as they can use me to hurt him and my beloved son. Another time will come, and you will rescue me, but if you stay now, all will be lost." The queen sighed and kissed Orestros on the cheek.

Tears fell across his face, as Orestros pulled the queen closer and broke into a full run, crashing through soldiers as if they were rag dolls, while others dove through the air to get out of his way. Covering her in his massive arms, he burst through the gathering lines of soldiers.

The queen cried out with all of her strength, "Please, Orestros, if you love me, then obey me. Save yourself tonight, that you may return another day."

Orestros heard her but could not obey, as he turned her over his shoulder and, wielding his knife, struck down two more soldiers blocking his way through the gate.

"It will be all right, My Lady," he said, as two long arrows hit his back shoulder. Queen Thalia saw the terrible grimace on his face and reached over to feel the large shafts

protruding from his back. After another long run, Orestros
slowed and fell to one knee. Queen Thalia could feel the
warm blood oozing down his back and soaking his shirt.
Not far behind them, they heard shouts and alarm horns
from every direction. Armed men bearing torches filed out
of the castle, seemingly without end.

"Another mile and we'll be safely in the forest, My
Lady," Orestros gasped, out of breath, as he gently laid her
down and pulled the arrows from his shoulder with a deep
groan.

"Another mile and my brave hero will be dead," the
queen said sadly and meekly as she tried to catch her breath.
"Orestros, I need you to listen to me. Am I your queen?" she
asked with all of the authority she could muster.

"Of course, My Lady," Orestros answered without
hesitation.

"I command you to leave me here and make your way
back to the palace. When the time is right, bring my son and
my husband with all their armies and free me along with all
of these poor enslaved people. Do you understand me,
Orestros?"

Orestros nodded in agreement. "I'm sorry, My Lady,
I've failed you."

"Dear sweet friend, you've not failed me unless you fail
to escape. Go, now! All will be well." Queen Thalia kissed
him on the cheek and pushed him away.

Orestros laid his knapsack beneath her head and gently
stroked her fevered brow before disappearing into the night.
Within minutes, dozens of torch lights surrounded her, as
hundreds of soldiers on horseback and on foot pursued the
howling bloodhounds into the foothills.

On a great black stallion with a raven perched on his
shoulder, Master Deimos looked briefly at the frail queen

53

and laughed, as she was dragged with ropes back toward the castle. Standing in the stirrups, his dark figure was silhouetted in the orange flickering torchlight.

"I want more dogs and more soldiers brought here at once. If the giant escapes, there'll be a terrible price to pay by all of you! Do you hear me?" he screamed. Several dozen men around him briefly bowed their heads and responded, "Yes, Master Deimos. He will not escape."

"What are you waiting for?" again he screamed, as all those surrounding him ran toward the road leading into the forest. The black raven on his shoulder leapt into the air and flew toward the torches slowly moving up the mountainside.

Deimos then kicked his stallion with his sharp spurs and charged off in the direction of the mountain, following the howls of the bloodhounds.

Chapter Six

Desperation and at last resignation filled the thoughts of the travelers in the chamber, as doom and death seemed certain. The chamber continued to fill, and everyone knew something was wrong, as giant bubbles erupted from the direction of the door and slowly disappeared in the dark blue fluid. Just as it was about to cover their heads, another even brighter light began to emerge. From out of the fluid, as sapphires began to explode randomly like charges from electric eels, Lady Arianne's image became clearer and clearer, though no one else was visible.

Ammon grasped Aleah's hand firmly, as he looked into the changing colors and saw only Lady Arianne's image clearly forming. A strange luminous aqua-green light clouded her eyes and then shone forth like tiny distant beacons. At the same time, an aura of the same color surrounded her entire form. She at last appeared glowing and serene as if in a trance.

A sudden almost blinding flash of the green light exploded in the chamber, leaving everyone but Lady Arianne collapsed on the gray stone floor trying to regain their senses. The aura surrounded her for a few seconds longer and then disappeared as she too collapsed, falling hard onto the floor, unconscious.
Unlike before, all but Lady Arianne were soaked from the blue fluid.

Aleah, still unstable, managed to crawl slowly to her side and moaned in pain with every exertion. Despite the pain, she tried but could not arouse Lady Arianne. The king was able to sit up with great difficulty, and the prince crawled unsteadily to his side, also moaning in pain.

"W h a t   h a p p e n e d ?" Ammon asked, speaking slowly and stretching his words out. As he reached out to his father, his effort seemed to be in slow motion, causing him to grimace from the pain.

"Everyone, sit still," the king said in a low, slow voice. "We must all sit still for a few minutes."

Ammon looked up and saw the clear walls of the chamber and the Grand Reception Hall. He noticed the various counselors, knights, and Royal Guards that had been present at their departure, though now they were shielding their eyes and not moving at all. They appeared frozen, completely suspended in time and motion.

Aleah called out slowly, "Something's terribly wrong with Lady Arianne. Please help her, King Hyperion!"

The king turned toward Aleah and Arianne. "She will recover if we all remain still for a few more minutes."

"What's happening, Father?" Ammon asked, as he slowly pointed toward the hall.

"Lady Arianne has caused time to stop outside the chamber. In a few minutes, it will begin to resume. Until then, we must remain still or Lady Arianne and all of us will be damaged in the motion of time returning to its own space," the king said and, looking more tired than Ammon had ever seen, he rested his head against the chamber wall and closed his eyes.

Ammon slowly placed his folded cloak under the king's head and, looking across the chamber at Aleah, offered a tender smile as sleep began to overcome them both.

❧ ❖ ☙

They awakened to sounds, as knights and Royal Guards peered through the walls of the chamber and called out to the king and the prince. They all moved as if everything were normal again. King Hyperion stood and offered his hand to Prince Ammon, gesturing for him to stand. Aleah had also awakened, but Lady Arianne remained strangely still. The king led Ammon to Lady Arianne's side.

"Help me," the king said, as he took her in his arms and walked toward the door. "Open the chamber door, Ammon," he ordered as Aleah stood nearby.

Ammon grasped the door and opened it with ease. Royal Guards immediately, though ever so carefully, took Lady Arianne from the king and awaited his exit and instructions.

"Take the lady to the infirmary at once and be certain that my personal physician cares for her. She has saved the lives of Prince Ammon, Mistress Aleah, and me. Care for her as you would care for your king. Make haste!"

The Royal Guards laid her on an elegant stretcher and carried her out of the hall in a procession with several other guards on either side. Ammon and Aleah followed closely all the way to the infirmary.

When they arrived, Ammon noticed that the younger guard was no longer there and asked the physician what had happened. The physician led him back into the corridor, while speaking in a soft whisper. "I'm sorry, Prince Ammon, but he died this morning shortly after you departed in much the same way as his fellow guard did yesterday. Before he died, he screamed that you and the king must be warned, something about green eyes and a witch. I'm sure he was delirious from the fever, but he repeated it over and over until he finally passed away. There was nothing more I could do for him. Because of the infection and the strange green pallor to their skin, we had both bodies cremated."

"Thank you. They were good men and will be missed," Ammon said, slowly shaking his head and looking at the empty beds where his friends had lain. "Please make sure that their families have all they need to be comfortable. Also, tell them that I will visit them as soon as time allows.

Send food and fresh fruits for their children. Can you have these things taken care of for me? Any cost will be met by my family."

"Of course, Prince Ammon," said the physician. "I'll have my assistants do so without delay. The prince started toward Lady Arianne's bed. "One other thing. Do you recall the green pallor on the faces of the guards?"

"Of course, it was strange, as well as the horrid smell of the wounds," Ammon said dryly.

"I know it must sound strange but at the cremation, as the bodies were burning, the green color seemed to vanish from their skin, and the terrible odor disappeared completely. Some of us heard what we thought sounded like sighs of relief come from the mouths of both men. I've never seen or heard anything like it in all my years. I just thought you should know."

"Thank you, Physician. Thank you for caring for them. Please apply all of your knowledge and wisdom to the care of Lady Arianne now. She somehow saved our lives before she finally collapsed. Please do what you can. She must travel a great distance soon, and we need her desperately."

"I will do all I can for her, Prince Ammon, and I will make sure that the fallen guards' families are cared for, according to your instructions." The physician bowed slightly and joined his assistants at Lady Arianne's bedside.

Ammon followed and stood at Lady Arianne's bedside with Aleah. Then he took Aleah's hand tenderly in his own and said, "She'll be all right, Aleah. My father said she just needs time to rest."

Aleah took a handkerchief and wiped the tears running down her cheeks. She then looked at the prince and saw a tear forming in the corner of his right eye.

"I know that she did something, something that saved the lives of us all. Do you know what it was, Aleah?" Ammon spoke in a soft and caring voice.

"She knows how to change things. I don't understand it myself. Once when I was very young, no more than four or five, I fell from the top of a cliff while we were having a picnic with your mother, the queen. I would have died from the fall. While I was mid-air, Lady Arianne appeared above me. I saw a bright, almost blinding, flash of aqua-green light. The next thing I remember I was standing on the edge of the cliff again, just about to fall when Lady Arianne pulled me back from the edge. She laid down on the edge afterward and seemed very tired. Your mother and I had to help her to a soft bed that we made from pine needles. After we laid her down, she slept for hours. Until today, I've never seen her behave so, nor have I seen that strange green light again."

"How could such a thing be possible?" Ammon wondered aloud.

"She's a wonderful lady with a great capacity for love," Aleah said softly, while taking Lady Arianne's hand and squeezing it tenderly. As Aleah squeezed her hand, Arianne stirred and slowly opened her eyes. "Is everyone all right?" she managed to whisper.

"Thanks to you, My Lady," the prince said and brushed a stray hair from the side of her face.

"And your father, the king?" she asked, again in a soft whisper.

"We are all well, My Lady. We're worried about you. Are you well?" Aleah asked.

"I will be fine in a little while. Prince Ammon, you must send a message to your father at once."

"Of course, My Lady. What shall I tell him?" Ammon asked readily.

"The travel chamber can never be used to return to my home world again or to the Dominion of Deimos!" Your father must understand this: such a journey would be a catastrophe; all within the chamber would surely perish!"

"I understand, My Lady. I will tell him without delay. May I also tell him that you are well?"

"Yes, My Prince. Now go and waste no time."

Ammon leaned over and softly kissed Lady Arianne's cheek, and squeezed Aleah's hand gently, then quickly left the infirmary.

�❖�

As he walked through the long passageways and corridors of the palace, he thought about all that had happened in the past few days. He relived meeting Lady Arianne and Aleah and his first experience with his father in the travel chamber. It seemed as if it had been a dream, until he remembered the enormous axe striking the wooden door of the chamber, and their narrow escape. A shiver ran up his spine and goose bumps appeared on his arms as he recalled the pounding on the travel chamber door and the feeling that death was about to consume all of them as the fluid rose over their heads.

At last, he found himself seated on the tower platform where only a few days earlier he had been flying a kite. He walked to the edge and peered into the Prism sky. Far in the distance, he could see the tiny outline of a small image becoming larger and larger as it approached. He rubbed his eyes to be certain that what he was seeing was real, as it continued to make its way steadily toward the platform. He finally sat cross-legged on the stone floor and watched the image, as it glided on the wind currents approaching the tower where he was seated.

Soon, he was able to distinguish some kind of large white bird, larger it seemed than any bird he had ever seen before.

After a few minutes, the great white bird circled the platform several times, as if it were identifying him. Then it came to rest in front of him and stood a few feet away. It had great yellow eyes that very slowly blinked, staring directly at Ammon. He recognized it as a great arctic owl. He had never seen such an immaculate creature, standing more than two to three feet tall. The owl was beautiful, stark, and white.

As he reached out to touch the owl, it stepped away and off the platform, disappearing, a moment later rising into the air above the prince. Without hesitation, it flew through one of the large open windows into the corridor to the Grand Reception Hall.

༄ ❖ ༄

As Ammon arrived in the hall, he found his father and several Royal Guards, along with a physician attending the king. Looking around the high ceiling, the prince could not see the owl anywhere. He hurriedly related Lady Arianne's warning to his father and sat beside him, carefully observing him, while looking everywhere for the owl.

"Don't worry, son. I'm feeling much better." As the king finished speaking, he smiled reassuringly at Ammon.

"Your Majesty!" one of the guards said with alarm, as he pointed toward the top of the hall. The owl had left its perch on the highest rafter and, with its impressive six-foot wingspan, dove through the air at a great speed, landing on the long table directly in front of the king, and then blinked slowly. The Royal Guards were taken aback and immediately drew their swords.

"Put those swords away!" the king commanded, as he reached out and gently stroked the beautiful white bird.

The prince immediately smiled in wonder at the sight of the great owl. "Ammon," the king said, as he stroked the great owl again, "meet our friend and messenger, Hermes.

He is the friend and companion of Orestros, and if I'm not mistaken," the king said, reaching under the feathers of the owl's leg, "he has brought us word from our true and very brave friend." King Hyperion paused and revealed a small rolled note.

"Guard, go to the royal chef and ask him to prepare some choice strips of rabbit for our friend. He has no doubt traveled a great distance to bring us word from Orestros, and he must be hungry. Make haste." The guard immediately left the hallway and sealed the door behind him.

The king then motioned the prince to move closer, as he carefully unrolled the note. The owl flew to a large beam, far above the table and watched everyone carefully. The king pulled one of the candleholders closer; the large ivory candle burning in it brightly illuminated the table in front of them. He looked at the note briefly and then handed it to Ammon, "Tell us what Orestros has said, son."

The prince began to read aloud, "Your Majesty, our worst fears have been realized. Master Deimos has been consumed with his evil magic and is laying waste to his dominion and all those with the misfortune of falling into his hands. Even more tragic, I found Queen Thalia in his darkest and most dreadful dungeon. My attempt to free her was unsuccessful, and she ordered me to escape and send word to you and the prince. For now at least, she is alive and safe. Forgive me, sire, for failing to free her. I will be arriving at the palace soon after you receive this. Forgive my failure. All will be explained. Your loyal subject, Orestros."

"If Orestros failed, it was not for lack of trying," the king said. "He is the bravest of any man I know. I pray he is not gravely wounded and will be prepared for the journey ahead." He then took the note from Ammon and tucked it into his sleeve.

"What now, Father? Where will you send Orestros next?"

"To the surface of Earth, Ammon, this very day, if possible. You, Orestros, Lady Arianne, and Aleah will depart as soon as he arrives and Lady Arianne is ready to travel."

"But what about Mother? Won't you go after her now that we know where she is?" Ammon asked, fearful and confused.

"For now, I must know that you are safe. If Orestros failed in his attempt to rescue her, the task and method of our next attempt must be without error. I firmly believe that Deimos will not harm her, at least for the time being, and that he will most certainly send spies and assassins for you and me. I'm doing what's best for all, Ammon. You must follow my instructions to the letter. When the time is right, I promise, you will be present for your Mother's rescue and the well-deserved justice for Master Deimos."

Chapter Seven

Deimos prodded and spurred his black stallion toward the high mountains until it stumbled and nearly collapsed. Heavy sweat saturated its dark black mane, and heavy white foam saturated the silver bit in its mouth. The stallion's ears were drawn back in fear and exhaustion, as it gasped for air amid the black smoke from hundreds of torches and fires raging throughout the countryside. Deimos repeatedly dug his sharp spurs into the magnificent stallion's sides, as he commanded it from one direction to the next, shouting orders and lashing his long black whip at soldiers hurrying from one search area to the next.

Soldiers called out sightings of Orestros in two or three different directions at once; until they finally agreed he must have taken a difficult path, a terribly steep and treacherous one, especially in the night. Stumbling and out of breath, most of the foot soldiers soon fell behind, as horsemen whipped their horses to try to keep up with Orestros. Bloodhounds were the closest but even they stopped and rested, unable to overcome the tall cliffs, where the scent disappeared, though horsemen had seen glimpses of the giant using ropes to scale the high stone cliffs. Foot soldiers, horsemen, and dogs eventually gathered further up the mountainside at the large opening of a cavern, where Orestros had disappeared.

Arriving there, Deimos dismounted and called for large kegs of black powder to be placed at the entrance and in the snow on the high ledge above it. As the fuses were lit, he mounted his horse, rode to a safe distance, and then watched as the explosions thundered through the mountainside and sealed the opening. A few minutes later, an even larger explosion sent shockwaves through the air. Dozens of his soldiers and horses perished in the fall of boulders and rocks.

A slow and deep rumble began after the second blast of explosions and, looking far above the cavern's rubble where the opening had been, Deimos could see entire ridges of snow cascading down the mountainside, as one after another avalanche covered everyone and everything in their path. Deimos smiled, his eyes gleaming in the glow of the Prism's night sky, as torches and more fire spread into the forest from the explosions. The faces of men dying and screaming were illuminated all around him.

An unexpected final blast shook Deimos and, as his stallion reared up, he was thrown to the ground. He climbed onto its back again and laughed, "No one could survive that!" With his tarnished silver armor gleaming in the torchlight, he was heedless to the moans and cries coming from his own soldiers, many injured and some dying from the repeated concussions.

He reined the black stallion around and dug his spurs into its sides. As his stallion reared in agony and fear, its nostrils flaring, Deimos lashed several of his own men needlessly with his whip, while laughing maniacally. "Search the rubble and the surrounding trees!" he shouted. "If there's a body, I want it found! If there's a piece of the giant's body, I want it found!"

Reining his stallion in a complete circle, Deimos then released a frightful scream, which echoed throughout the forest, as the dust and snow were still settling. Again digging his spurs into the stallion, he raced toward his dark and ominous castle in the distance. As he rode, he tried to remember an old friend's advice, but it eluded him.

❧ ❖ ☙

When Deimos arrived at the castle, he turned his spent stallion over to the stable master and, throwing his gloves to the ground, proceeded to his private chambers where he bathed and dressed in his most becoming robes. Combing his long blonde hair, he spread scented oil on his arms, legs, and chest. His valet carefully shaved him, removing his scraggly dark brown beard and leaving only a well-groomed mustache.

Deimos then put on a blue-and-white silk shirt which gave him the impression of a fine gentleman and knight. Over the shirt, he wore a highly polished silver vestment of chain mail. His knee-high, highly polished black boots were adorned with bold silver buckles. Around his neck he wore a long ornately crafted silver chain with a medallion, inset with the symbol of his authority: a very large and brightly shining diamond, shaped like what once was called a 'star' from ancient legends of Earth.

As Deimos looked into a brilliantly polished platter of pure silver, which reflected his image perfectly, he admired himself for nearly an hour. He donned a large dark blue calotte, a skullcap, with a small single white feather attached to one side.

He walked confidently toward the dungeons. Upon arriving on the long ledge above the leech-filled pools, he summoned the lead guard and spoke to him softly in a very reasonable tone. The guard had never seen such behavior from Master Deimos, nor had he ever seen him dressed in such a fashion.

As the guard accompanied Master Deimos to the row of cells near Queen Thalia, Deimos spoke to several other guards requesting certain things be done. His voice was calm and his speech polite, rather than his usual screaming and shouting. The surprised guards followed his directions without delay, and

Deimos quietly returned to his suite in the castle tower, far above the wretched squalor and stench of the dungeons.

The personal guards of Master Deimos approached Queen Thalia's cell door. These guards were well-groomed and conducted themselves as gentlemen.

"Lady, please come with us. Master Deimos has demanded your immediate release," one of the two guards offered as they opened the heavy rusted door.

Sitting in a corner on a thin layer of straw, Queen Thalia struggled to stand but held her head regally, as she stepped awkwardly toward the doorway. The two guards ran to her side and assisted her, as she stepped through the doorway, simple steps which she had thought she would never make. Aside from her brief and hurried exposure to the outside world with Orestros, she had not seen the Prism light of day or night, cascading through the emerald sky, in nearly two months. Still, in the dark recesses of the dungeon, she dreamed from memory of how it would appear.

Unable to walk far without assistance, the guards respectfully helped her up the long winding staircases, allowing her to rest at times and offering her sips of fresh spring water. She didn't understand what was happening or why the guards had changed, but she recognized that their voices were different, kinder, and gentler than the harsh, angry voices she had heard during her long imprisonment.

As she stumbled and nearly collapsed, after ascending a particularly long staircase, the guards again offered her assistance and fresh water. The younger guard produced a clean cloth and wiped her brow as he knelt down beside her. The reason for their kind treatment finally occurred to her. 'They are taking me out for my execution,' she thought, carefully looking into the eyes and faces of her guards.

"Why are you doing this to me? If you want to execute me, why not do so in the filthy dungeon where you've imprisoned me? Must you display my death for all to see?" she managed to speak with one of her last threads of dignity.

"Queen Thalia," one of the guards replied, "Master Deimos has returned and upon learning of your imprisonment has ordered your immediate release. We're not taking you to an execution but rather to special rooms that are being prepared for you. Please, Your Majesty, help us if you can, but we are prepared, if necessary, to assist or carry you. A physician is waiting for you in your private rooms. Master Deimos is terribly concerned about you and awaits you at your earliest convenience."

Queen Thalia looked at the two guards in disbelief, "Thank you, "she said with a fervent authority and natural dignity, "but since your master has decided to take my life, I would prefer to maintain what dignity I still possess by walking." She then raised her full-length, tattered, and dirty white lace-embellished skirt, so that it did not brush against the grimy stone steps.

∾❖ৎ

When Queen Thalia finally arrived in the rooms that Master Deimos had prepared for her, she found two young and very beautiful maidens waiting for her. Dressed in long, sheer white raiment, they immediately approached her, stated their names with delicate and articulate voices, and then bowed and presented themselves on one knee, awaiting her acceptance and response.

"Please rise," Queen Thalia said, as she motioned them to stand and then seated herself at a dining table filled with freshly prepared melons, fruits, sweetened breads, and cheeses of many varieties and colors, intended to please the eye as well as the palate. She removed a white linen napkin from its silver ring and placed the napkin in her lap. With a small fork, she placed several slices of honeydew melon on her plate. Taking a small bite, she turned toward the guards.

"May I assume that you have been instructed to remain with me until the execution?"

"My Lady," said one of the guards with a genuine and warming smile, "allow me to assure you once again you that there will be no execution. Since there is nothing further that we can do for you, we will retire to the corridor outside and await any request that you may have. Until then, we leave you in the very capable hands of these two maidens." He then dropped to one knee, and side by side the guards bowed and left the dining area, closing the heavy double doors behind them.

"My Lady?" asked one of the maidens

"Yes, Alexandra, isn't it?" Queen Thalia replied.

"Rosalyn," she replied. "That is Alexandra," motioning to the other maiden.

"Of course, excuse me," Queen Thalia replied.

"We have drawn a bath for you and laid out clean clothes for you, if you'd like to follow me."

Queen Thalia took several bites of melon and then drank from a blue glass goblet of fresh water. "I would like that very much," she replied and followed Rosalyn through a white linen curtain, where she found a large black and white marble bathing pool. Several beautiful dresses and robes were laid out on a table near a balcony overlooking the village far below.

"If you'll leave your garments beside the table, I'll have them cleaned and returned. I believe you'll find soaps and oils, and lotions and combs for your hair, beside the pool. If you require anything more, merely call out. I'll be seated there," Rosalyn said, pointing to an ornately upholstered chair beside the linen curtain.

"Thank you, Rosalyn. Do you have the authority to get me a large glass of fresh water and an orange?"

"Of course, My Lady. I'll get them immediately. Will there be anything else?"

"No, thank you, Rosalyn. I'm afraid that it will take some time to wash the filth of your master's dungeon from my hair and body."

"Of course, My Lady, take all of time you need. Master Deimos is anxious to see you, but he instructed us to make certain that you are not rushed and have everything you need."

"I see," Queen Thalia responded, as she removed her ragged clothes and threw them on the floor before slowly entering the bathing pool. "Rosalyn?"

"Yes, My Lady?"

"Please burn these clothes and be careful not to allow anyone to touch them without taking precautions."

"Of course, My Lady. I'll return with fresh drinking water and an orange in a moment," she answered and disappeared behind the curtains, ruffling in the gentle breeze from the balcony.

Queen Thalia submerged her head and body in the soothing water of the scented pool and, rising up, pulled her long brown hair behind her ears. She noticed a goblet of cool spring water and a peeled orange sitting on the ledge of the pool and took a large drink, then separated a segment of the juicy orange and took a bite. The orange refreshed her palate. "Thank you Rosalyn, it's been so long since I've had fresh water and fruit."

"You're welcome, Queen Thalia," replied a deep voice.

Queen Thalia quickly turned around.

"I didn't mean to startle you, Your Majesty. You can relax. I'm facing the other direction. I came just to make sure that you are being taken care of."

"Deimos!" Queen Thalia gasped in fear, as she pulled a towel into the pool water and covered herself.

"As I said, I didn't mean to alarm you. When you've finished bathing, I hoped you might join me for supper. Merely send word with Rosalyn or Alexandra."

Queen Thalia tightly wrapped the towel around her under the water, but when she looked up, Deimos had vanished. "Rosalyn!" she screamed.

"Yes, My Lady," Rosalyn responded, as she entered with a goblet of fresh water and a peeled orange.

"Is he gone?" Queen Thalia asked frantically.

"Is who gone, My Lady?" Rosalyn offered, looking around the curtains and then back toward the room. "There's no one here, except the two of us. Alexandra has gone to gather more clothes for you."

"Your Master Deimos was here. Look! He brought water and an orange," Queen Thalia pointed to where she had set the goblet beside the orange, but the only goblet and orange in sight were those that Rosalyn held in her hands. "I don't understand. I must be losing my mind. Please gather my clothes and bring them here at once."

Rosalyn set the goblet of water and the orange beside the pool and retrieved towels, which she also placed on the edge. She then assisted Queen Thalia from the pool and into the cover of the soft, plush towels.

"Did you actually see Master Deimos, My Lady?" Rosalyn asked, hesitating when the curtains nearly covered her as they fluttered in the cool breeze.

"No, but I heard his voice as clearly as I hear yours now," Queen Thalia replied sharply.

"Excuse me, My Lady," Rosalyn said, as she stepped quickly toward the balcony and shouted, "Shoo! Get away from here!"

"What is it?" Queen Thalia asked urgently.

"It's a large black bird, a crow I think. He comes around from time to time. Nothing to be worried about. Let me help you get dressed. I'm sure Master Deimos would not enter your bathing room unannounced. He's always so very polite to all of the women in the towers. He has ordered that you be cared for, above all."

"I heard a voice. We'll see about Master Deimos," Queen Thalia said flatly, as Rosalyn assisted her into a clean white gown and a soft, green and white robe which fell all the way to the floor.

"Will there be anything else, My Lady?" Rosalyn asked shyly.

"Not for now. You've been kind. Can you tell me what Master Deimos has in mind for me next?" Queen Thalia whispered.

"After I have assisted you, I'm to inform Master Deimos and, when you're ready, escort you to his dining chamber."

"Give me awhile to rest if you can," Queen Thalia requested.

"Of course," Rosalyn bowed slightly and left the room, closing the doors behind her. Queen Thalia could hear the door lock a moment later.

She walked to the balcony and leaned on the railing, looking up into the azure and emerald green of the Prism sky. Torch lights cast a yellow-orange glow far below. In a lighted window in another tower not far below her, she saw a large black raven fly through the open window. A moment later, the dark image of a black-bearded man, dressed in black robes, leaned out of the window and looked up directly at the queen.

She immediately stepped away from the balcony, as a sense of fear and peril overcame her. She started to slowly return to the balcony to see if he was still there. As she peeked over the railing, she finally saw the window, but no one was there. Suddenly the light of the window's room went out.

She ran to the doors and struggled, trying to open them, but the locks were secure and the doors did not budge. She returned to balcony and looked to the distant mountains, wishing that Orestros had escaped and would bring help soon.

From the window below, she saw a brief glimmer of light and, a moment later, the glow of embers slightly illuminating a face. It then disappeared, followed by the trail of smoke as if someone was smoking a pipe. She was certain she was being watched and quickly looked back toward the mountains, before leaving the balcony and the prying eyes of the man in the window.

Chapter Eight

Orestros had managed to descend far into the cavern before the first explosion sealed the entrance. Fire roared into the mountainside, sucking and burning the air from within. Orestros gasped for air, as the second explosion and avalanche forcibly threw his body still further into its depths, rendering him unconscious for what he guessed to be several hours.

Finally awakening to the utter silence of the underground cavern, he groped through the absolute darkness and felt snow and broken tree limbs but no trace of his climbing ropes. His knapsack still hung by one strap to his back and, rummaging through it, he found enough dry cloth to fashion a torch by wrapping the cloth around one of the broken tree limbs.

A warm, steady stream of liquid clouded and burned his left eye. Reaching up, he tasted blood and felt a deep wound on his forehead. Taking a large handful of snow, mixed with mud, he packed it onto the wound and held it tightly for several long agonizing minutes until the bleeding finally stopped. With his head throbbing and his legs unable to move beneath the weight of snow, rock, and mud, he managed to find his flint and quickly lit the torch. As it finally produced a flame, he held it into the space above him.

The cavern opened up nearly twenty feet overhead. He looked for familiar signs and formations of rock but found none. He carefully watched the flames and smoke from his torch, hoping they might indicate a breeze or an opening where fresh air might be entering the cavern, but they went straight toward the ceiling. The air was fresh and he was relieved but looking up along the walls of the cavern, he saw no possible way to climb out.

It took nearly two hours of digging to uncover his legs. At last able to stand, he extinguished his torch and, using the limb as a makeshift cane, slowly made his way further into the cavern. Lost and disoriented, Orestros constantly looked for any small gleam of light from above.

He tried to estimate the passage of time, to know when the Prism sky would be the brightest and possibly show him a way out. He walked and stumbled forward, hoping his estimations of day and night were correct. Before collapsing after each prolonged march through the darkness, he marked the direction he was traveling, so as not to retreat when he awoke.

He figured that he had traveled nearly two days and nights in the darkness of rugged rocks where no path could be found, when he withdrew a small, hand-carved whistle from the inside his boot leg. He cleaned the whistle by his fading torchlight and blew into it. No sound came forth, and he was pleased, knowing that only one creature could hear the silent call. He replaced it in his boot again and re-lit his makeshift torch from time to time to find a clearer way through the ragged stones which cut and bruised him with nearly every step.

The first day, he consumed the last of his dried beef and water. He found small droplets of water falling from hanging stalactites from time to time, as he continued his trek through the cavern. On the second night, he crossed a luminescent pool, and when he touched its water, it reflected a lime green hue. He filled his water pouch with this precious fluid. He saw aqua-green serpents, no longer than one or two feet, slithering around the edges and into the deeper pool.

The course Orestros traveled at last ceased its descent into the mountain, and he could feel the strain of his steps taking him up a steep ascent. He made his way for what he believed to be another day and night. The cloth used to burn his torch came to an end, and he cursed that his ropes had been lost in the explosions and avalanche. Exhausted, and again out of water, he blew his silent whistle with great effort and fell asleep on a large smooth slab of cool rock, awaiting whatever chance or destiny had in store for him in the darkness.

From out of a dream, he heard the first sound of hope and sat up abruptly. He listened hopefully but heard nothing. He blew his whistle again, standing and turning in all directions. At last, "Whoo, whoo" echoed the distant sound of Hermes from far above him. He stepped down from the cool slab of rock and stumbled through the darkness toward the sound, until he reached the wall of the cavern and then followed it, as the distant sound grew a little closer. He blew into the whistle again, and again he heard the reply, "Whoo ... Whoo," closer still. He held out his arm in the darkness and at first heard and then felt the cool swift flapping of air. Finally he felt the heavy bird land on his arm, as its enormous yellow eyes shone and blinked in the semi-darkness.

"Hermes!" Orestros said, as he smiled and stroked the massive white owl.

Orestros emerged from a small opening in the mountains above King Hyperion's palace, before the first bright orange light of the Prism morning.

꧁ ❖ ꧂

Ammon was awakened by his father's personal guards and escorted to the reception hall, where he found the king seated beside the tallest and strongest-looking man he had ever seen.

It had been nearly a year since he had seen Orestros, but there was no mistaking him. Ammon ran the distance of the hall, and Orestros leaned over to embrace him as an old friend. Ammon took a seat near his father and noticed that beside a large plate of fresh fruits and dark brown sweet breads and cheeses in front of Orestros was a small plate containing strips of raw meat.

He stretched his massive arm into the air, and the great white owl swooped down from a beam in the high ceiling. He placed a strip of the meat near the owl's beak, and it was immediately devoured. He placed another piece before the great owl, and the owl took it in its very large and sharp talons, before taking several steps down the table. With three great flaps of its enormous wings, it rose into the air and landed on a wooden beam far above them.

As all three men were seated at the long table, a most serious expression came over the faces of the king and Orestros. The king looked at Orestros and then nodded toward Ammon. "He has a right to know."

Orestros leaned forward and, resting his hands on his forehead for a moment, looked up with a pained expression and proceeded to tell the prince what he had seen and how he had attempted to rescue the queen. Ammon fought back his anger, as Orestros described the dungeon, the leeches, and the horrible sights he had seen in the countryside. "I watched from above as long as I could," Orestros said, "and I'm sure they took care not to injure her."

The king placed his arm around Ammon for a moment. He leaned his elbows on the table and covered his face in his hands.

"Our course of action is clear," the king said, as he stood and scratched his chin. "Tomorrow, Orestros, if you're able…"

Orestros interrupted, "I'm able now."

"Still," the king continued, "you and Lady Arianne shall rest while Ammon, Aleah, and I secretly gather supplies and implements for a journey to the Earth's surface, one which may be extended."

"Earth!" exclaimed Orestros, as Ammon looked up with equal surprise.

"Yes," the king said with authority. "There's no doubt in my mind that Deimos will make attempts on my life, as well on the prince. From what you tell me, I'm also convinced that he believes that you, Orestros, have died in the explosions and avalanche. That will be to our benefit. Until the armies are gathered; until a plan is formulated to enter those regions of the Prism that Deimos controls; until we know who his allies are, the safest plan is to send you to Earth until the time is right for your return. In the event of disaster, we may need to retreat to Earth and re-gather our strength. A passage must be found beyond the limits of the travel chamber, Orestros. I leave that to you and Ammon."

"Your Majesty, there is so little known of Earth's surface. Might not our energies be better used in stopping Deimos here and now in the confines of his own dominion?" Orestros argued.

"My decision has been made. With the first bright orange of Prism light, the four of you will depart with ample supplies and return only when I send word through the travel chamber, whether it is a day or a year. With grace and luck and careful thought, Deimos will be in chains upon your return, and the queen will stand before you in welcome. All must be ready at the appointed hour."

As the three walked toward the door, Ammon paused a moment, trying to remember something he wanted to tell his father, but the anticipation of the following day's journey clouded his mind.

Orestros called out to him from the corridor, "Prince Ammon, come along. I'll help you gather the supplies we'll need."

Ammon wanted to stay and think for a moment, as he turned back toward the green drapes that enclosed the travel chamber, and then part of the thought returned to him as he ran to catch up with his father.

"Father, what of Axel? Will he be joining us tomorrow?"

"He has not been seen in many days, Ammon. It is thought that he has gone somewhere with Princess Leda. Either way, we cannot delay. When he does return, he will be severely punished without an explanation. Perhaps we can send him afterward, if all is well."

"Do you suspect that Deimos is responsible for his disappearance?" Ammon asked, fearful that Axel and even Princess Leda might be held captive in Deimos's wretched dungeons.

"Anything is possible. Time will no doubt reveal all," the king said, his mind consumed with all that had occurred in last few months, and the preparations necessary for the trials yet to come.

Chapter Nine

As the bright orange Prism sky broke into the emerald and blue hues of night, large droplets of moisture fell like crystal snowflakes, cascading and disappearing as they scattered across the horizon. A subtle change began to sweep across the villages. Millions of souls throughout the Prism arose from their beds, wiped the sleep from their eyes, and splashed fresh aqua-green water on their faces, still yawning and considering the day before them.

In the palace above, the lower gates were opened wide, as messengers came forth and were received, as the king's guards and workers carried load after load of food and newly hemmed garments to and from the village squares for those in need or hungry. Those without means, after eating their fill, followed others into the lush open fields, where they cultivated and planted seeds in the rich brown soil, revealing tiny white granules and glittering nutrients from deep within the mountain's caverns. The seeds grew rapidly in the enriched soil, and green lush crops thrived and rustled as their dark green leaves waved in the breeze, beneath the light of the glowing Prism skies.

Ammon, having awakened early from a restless sleep, looked from his tower window and imagined the lives of the people below, whom he knew were unaware of the dangers and struggles he and his friends were about to undertake. Firm knocks at his door returned him from his thoughts, as Orestros entered his sleeping chamber and joined him at the window, placing a firm hand on Ammon's shoulder. The prince felt comfort and security having his friend beside him.

In a voice aged with experience and wisdom, Orestros said just above a whisper, "I often wonder how such terrible things can happen in a world which holds such beauty and promise." He grasped Ammon's shoulder firmly, still staring into the distance. "Perhaps it's up to you, the prince, to make these things right."

"What can I do?" Ammon asked, looking up at Orestros, still gazing into the distance.

"The right thing, Young Prince, not just for yourself but for all of those below that depend on you," Orestros said, looking down at the prince and smiling gently. "I'll be here to help you when I can, and if you are true and wise, others will follow."

"I don't think I'm ready," Ammon said distantly, as if speaking to himself.

"No one is ever ready, Prince Ammon. Have faith in what you've learned and know what's right and what's wrong. Make that choice and all will be well. Sometimes you may feel that all is lost, but it never is as long as you know the truth and care for others," Orestros said and then waved his large hand, gesturing to the villages below. "Their lives will depend on your faith and commitment to peace and compassion, the same commitment that your father has shown them throughout his life."

He then turned Ammon away from the window. "It's time to get going. We still have preparations to complete. Shall we begin?"

Ammon looked at Orestros. "Will you help me?"

"Of course, come on, let's get started." He smiled and placed his massive hand on Ammon's shoulder as he quickly grasped his dagger from the footstool by his bed and put it into his belt.

≈ ❖ ≈

When Orestros and Ammon entered the hall, King Hyperion, Arianne, and Aleah were already present. Looking at the travel chamber, Aleah was noticeably nervous but showed some relief, as she saw the prince and Orestros arrive. Two Royal Guards and Orestros loaded several more heavy boxes into the chamber. The guards, well-known to Ammon, were armed with swords and packs containing their own travel provisions.

No one noticed a small corner in the back of the chamber, surrounded by crates and boxes, where a large cloak covered a form which moved slightly from time to time. From beneath the cloak, muffled sounds came forth but were undetected in the sounds of the travelers' activities, as they moved their personal belongings and talked among themselves.

Before closing the door, King Hyperion stepped into the doorway. "All of you know what's expected of you. Above all else, you must remain safe until I send for you. It may be a day or a year, but I will send messages. In the meantime, Orestros will attempt to secure another path which was written about before the Prism was created. Remember, be safe and help one another."

Ammon embraced his father briefly, before he closed the door to the chamber. Ammon grasped Aleah's hand, and then pulled his medallion from beneath his silver chain mail shirt and held it above his head. The crystal inside the medallion began to shine brightly. Everyone, especially the guards, who had never been in the chamber before, looked nervously at one another as the medallion shone with an almost blinding white light, causing the glowing light blue fluid to fill the chamber.

As the sapphire blue eruptions began to randomly fill the fluid and quickly cover their heads, something odd began to occur. Instead of the soothing fluid that had covered them each time before, the temperature was cold and becoming colder by the moment. Ammon looked through the fluid but couldn't see any of the other travelers. He slowly felt

Aleah's hand slipping from his grasp, until she was gone. He reached wildly through the fluid, but it had become so cold that he had difficulty moving his arms at all.

Large bubbles emerged from the bottom of the chamber, forcibly propelling Ammon into one wall after another and pushing him into bodies and crates, although he could not distinguish who or what they were. Grabbing hold of something, which seemed to be moving beside him in the swirling fluid, he pulled it closer to his face to see what it was. Finally focusing through the freezing blue fluid, he saw two red eyes and then the sharp teeth of a large rat as it tried to bite him. He pushed it away in fear and horror.

A moment later, as he was again hurled into a wall, the corner of a very large crate strike him in the head and, afterward, all that he sensed was his body shivering from the freezing cold. As he felt a deep gash on the side of his head, small shining points of light seemed to appear in his peripheral vision. He felt very sleepy, when suddenly a firm and powerful hand grabbed hold of his arm.

The next thing he felt was a cloth, wiping the blue fluid away from his face, as he coughed more of the fluid from deep within his lungs. He managed to turn on his side as he curled up and felt a soft substance. His eyes began to focus, and he could see the green surface below him. As he felt it, a powerfully bright yellow light consumed everything around him.

"Orestros!" he called out, his voice quivering from the cold.

"I'm here. We're safe, perhaps," Orestros said with caution and acute awareness, as he used all of his senses to see the strange world around them. "You need to awaken. Something terrible has happened, and I'm not sure if it's safe here." Orestros tried to shield his eyes from the bright, intense yellow light.

"Are we still in the chamber?" Ammon asked, still shivering and unable to see clearly, as he raised his arms to protect his eyes from the burning light. "Where are Aleah and Arianne? Are the guards all right?" he feverishly asked, as he felt the ground around him and tried to see through the blinding light.

"Cover your eyes, Prince Ammon. I've never seen light like this. I don't see anyone else, but I'm certain that we are not in the chamber." Orestros's voice registered deep concern.

He pulled his backpack to the ground and rummaged through it for his water pouch. Using a knife from his belt, he dug into the soft ground beneath them. Out of the small hole he had dug, he poured a small portion of aqua-green water and with his hands mixed the water with the substance into a smooth muddy mixture. He closed his eyes and rubbed the mixture on his eyelids, and then repeated the same to Ammon's eyelids. They both continued to shield their eyes, though the mixture seemed to help them see the world around them.

"What place is this?" Ammon asked, looking around at the strangely colored sights, while still shielding his eyes.

"I've never seen it before, Prince Ammon, but I believe this is Earth." Orestros looked in wonder at the different colors and at the blue sky.

"Why is it so bright? I can barely see," the prince asked, looking toward the ground.

"It's the sun. You can never look directly at it, the legends say. If you do, you'll be blinded forever."

"I don't like this place, Orestros. It's not what I expected. I thought Earth would be beautiful but now I can barely see. We should go back; we can't survive in this place."

Ammon looked along the ground he was laying upon and noticed the form and tunic of one of the guards. "Do you see him over there?" He pointed to the figure in the distance.

"Stay here," Orestros whispered, as he ran to the figure lying on the ground.

Ammon watched Orestros carefully try to rouse the guard and then lay the guard's tunic over his face, before running back to the prince.

"He's dead, isn't he?" Ammon said sadly.

"I'm afraid so, but he left us with more food and water, also tools," Orestros said, as he looked through the guard's pack.

"If he's dead, what about the other guard and Aleah and Lady Arianne?"

"We'll begin searching for them, as soon as you're able to travel or I can find a safe place for you," Orestros said, still alertly watching in every direction for danger or the remote possibility of help. "Do you hear the sound of water over there?" He motioned to a distant ridge.

"I think so," Ammon replied. "We've got to find the others."

"As soon as we're safe, I'll begin the search," Orestros said with authority.

"Don't let me slow you down. I can take care of myself," the prince said, as he struggled to his feet and tried to take a few steps before becoming dizzy and grasping his wounded head. Orestros held him up until he could stand on his own. "I'm all right. Let's go." The prince stepped awkwardly but managed to pick up the guard's pack and continue toward the sound of the water.

With each few steps, his sight improved, and he realized that they were walking through a field of lush green grass up to his knees. He had seen grass before but never as green as this, nor as tall. All of the colors seemed similar but different. Blue flowers grew out of the long grass in a color he had only seen in the Prism skies.

"My eyes are getting better. Have you noticed the colors?" Ammon asked, as he noticed that Orestros was no longer at his side. "Orestros?" he called out.

A few feet away he heard, "Shhh! Stay down low! There's something out there and getting closer."

Ammon crouched in the grass, looked in the direction of his friend's voice, and then slowly crept toward it.

"Where are you? Maybe it's Aleah, and the others," he whispered but before he could say another word, Orestros's massive hand covered his mouth.

"It's not them! Stay perfectly still and quiet," Orestros whispered into Ammon's ear. He could hear the grass being trampled on, as several large creatures moved in from several directions. Suddenly, he heard a wild screech erupt from the silence. It almost sounded like a scream, but something about it sent a shiver down his spine and raised goose bumps on his arms. As he pulled the guard's pack onto his shoulder, along with his own, it caused a slight rustle in the grass. Immediately several more violent shrieks came from a short distance from where he and Orestros had been huddled close to the ground.

A large creature flew through the air and landed on Orestros's back, sinking fangs two to three inches long into his shoulder. Blood sprayed into the air and across Ammon's face. Orestros hurled the creature to the ground with such force that it did not move again.

"Quickly, Prince Ammon, go to the water. Don't wait for me. The other creatures will be on us in a few seconds. Swim until you are in deep water far from the banks. That's your best chance at survival." Orestros pulled a long knife from his belt and pushed Ammon, pointing in the direction of the running water. "Run, now! Run like you've never run before and don't stop, no matter what!" he shouted, as another one of the large creatures flew through the air, its fangs exposed, and attacked Orestros.

Ammon ran and stumbled through the grass, all the while hearing strange growling and heavy breathing not far behind him. Though it was still difficult to see in the bright yellow light, he finally reached the banks of a body of flowing water and leapt into it without hesitation. Looking back, as he swam deeper into the water, he saw one of the creatures standing upright and screaming at him. He had never seen such a creature. It stood nearly five feet tall and had a bright red face and mane with large tufts of silvery gray fur on either side of its deep-set black eyes and over the rest of its body. It exposed long, sharp fangs, screaming as if in a murderous rage.

The backpacks helped to keep Ammon afloat, as he swam with steady strokes toward the opposite banks of the water. He finally lifted himself and his packs onto the muddy shore. After carefully looking in all directions, he pulled himself onto the grass. He could no longer see the strange screaming creature, but more importantly, he could see no sign of Orestros.

He tried not to think of what had happened as he drained water from the packs and began to look for some form of shelter from the bright light. Noticing a large stand of somewhat familiar-looking trees in the distance and keeping low as his friend had told him, he began to make his way through the grass. Overwhelming fear began to grip his mind, as he kept alert for the movement of other dangerous creatures. Not yet understanding what had happened or what might happen next, he was certain of one thing: he was completely alone in a very strange and hostile world.

Chapter Ten

In the reception hall, the king, his advisors, and counselors stood before the large green drapes dumbfounded at what they had just seen. The travel chamber lay in complete ruins with no evidence of any survivors or clues as to what had happened to them when everything went wrong. The blue glowing fluid that once filled the chamber now covered the floor of the hall.

Everyone had watched the turmoil within the chamber, as it began to transport its travelers and their supplies to Earth, but there was no way to know what had happened to them after the chamber cracked and shattered into pieces. As they began to talk among themselves, the king returned to his chair at the head of the long table and sat with his hands covering his eyes. The counselors and advisors quickly took their places and silently awaited his instructions.

After a long silence, the physician finally stood and addressed the king, "Your Majesty, I'm not certain if everyone here saw what I did, but I believe I may know the cause of this terrible disaster." He then awaited the king's response.

"If you know something, then enlighten us! That applies to all of you!" the king said, raising his voice with authority.

"It hadn't really occurred to me until I saw something which may confirm it," the physician began.

"Out with it, man! If you know something, tell us!" the king shouted, slamming his fist on the table.

"For just a moment, when the travelers were being thrown about the chamber, I thought I saw that old woman among them. Also, I would swear that I saw a large rat."

An advisor seated near the king stood immediately. "That's not possible. She's not even permitted in this part of the palace, nor was she there when the chamber door was closed."

"Perhaps she was there but not visible. You'll recall there were crates and supplies. She may have hidden amongst them," the physician continued. "If so, and if she's up to her old mischief again, it would certainly explain the problem. What I'm saying, Sire, is that this may have been deliberate and, if so, the travelers probably arrived safely. For her to get to Earth, everyone in chamber must also get there. It's just our ability to pursue or intervene that's been damaged."

"Find the old hag Morgana at once and bring her here!" the king commanded, again slamming his fist onto the table. Several guards walked briskly out of the hall. "Is there anything else?" he asked, looking at the men seated around the table.

"One other item, Sire," the physician said, standing again. "One of the two guards that died said something rather odd. We didn't give it much thought at the time, because he was raging with fever, but he sat up suddenly just before he died and said he saw a pair of green eyes and something about rats. He also mentioned that you, Sire, must be warned. Prince Ammon was there at the time. I felt he would relate that to you if he felt it important." The physician cleared his throat, awkwardly took a drink of water, and returned to his seat.

The king began pacing in back of his chair. "Confine yourself to the infirmary, Physician, for if you are not out of my presence within the next few moments, you will surely be in the dungeon," the king said with absolute authority. He turned to the green drapes where the chamber once stood. "All of you, save the wizards, sorcerers, and any others with the powers of necromancy, be gone or face the penalty of death!"

❦ ❖ ❧

The hall quickly cleared of all but three old men, two of them with long beards and gray hair. The one seated to the left of the king had long streaks of stark white in his hair and a light beard and mustache but was considerably younger than the other two.

"Seal the doors!" the king commanded, and the guards immediately followed his order. A moment after the doors were sealed, the king sat in his chair and glared at the three old men. "Deimos is mounting an army against me. My son, the prince, is lost and may have perished along with three others, all very dear to me as well as important to our future. I would like an explanation! If the prince is dead, all of you know that this Prism world will collapse with all of us trapped within it."

Pelos, the wizard sitting closest to the king, leaned forward, his cat-like yellow eyes gleaming against his gray beard. "Sire, all of us at this table advised you to tell Prince Ammon of the prophecy, that he might understand the need for safety, but you declined to heed our advice for another year. Perhaps your wisdom in this matter has escaped me, though I have witnessed the young prince in reckless behavior on more than one occasion. Still, and more importantly, I believe that he is safe for now. No one knows what awaits him and his fellow travelers on Earth, but at this time, despite our shared concerns, we must direct our attentions to containment of Master Deimos and the rescue of Queen Thalia, else all will be lost."

"I want some assurance that my son is safe. If magic and sorcery must be used, then so be it," the king said, glaring at the three men.

The wizard named Antare, sitting beside Pelos to the right of the king, leaned back into his chair. "We've used the magic of the travel chamber twice, and look at what has happened. Sire, you know the law. If we use magic and ancient incantations, it will surely come back on us!" He leaned forward and stared at the king.

"If we lose the prince, we may all be lost anyway!" the king shouted. "Xandros, you are the necromancer, like your father and his father before. Have you no ideas or sight into how we may see onto the surface of Earth and at least know the condition of the prince and the others?"

Xandros, the third sorcerer, was by far the most mysterious of the three, not merely because of the stark white streaks running through his hair but by the strange aura that seemed to surround him. His robes were gray in the lighted hall but turned as black as a shadow, almost making him invisible, when the lights were dimmed or out. He rarely spoke and was neither trusted nor liked by his fellow sorcerers, though greatly respected and feared, despite his youth.

He at last spoke softly and elegantly, which caused everyone at the table, including the king, to lean forward and listen carefully. "Perhaps if we gather this fluid into a new and much smaller chamber which I can devise, along with ancient incantations, which have unfortunately been outlawed for centuries, it may give us a glimpse into what is occurring on Earth and elsewhere. Meanwhile, let us gather our powers to deceive Master Deimos into the belief that our armies and allies are awaiting his invasion like a trap about to be sprung. Where there are ten soldiers, they will appear to be a hundred. Where we have a hundred, they will appear to be a thousand. Even Deimos will not attack such a formidable force and, if all goes well, we shall have the time needed to bring the illusion into reality, with my guidance and, of course, the king's permission. On the other hand, the prince will soon realize his powers, of this I am certain."

Xandros smiled a cunning smile, closing his eyes ever so slightly, as he looked at those sitting around him. Beneath his thin eyelids, his eyes shone like gleaming steel. "Let us have faith in this vision until we can recall him. Sire, build your armies, we shall create a way to see Earth and use all of our powers to bring about both goals within the passage of one month. With cooperation from Pelos and Antare, I will complete a viewing glass—an imaging board, if you will—to see Earth in a matter of days."

Pelos leaned back from the table and spoke in what seemed to be a loud voice, though normal, after Xandros's soft whispering, "The ancient incantations of which Xandros speaks were destroyed centuries ago. Sorcerers that tried to hide them paid a terrible price, as we all know. Are you saying, Xandros, that despite the law and the penalties, you are in possession of these ... these spells?"

Xandros leaned forward and spoke softly, as if divulging a secret, "If it is the king's will, I will produce these incantations. Is it your will, Sire?"

"Xandros, it is our will. The others will assist you in any way you may require. I want to be advised of your progress and witness as much of your activity as I may. If successful, you will be rewarded above all others."

Xandros merely leaned back in his chair and nodded in agreement. He then expressed the hint of a triumphant smile, while the other two sorcerers looked at one another in surprise and growing suspicion.

After a short silence, one of them finally spoke, "Sire, we are at your service, but there's a reason that those incantations were made illegal and were thought to be destroyed," he said nodding toward Xandros. "If we use this black magic—and, make no mistake, black magic is exactly what it is—then we risk much. I plead with you to at least allow us a few days to forge a plan that extols our goodwill and compassion, not the ancient history of treachery and deceit."

"Show us a plan, sorcerer, and we will take it under advisement. Until then, I command you to assist Xandros in his plan, withholding nothing. Time is quickly running out, and action outweighs consideration." The king pushed his chair from the table and walked resolutely out of the hall.

After the doors were closed behind the king, Xandros stood and addressed his colleagues, "If you two will collect the chamber's fluid in a temporary container, I will retire to my tower and begin work on the glass imaging board."

He began to walk toward the door, when Pelos interrupted him. "How do you propose we collect the fluid from the floor?" he said, smiling, considering he had finally outwitted Xandros.

"Undoubtedly the palace cleaning servants will loan you both mops. That would be my suggestion, but you may of course design another approach if it better suits you. I believe the king would frown, however, at allowing cleaning servants to accomplish such an important task. Thank you. I will return shortly to inspect your work and the clarity of the fluid." Xandros smiled mischievously and exited the hall.

Chapter Eleven

Rosalyn found Queen Thalia asleep when she returned and promptly informed Master Deimos that the queen was exhausted and difficult to arouse, probably due to her experience in the dungeon. She then suggested very humbly that Deimos allow her to sleep. He agreed with his servant.

Rosalyn remained at the queen's side throughout the night and gently awakened her with tender reassurances when she observed the queen experiencing frightful nightmares, frequently calling out, "King Hyperion" and "Prince Ammon."

When the queen fully awoke to the deep orange mixed with dark and bright blue hues of the Prism's morning sky, she sat up and stretched her arms. Rosalyn appeared and placed freshly peeled oranges from the palace gardens on the bed beside the queen, and hot tea on a small table next to her bed. Queen Thalia looked carefully at the delicate white dishes with their dark and richly defined red borders. Remembering where she was, she looked around suspiciously, as she sipped the hot tea and ate small bites of the juicy oranges.

"How long have I been asleep?" she asked Rosalyn.

"Since early last night. I thought it best that you sleep and regain your strength. I told Master Deimos, and he agreed that it would be for the best," Rosalyn answered. "He's very concerned about you and is determined to find those responsible for your inconsiderate treatment and imprisonment."

"And when did your master return to the palace?" Queen Thalia inquired.

"I'm not aware of the exact time, though I did see him ride through the gates last night. You were brought here to this tower not long afterward, and he instructed all of us that you were to receive the very best care. He was also seen harshly scolding several of his advisors and guards. I assume because he found out that you had been imprisoned and treated so badly in his absence." Rosalyn smiled sweetly and poured Queen Thalia more of the dark tea from an exquisite white ceramic pot, also decorated in the same deep red colors.

"That sounds beautifully rehearsed. Is that what your master told you to say?" Queen Thalia whispered to Rosalyn softly, as if exchanging a secret between two close friends. She then sipped her tea and looked at Rosalyn and her surroundings with suspicion.

Before Rosalyn could respond, a firm knock came at the door across the room. "Shall I answer, My Lady?" she whispered, as she helped Queen Thalia into a luxurious red robe.

"Of course," Queen Thalia responded in a normal tone. "No need to avoid the inevitable. I believe we both know who it is." She then stood in a very dignified manner and walked confidently to the balcony with her teacup in hand and looked down onto the open palace grounds. She noticed a large number of well-armed soldiers coming and going through the gates.

Rosalyn walked briskly across the room and opened the door, and then bowed respectfully, as Master Deimos entered and walked directly to Queen Thalia. He bowed his head and lowered himself to one knee, conspicuously dramatizing his submission and unwavering loyalty and respect. The queen acknowledged him, but she withdrew her hand before he could kiss her ring. At the same moment, again she heard the pounding hoofs of a large number of horses entering through the gates below her balcony.

"Thank you, My Lady, for receiving me. I'm glad to see that you are recovering from your ordeal," he said, standing proudly a few feet from her. She looked at him sternly before returning her gaze to the snow-capped mountains. "I trust your needs are being met?" he asked humbly.

"After a very unpleasant stay in your cruel dungeon, anything would be an improvement," Queen Thalia stated firmly, without looking back at Deimos.

"Queen Thalia, that such an offense has taken place is beyond understanding and, though I was away pursuing an army of very dangerous raiders and rebels, ultimately I am responsible for all that happens here. I humbly ask your forgiveness and pray that you'll allow me and all of the subjects at my command to serve you and to show you our unending affection and celebrated capacity for hospitality."

Queen Thalia placed her teacup on the balcony ledge and turned to face him. "Master Deimos, do you actually expect me to believe that this is a terrible misunderstanding and that you had nothing to do with my kidnapping and imprisonment?" she said, glaring at him.

"My Lady, that my men were able to rescue you from the raiders was nearly a miracle. I interrogated the officers responsible for your rescue. They assured me that they had no idea as to your identity, and assumed that you were one of the rebels. Fortunately an officer in the prison suspected that you were far too refined to be a rebel and reported your presence to me when I returned from battle with the raiders last night."

"You're saying that these raiders or rebels were responsible for my kidnapping?" Queen Thalia asked, raising one eyebrow skeptically.

"I'm afraid so, My Lady. We are in the process of interrogating the rebels that were captured with you at this very moment, but they have not been of much help in the past," Deimos responded as he stepped beside her and gazed at the mountains. "It may be of some consolation for you to know that I've sent a small group of my best soldiers and diplomats to the king to inform him that you are safe and under my protection. Unfortunately, it will take them at least a week to travel the distance, assuming they are able to get through the rebel territory."

"Master Deimos, why is it that the king and I have heard nothing of these so-called rebels before? Need I remind you, it is your sworn duty to inform the king of any such rebellion? There has never been such a rebellion in the entire history of the Prism, because rebellions are generally formed as a last resort to injustice. If such a rebellion has arisen, one must ask oneself 'Why?' Have you engaged these rebels in a reasonable dialogue or determined their reasons for such extreme and deliberate acts against the king?"

"My Lady, these rebels are barbaric! Their goals are looting and lawlessness. I have sent messages to the king on at least three different occasions; unfortunately, I can only assume that none survived the journey. If they had, my pleas for help from the king would have been answered.

"I have been forced to begin military conscription of our once-peaceful domain to deal with the rebels alone. That they were able to kidnap you shows how far-reaching their grasp is and how dangerous they have become. Perhaps now you can understand what a miracle of chance occurred when we rescued you. I believe that their plan was to hold you for ransom and eventually murder you, as they have so many others." Deimos finished speaking and sat on the ledge of the balcony, conveying a sincere and concerned expression.

"Master Deimos, I'm sorry. But neither the king nor I have received any such reports. If this is all true, then why did your guards attack my dear friend Orestros last night as he tried to rescue me from the dungeon?"

"Orestros? Your friend? Do you mean the giant?" Deimos asked with a surprised expression.

"Yes, my loyal friend. Can you bring him to me?"

"Queen Thalia, if he had announced himself as a representative or messenger of the king, he would have been welcomed. Despite my absence in battle with the rebels, you would have been freed from the prison and cared for immediately. Unfortunately he did not and chooses to circumvent all authority."

"May I ask what has become of my faithful subject?"

"He disappeared into the high alpine regions," Deimos said as he gestured to the mountains.

"Then I can assume that he escaped," the queen said, grasping at hope.

"Now that I know he was one your servants, I'm glad to tell you that he did indeed elude capture," Deimos said with a smile.

"And you say that you have already sent word to the king and to my son, Prince Ammon?" Queen Thalia asked, watching the facial expressions of Deimos carefully, looking for any sign of deception.

"As I said, My Lady, I'm concerned about the safety and survival of the messengers as they travel through rebel-controlled territory. I am confident that the king and the prince will soon be aware of your presence here and of my protection."

"Thank you, Master Deimos," Queen Thalia said and offered her hand. Deimos again bowed and then lowering himself to one knee and kissed her ring before standing.

"My Lady, I am leading a small force in search of a suspected rebel leader and must take your leave. If you are in need of anything, young Rosalyn will be nearby. Perhaps we can talk further upon my return." He bowed slightly and left Queen Thalia at the balcony, closing her doors quietly.

Rosalyn met Deimos in the corridor with a basket containing six newborn puppies.

"Master Deimos," she said excitedly, gently lifting one of the wavy blonde pups out with her hands and offering it to Deimos.

"Cute little pups. Why not take one to Queen Thalia? Perhaps it will amuse her for awhile. Give me the basket with the others, and I'll find homes for them."

"You're such a good man, Master Deimos."

"Thank you!"

Rosalyn took one pup and handed the basket of puppies to Master Deimos.

"Shall I give her the pup now, Master?"

"As you please, Rosalyn," he said and walked away.

As Rosalyn excitedly ran down the corridor toward Queen Thalia, the black raven flew through a window in the corridor. It landed a few feet in front of Deimos, and with a flash of lightning, similar to one in a thunderstorm, transformed itself into a black-robed wizard with a long black beard.

"You summoned me, Master," the wizard said in a dark voice which echoed with each word.

"Keep an eye on the queen and make sure she communicates with no one except Rosalyn. If she does, kill them both!" Deimos looked sternly at the wizard as he gave him orders, and then handed him the basket of puppies.

"I've told you, no dogs will be born or allowed to live. No servants may possess them, and no people from the countryside shall have them to warn of our arrival. Make sure that these never reach the hands of the people!" Deimos then turned abruptly and walked away.

The wizard took the basket and, a little further down the corridor, pushed them into a burlap sack and dropped it from the window into the moat surrounding the palace. A whimpering sound was heard as the sack slowly sank into the stagnant water.

Rosalyn, who had returned to thank her master for his kindness, observed the whole exchange and, leaving the puppy behind a large, cushioned red chair in the corridor, stepped carefully through the open window and disappeared into the murky water. After coming to the surface several times for air, she finally emerged with the burlap sack and swam to the bank of the moat, struggling to drag herself onto dry land. With all of her might, she ripped the sack open.

Chapter Twelve

Arianne and Aleah sluggishly awakened amid the debris and broken crates of what had once been the travel chamber. As they slowly became aware, they found that they were soaked in the once-glowing blue fluid, though still partially blue, that had become a thick, slimy substance with an unpleasant odor and a green haze. Aleah reached out toward the vague image of Arianne. The light from the sky was almost blinding. She could see that Arianne's body was shaking, as well as her own, from the cold fluid still covering them.

"What happened?" Aleah finally asked, wiping the thick substance from her eyes and face.

"The travel chamber collapsed," Arianne managed to say as she coughed, desperately trying to clear her nose and lungs of the foul-smelling substance.

"Can you see the others?" Aleah continued in a raspy voice, as she coughed and tried to wipe more of the fluid and tears from her own eyes.

"No, but I have a feeling this is not a safe place. Do you see a way to get to some sort of cover?" Arianne said just above a whisper.

"Some supplies are over there," Aleah said, motioning to the wreckage of several crates in the grass not far from them.

"Is it safe?" Arianne asked in a low whisper, looking cautiously around them and deliberately smelling the air.

"Something has gone terribly wrong. We need the supplies and a place to hide until the guards and the others find us," Aleah said, carefully gathering as many supplies as she could get into two large packs, before returning to Arianne's side.

"I have a bad feeling," Arianne said with a little more clarity and certainty. "We must leave this place quickly!" She spoke gruffly as she grabbed Aleah's arm. Keeping very low to the ground, Arianne pulled her until they both ran together with the supplies in their arms. Arianne stumbled after she struck her leg on a large pile of stones. The pain immediately overcame her, and she collapsed onto the ground.

Aleah knelt besides her, shielding her eyes from the light while trying to see how badly Arianne was hurt. "Are you all right?" she asked, as she noticed Arianne's leg oozing dark red blood and strange green pus at the edges of the cut.

"It's nothing," Arianne replied, despite the pain. "This appears to be a wall of some sort. If we follow it, we may find some refuge. Then we can come back for more supplies."

Arianne winced from the pain, as she crouched down and followed the crumbling row of layered stones.

"Arianne," Aleah said, as they tried to hurry, "do you think this is Earth?"

"I'm afraid so, my dear, though it's not what I expected," Arianne responded, moving as quickly as she could and looking fearfully in all directions.

After another fifty yards, she paused to rest against the stone wall which was now taller and more regular. As they began to leave the grassy meadow and climb more steeply upwards, Arianne could feel her body temperature rising. In the skies, a strange gray mass slowly began to cover the bright yellow light and, at last, Arianne and Aleah could see the world around them. Behind them, they saw a field of lush green grass, higher than their waists, which seemed to go on for miles. Ahead of them, they could definitely discern the remnants of the stone wall they had been following. It had been man-made but was very, very old and in terrible disrepair.

On the ridge above, there appeared to be a stone house, though it was difficult to see more than its outline. Beyond that, they could see heavily forested mountains, the summits of their tallest peaks covered with snow.

"Do you see it?" Arianne asked.

"I see something this side of the forest and the mountains. It looks almost like a house," Aleah answered excitedly.

"Perhaps it's what used to be a house a very long time ago," Arianne added cautiously, as she stopped long enough to raise her green skirt and look at the gash just below her knee. It was still bleeding. She rummaged through one of her packs and found a clean bandage. Aleah helped her quickly wrap it around her leg.

She cautiously raised her head again to get a better view of the structure on the ridge above them when in the distance, deep within the meadow behind them, she heard several strange sounds. At first, it sounded almost like someone or something screaming, followed by silence, except for the rustling of the grass as a warm breeze passed over the fields.

"Did you hear that?" she asked Arianne.

"Yes, something in the tall grass. Until we know what it is, we'd better assume that it's not a friend. Hurry now. You go first, and let's hope that the old house can offer us some protection."

Aleah picked up the supply packs and continued quickly along the stone wall. Arianne reopened the pack from which she had found the bandage and produced a small bottle of a black and gray powdered substance, mixed with innumerable tiny granules of the same color. As she struggled to catch up with Aleah, she shook the powder onto the ground behind her every few feet.

"Arianne!" Aleah called out from the edge of the ridge. "It is a house but bigger. It must have been a castle or something, though not much of it remains. Come and see!" Aleah's voice, though still hushed, was filled with excitement as she ran through the short grass surrounding the stone ruins.

"Wait for me!" Arianne called to Aleah, but she had already disappeared among the fallen stone walls. As Arianne hurried to catch up, she noticed that blood had soaked through her bandage again, and the pain and swelling was increasing. She looked back along the wall to see if anyone or anything might be following them and, seeing nothing, she sat on the ground beside the wall to rest.

Aleah reappeared a few minutes later, no longer carrying her packs. "Arianne, we were right. No one has lived in this house in a very long time, but it will shelter us and with a little work, I think we can secure a door to one of the main rooms to keep us safe. There's also a well in the yard, but I don't know if there's water still there."

As Aleah finished speaking she noticed Arianne's leg and the bloody bandage. "I'm sorry; I was so excited that I almost forgot about your leg. It's only about another fifty yards. If I carry your packs, do you think you can make it?"

Arianne slowly stood, while steadying herself with one hand on the stone wall and replied, "Yes, yes, of course I can."

Aleah quickly ran toward the ruins of the structure, returning with a long black metal pole that had been sharpened at one end. She handed it to Arianne, "I thought you might be able to use this for support," Aleah said, with a gentle smile. Arianne smiled in return.

"For protection, as well. Thank you, my dear!" Arianne reached out and pulled Aleah closer, embracing her for a moment. "Are there any more of these?"

"Lots of them. I thought we could use them to secure the doors, but you'll see when we get there." She was pleased at Arianne's response and excited that she had found the refuge that Arianne told her they needed. She gathered the supplies that Arianne had been carrying into two packs and slung them over her shoulders, and then helped Arianne to her feet.

Walking fifty yards to the stone ruins became increasingly difficult for Arianne as the pain and swelling increased. "Perhaps when we arrive safely, we can find some medical supplies among the packs. If not, I'll go back and try to find them in the wreckage," Aleah said, as she helped Arianne through the final distance and into the room that Aleah had thought to be safe. She then helped Arianne to lie down and examined at her swollen leg. She quickly began to rummage through the packs in search of medical supplies but found only bandages.

She felt Arianne's forehead, after noticing beads of sweat appearing and, using water from their drinking pouches, applied cool cloths. Arianne's fever continued to worsen as the afternoon passed. The bright yellow light—they now knew it to be the fabled but very real sun—began its descent on the horizon.

Aleah worked tirelessly, setting the metal poles across each opening in the stone refuge and securing each one. She managed to construct a gate of sorts, which could be opened and closed and locked from the inside, by sliding a long pole through several others which were solidly locked in place. She wanted to test her devises, but Arianne was in no condition to assist her.

Before she locked herself and Arianne in for the growing darkness of night, she climbed to the top of what must have been a tower at one time. As she looked down across the expansive lowlands, she noticed small, gray apparitions appearing and then disappearing in the tall grass, each time moving a little closer. She thought it odd, but she had never been on the surface of Earth before, and she wondered if such occurrences might be natural phenomena. As the sun set, she once again heard the strange screams, though this time they were much closer. She remembered what Arianne had said about considering them unfriendly until proven otherwise.

A sudden burst of fear filled her body, as she quickly ran to the room where Arianne lay asleep. She secured the poles and tried to reinforce them to make certain that her makeshift door would hold but, with each passing moment, she grew more and more distrustful of her own invention. She threw a few more pieces of broken sticks and wood onto the small fire and sat beside Arianne, once again applying a cool cloth to her forehead and observing the swelling of her wounded leg.

She had gathered all of the remaining poles into the room and wrapped torn clothes around some of them to use as torches. She heard the strange screams again, this time no more than a few hundred feet away. From the sounds, there seemed to be many more of them. Aleah had never heard anything like it before, and she tried to arouse Arianne who finally stirred from her feverish sleep. "No matter what, don't let them in here," she said, trying unsuccessfully to sit up.

"What are they? What should I do?" Aleah asked frantically, but Arianne had collapsed back onto the pallet of blankets. She managed to mutter the word "fire," before closing her eyes.

The screams approached Aleah's makeshift door, before everything became quiet. Looking outside, she watched the sky grow darker. She remembered the Prism skies at home, desperately wishing she was still there and safe. She changed Lady Arianne's bandage, now soaked with a foul-smelling green drainage.

She was startled as something heavy struck the door, causing it to shake and dust to fall from the stones that covered the ceiling. A piercing scream came from the other side of the door, and she cringed as her muscles contracted involuntarily. She fell back from the shock as she noticed black hairy fingers slipping beneath the door and in-between the metal poles. The screams became even louder, as several of the creatures dug from beneath and pulled at every opening. Aleah lit one of her torches and, despite her sense of panic, repeatedly burned the hands coming through the doorway.

For several moments, everything turned quiet and then it started again, more violently than before. Aleah ran back to Arianne's side and covered her ears to keep her from hearing the shrieks. They only increased in fury and volume, as the door slowly began to give way. She lit another torch, but as she reached toward her attackers, they managed to take it away from her and drop it onto the ground.

At last, she took one of the sharp poles and, sitting beside Arianne, waited for them to finish breaking through the door. A moment of calm and resignation came over her, as she gently wiped Arianne's forehead, almost unable to hear the furious screams and growls a few feet away.

Chapter Thirteen

Orestros managed to fend off the creatures, and they finally retreated in fear upon realizing his size and strength. He carefully observed his wounds and buried the guard's body. He also collected and filled two large packs with supplies that were scattered across the grass, before tracking Ammon to the edge of a small river. His eyes, still sensitive to the sun, were slowly adjusting as evening began to fall across the open plains.

He prepared to cross the river but looked back momentarily, almost as if he had heard something cry out from a long distance away. Looking to the ridge above the grassland, he could dimly see the glow of a small fire nearly a mile away on the darkening horizon. He carefully hid his packs among the willow trees and reeds growing beside the river bank and started walking toward the glowing firelight on the distant ridge. For a moment, he considered that Ammon had come back ashore and was journeying toward the mountains.

His pace quickened, as he realized that Ammon would not light a fire, knowing it would attract the creatures but thought that perhaps Aleah and Arianne might make such a mistake, if they had not yet encountered the wild beasts.

As Orestros proceeded boldly, he heard the screams of the creatures in the distance. He began to run with all of his might, taking strides that would require three large leaps from an ordinary man. As he saw the ruins and heard the violent screams of the creatures, he released a yell which echoed through the lowlands and reached the ruins and firelight above him. The eerie shrieks stopped as he trampled the grass and, at last, followed the decaying wall leading to the ruins.

❦ ❖ ❧

Reaching the small, enclosed room where the fire was burning, he found Aleah's makeshift doorway completely torn apart. Two of the large creatures lay dead, impaled with sharp poles. Arianne lay undisturbed on several blankets, covered partially with another, along with wood and sticks apparently laid there to conceal her.

Orestros quickly dropped to his knees and uncovered her, then pressed his ear against her chest, listening for a heartbeat. It was rapid, and he could feel the heat and perspiration of fever raging throughout her body, along with a strange green hue which seemed to be overtaking her pale white skin.

Looking around, a few feet away, he saw Aleah crouched in a dark corner of the room, holding her hands over her ears and shaking as she stared wide-eyed into the remnants of the fire.

Crouching down, he gently pulled her hands away from her ears and rubbed them together in his own hands. Her hands were as cold as ice.

"Aleah," he said calmly, still warming her hands. "It's all right now, they're gone. You're safe and nothing here will harm you." Orestros then cupped her tender face in his massive hands and turned her head to face him, though she continued to shake and stare into the burning embers.

"Orestros?" she finally whispered.

"Yes, little one, I'm here and you're safe. We need to help Lady Arianne. Can you stand up now?" he asked in a very gentle voice.

"I think so," she answered. As she stood up with his help, Orestros noticed a long gash on her forearm. He helped her to sit near the fire and then quickly added several pieces of wood. As the room became illuminated more brightly, he retrieved a bandage from their supplies and wrapped it around Aleah's arm.

He returned to Arianne's side and, using his knife, cut the foul green-soaked bandage from her leg. The odor was almost overwhelming, and he had to turn his head away. He then pulled a leather pouch from around his neck, opened it, and poured the fresh water over the large infected wound.

Though still unconscious, Arianne groaned in pain as the fresh water streamed over the wound. From a pocket inside of his long black vest, Orestros then produced a small handful of dark green moss, with small splinters of what appeared to be tree bark. He splashed water onto it and carefully applied it to Arianne's leg, as again she moaned in pain. Finally, he wrapped a clean bandage around her leg and, pulling her up slightly, poured a small amount of water onto her lips.

Arianne squinted open her eyes. "Orestros, is Aleah all right?"

"She's a little shaken up, Lady Arianne, but she'll be all right. You're the one we're concerned about."

"My leg hurts. It's infected. Something in the travel chamber caused all of this to go wrong. I thought I saw an old woman and rats; they fouled the fluid somehow."

"Don't worry about that now. You need to rest. I've put some medicine on your leg that will help draw the poisons out."

"Take care of Aleah and Ammon. They are in danger. The creatures are killers."

"I'll take care of them. You need to rest and drink water. The creatures won't come back here for awhile, and I'll fix the door so that they'll never be able to get through it again," Orestros said, as he helped her to drink more water from his leather pouch. He took a clean white handkerchief from his vest and gave it to her to wipe her forehead.

"Thank you, Orestros. You're a very kind gentleman," Arianne said, smiling ever so slightly.

Orestros blushed and turned away, "I've never been accused of that before," he said gruffly, covering his mouth to hide his smile.

"That's because no one knows you," Aleah whispered

As she sat down beside them and placed her arms around Orestros's huge arm, he patted her on the shoulder and then stood up. "I'll fix the door and then I need to find Prince Ammon."

He then turned to Aleah. "Place a pinch or two of this into a small pan from your pack and heat it until it's warm. Lady Arianne must drink all of it at least twice before I return. If she drinks it all, she will begin to feel better by morning," Orestros said, seriously looking in Aleah's eyes as he handed her the pouch.

She opened it and felt the rough, reddish woody substance within. "What is it?" she asked curiously.

"Medicine, Aleah. Perhaps some day I'll teach you about it."

"Find Prince Ammon? Haven't you seen him?" Aleah asked, changing the subject.

Orestros pulled the spear-like poles from the bodies of the creatures and tossed them to the side, while observing the hands and feet of the ape-like creatures.

"He was with me when these creatures attacked us unexpectedly. I sent him across a small river not far from here and told him to wait for me," Orestros related.

"Then you really must leave us again?" Aleah asked with resignation and an understanding in her voice as she grasped the pouch he had given her.

"You'll be safe. It shouldn't take me long to barricade the door. I think those creatures won't return tonight." Orestros dragged the two bodies outside and began constructing another barrier. "You won't be able to get out until I return, but it's safer this way. Tomorrow we'll find a better refuge and some means to guard against the creatures."

"Orestros!" Aleah called out and ran to the door. "Thank you! Find Prince Ammon and come back soon." In another minute, the doorway was sealed and Aleah returned to Arianne's side.

∞❖∞

Outside, Orestros climbed to the remains of the tower and looked toward the river. He couldn't see any movement but in what appeared to be a forest beyond the river, he could see thick green smoke rising from the trees. He gazed around the ruins, as his eyes continued to adjust in the dimming of the sun's light. He noticed another light not far from the room where Aleah and Arianne had lit their small fire.

Orestros slowly descended from the tower and stepped quietly toward the glow of its blue fire. He realized that it was indeed the light that he had seen from the banks of the river. He crept among the ruins of huge monoliths and empty chambers that had once been the homes of an ancient people. Broken pottery and fireplaces lay in ruin all around him; still in the distance, a glowing flame continued to burn.

He reached a carved and decaying set of steps. Time had aged everything, and ivy, which he knew from the Prism, covered the walls and passageways. Tall columns rose on either side of a gray marble alcove above the single blue flame which illuminated the entire structure. On it were chiseled words that simply read: Remember us.

Orestros wondered about what Lady Arianne said she had seen in the travel chamber, and if it was the fever or really something she actually witnessed, as Morgana once again entered his thoughts. He stopped thinking and leapt to the ground, then jogged at a steady pace through the deep grasses toward the river. Pausing momentarily, he looked at the darkening blue sky and witnessed something he had known only from ancient myths. Tiny points of white light sparkled in the sky as if they came from far away, further than he had ever imagined.

"Stars!" he whispered aloud. Again he pulled the whistle from inside of his boot and blew into it several times. He searched the deep blue sky, filled with more stars than he could count, but there was no sign of Hermes.

Chapter Fourteen

Ammon found the cover of large bushes near a stand of trees he had seen from the riverbank. They were the largest trees he had ever seen, and he spent most of the afternoon resting in their shade while he tried to understand what had happened and where Orestros might be. Birds of nearly every color, most of which he had never seen before, flew about in every direction, some landing within a few feet of him and looking at him curiously. Red birds and blue birds, small black birds with small stripes of red and gold on their wings, and orange birds with black hoods and stripes delighted him to no end, just as their songs did that filled the air.

The sun slowly lowered behind the mountains, and enormous white billowing masses blew across the sky. Ammon tried to remember their name, but the word eluded him, for no such things existed in the Prism world. There was an ancient book, which his father King Hyperion had sent with him, identifying such things and many animals that were said to exist on Earth, but he feared the book was lost in the wreckage.

Ammon considered swimming back across the river to retrieve the book and supplies, but he recalled the screaming, growling creatures that had chased him to the river's edge. He also knew that Orestros would look for him where he was and not in the dangerous tall grasses from which he had escaped.

With the setting of the sun, he was able to wash the mud from his eyelids. To pass the time, he carefully sorted through the packs he had salvaged from the wreckage of the travel chamber and inventoried each item. He was careful to eat only a small portion of food, not knowing where or when he would find another source. He watched carefully in every direction for any sign of the creatures that had attacked them so soon after their arrival, but he saw no more of them, nor did he find any of their tracks on the side of the river where he now rested.

He sat in the shade of the tallest of the trees and watched the birds, while thinking of his comfortable home in the Prism and how very far away it now seemed. The great adventure he had imagined the day before had turned into a dangerous and even deadly experience. Though trying not to think about it, he considered the very real possibility that he would not survive.

As darkness began to cover the western skies, the twinkling of the first stars he had ever seen began to twinkle overhead. He thought he had never seen anything so beautiful, and he wondered if Aleah and the others were watching and wondering at the same sight. He gathered several large bundles of sticks and twigs, along with dried leaves which had fallen from the trees around him. Every time he was about to light the small camp fire, however, he remembered the screaming creature at the riverbank and hesitated. He finally decided to remain in the darkness. Using two blankets, along with several large and long branches, he constructed a small tent for himself in the shelter of the overhanging tree branches.

As night settled in and the sky became darker, Ammon lay on his back and gazed at the sky as more and more stars appeared. He could hear beautiful songs of strange night birds in the tree branches above him as he drifted in and out of a light sleep. His sleep soon became deeper and longer, and when he next awoke, a dark orange and yellow light was rising from the opposite horizon from where it had disappeared the day before. The light illuminated the fields and trees and, though bright, it did not hurt his eyes at all. It grew larger and larger until its full round shape could be seen. It was very, very far away, yet closer than the stars, and Ammon immediately knew that it was the moon. He looked at the sphere for hours, trying to recall the stories about it.

As he wondered at the moon's size, he noticed a small, thin trail of smoke slowly streaming in front of it. It was difficult to be sure, but the smoke had a greenish tint to it. His eyes followed the smoke to its origin, on the other side of steep hills, which appeared to be covered with tall trees. Large boulders and rocky cliffs were visible in the moonlight. He could almost make out the shadowy figure of someone looking in his direction but, after watching it carefully for several minutes, he decided that since it hadn't moved, it must be a tree.

He lay on his back again and watched the moon and stars with fascination. When he stood up again and looked to see if the distant figure was still there, it was gone, though he could still see the cliff illuminated in the moonlight.

"Orestros?" he whispered to himself. He began to consider that Orestros might have passed him in the darkness before the moon rose, but he dismissed the thought, knowing that Orestros was far too good of a tracker to make such an error. The longer he lay in the grass, the more his imagination began to run wild. He began to wonder if the creatures had overpowered Orestros. The more he considered that possibility, the less he believed it possible. He had witnessed Orestros easily throw one of the creatures to the ground.

As that thought finally left him, another one came to mind. What had happened to Aleah and Arianne? Had the creatures attacked them also? Of course he knew they could not fight the creatures very effectively; for that matter, neither could he. Everything depended on Orestros, until they could organize and construct a defense and some sort of refuge.

Ammon continued to worry about all of them and the other guard who had come with them, but all he could do for the time being was to worry. He realized he needed to make a plan for the next day. As he gazed at the stars and moon suspended in the dark blue sky, he fell asleep. Without realizing it, he had crawled into his tent and covered himself with a blanket as the night air took on a moist chill.

❦ ❖ ❧

Ammon awakened as a red glow began to rise where the moon had once been. He could still see stars in the sky, but the twinkling slowly faded the higher the glowing light rose in the sky. Sitting up and scooting out of his tent, he noticed that the moon was gone. Once again he heard the tiny songbirds singing to one another on their flight into the grassland. More importantly, he smelled smoke and the unmistakable aroma of frying fish. As he looked around, he saw a campfire with a small pan, containing two large fish, much larger than the fish he had seen in the waters of the Prism.

"Have some breakfast, Prince Ammon. We have much to do and miles to travel," Orestros announced, just before he appeared from the tall grass with several more fish on a line slung over his shoulder.

"I can't believe it's you!" Ammon said, with excitement as he joined Orestros by the fire.

"It's me. Now eat some fish for strength, and then we'll get moving. Aleah and Lady Arianne are waiting for us, and I'm sure they're scared and hungry."

The prince smiled broadly, when he realized that his hours of worry had been needless. He sat beside the campfire and quickly devoured the warm fish.

Orestros carefully laid a large, thick book beside Ammon, as he took the other fish from the pan. "I thought you might want to study this."

Ammon licked his fingers and wiped his hands on the back of his pants. He picked up the book and started to turn the pages. There were hundreds of detailed drawings of animals and plants with a description beside each picture. Some were animals that existed in the Prism, but most were strange and wild animals said to have existed on Earth. Although he had seen the book before, he never expected to actually encounter the creatures depicted in the drawings.

"Look at the page I marked earlier this morning," Orestros said as he ate tender bites of the fish. Using a cloth, he wiped his hands before handing the cloth to Ammon. He wiped his hands again and turned to the marked page. He was surprised to find a drawing of the creatures that had attacked them on the previous day. He then set the book closely beside him as he continued to eat his fish. He read aloud from the ancient writings, "Baboon: a member of Papio and other genera of large, ferocious, terrestrial, dog-faced monkeys. Usually found in large groups, called troops, which can sometimes number more than 200. Attacking in small groups of three or four, these fierce creatures can easily take down a man or other predator in minutes, leaving only pieces of their victim."

"We have to be very careful, Prince Ammon, these baboons will show us no mercy."

"What about the others?" the prince asked, looking up from the book and picturing the baboon that had chased him the afternoon before, while imagining the danger that Aleah, Lady Arianne, and his father's guard might be facing.

"Lady Arianne and Aleah are safe for now but the sooner we get back to them, the better off they'll be. I have not found your father's guard. We can only hope he's found some refuge," Orestros answered in a serious tone.

The prince quickly finished his portion of the fish and then wrapped the remainder in the cloth Orestros had given him and placed it in his coat pocket.

The two men quickly finished packing their supplies and blankets. The sun began to break above the distant mountain ridges, and a stream of white light passed through low-lying clouds to illuminate the spot in the tall grass where they began walking at a brisk pace toward the river.

Chapter Fifteen

The evil witch Morgana climbed once again onto the cliff above the ruins of a castle she had found. She peered into the moonlit sky toward the river. In the trees not far from the riverbank, she saw the slight movement of what appeared to be a man. Drawing a dark green glass from within her cloak, she peered through it and looked again toward the trees where she had seen the man moving. Through the glass, his image became clearer and closer.

"Prince Ammon!" she whispered in her gurgling, rough voice. She coughed, and her voice then changed to a much more pleasant tone. "So you've survived!" She smiled wickedly and continued to watch until she perceived that he was watching her.

She immediately climbed down from her perch on the cliff and returned through the crumbling gates to what once had been a beautiful castle. Crossing the courtyard, now overgrown with vines and young trees, she stood beside her green fire in the large hall. The roof had long since collapsed, but large pillars still stood, and the remnants of faded paintings still hung on the walls. Portraits of noble kings and queens stared from their dusty frames like ghosts from the distant past. Cobwebs seemed to droop from every corner of the hall. Morgana's green fire, and the glow of the smoke arising from her black caldron, illuminated it all.

Morgana herself was different; she no longer looked the old hag but was dressed in stark black robes and wore a black skullcap. Her face, though stiff and unforgiving, no longer showed the signs of old age but almost possessed dignity and evil charm. Her eyebrows were pointed and sharp and even crueler than the hint of her mocking smile.

Her eyes, larger than normal, were almost completely black except for the green reflection of the firelight.

Morgana sat on a stone pedestal by a small pool of water and looked at her reflection. As she did, the water began to swirl, slowly at first, then faster until it was moving without any ripples. She waved her hands over the water several times as if conjuring some faraway ally or friend, until an image began to appear. It was the image of a man with black hair and a long black beard. His eyebrows were black and bushy, and beneath them his eyes gleamed as black as hers.

She revealed a dark and sinister smile, as if she had expected the image. In a moment, from out of the small pool of water, the image of a large black raven flapped its long wings and, in a flash of dark blue light, the gleaming black bird was transformed into the black wizard of Master Deimos. The image was strangely different from reality, however, and Morgana could almost see through it.

"Morgana ..." the dark wizard said.

"I am here and safe," she answered.

"The travel chamber is destroyed?" the wizard asked with a sinister grin.

"It is destroyed, My Lord, just as we planned," she replied.

"And what of your fellow travelers? They are dead, I presume," he asked, still glaring from his transparent image.

"I killed one of the guards myself when he tried to interfere with my escape. The other is here." As Morgana paused, the guard slowly emerged from the darkest shadows and bowed in respect, as she continued, "Prince Ammon, however, has temporarily survived," she concluded.

"And what of the others?" the wizard inquired harshly.

"I assume they are dead, but I have not confirmed their deaths. I plan to do so today. The giant named Orestros was among them and has caused me to be concerned," she said humbly, afraid of the wizard's temper.

"Orestros, the giant? Impossible! Master Deimos buried him with explosions deep in the caverns several days ago! What are you saying? He's already dead!" the wizard screamed, emitting a dark blue vapor into the air as the words left his mouth.

"I'm sorry, My Lord, but Master Deimos is mistaken. The giant survived and accompanied us in the travel chamber. He was alive and well when the chamber was destroyed. Since then, I cannot say. I have commanded a troop of fierce baboons to attack and kill all survivors. By midday, I will know what success they have achieved." Morgana finished speaking and stepped away from the image of the wizard, as blood red streaks began to flow through his transparent image.

"Morgana, Master Deimos must never learn of his failure before we are ready, or you and I will surely pay the price with our lives," the black wizard said, his voice surprisingly calm, though she could see the violence in his eyes as they turned from black to red. "So what do you plan to do to correct your error?" he asked, arching his right eyebrow and glaring at her.

"I was awaiting your instructions, My Lord," she said and bowed submissively.

"At least you know that it is I who is in charge of this plan!" he said with his usual air of superiority, as treachery and threat lay just beneath the surface of each word and every gesture. "Never forget that it was I who freed you from the dungeons of King Hyperion, and I that have restored you to your youthful appearance and dark beauty, instead of the decrepit old hag you had become. It is also I who will give you your revenge upon King Hyperion and Prince Ammon."

"I am forever in your debt, My Lord, but what of Queen Thalia? May I know your plan for her?" Morgana asked, smiling wickedly.

"Queen Thalia will be the pinnacle of my success. I will deal with her in my own way when the time is right. First, I will slowly lure her to our side, though she will know nothing of it. She will then assist me in our other goal—the destruction of Master Deimos. All things in good time, Morgana, then the two of us will rule Prism and Earth unchallenged." The black wizard's eyes glowed red as sparkles of dark blue surrounded his image. Morgana dropped to her knees before him.

"I am your servant, my beloved. How shall I proceed to bring your plan to life?"

"Where is the king's guard?" the wizard shouted.

Morgana stood beside him and beckoned the guard, still dressed in his yellow tunic and holding his spear at his side.

"I am here," the guard said, bowing submissively to the wizard and Morgana.

"What is your name?" the wizard asked in a sly, treacherous voice.

"They call me Bartholomew, My Lord; it is the name of the guard who met with an unfortunate accident some years ago. My true name is Akred. At your service, My Lord and Lady." The guard removed his hat and bowed in an absurd manner, wickedly smiling to reveal dirty yellow teeth that were broken and sharp.

The wizard and Morgana laughed, knowing he had murdered the real Bartholomew, in order to take his place and credentials before Bartholomew was to report for his first day of service to King Hyperion.

"Akred, this is what you shall do to serve us and insure your position in our New World order," the wizard began. "First, you will continue your masquerade a bit longer. You will find Prince Ammon and relate the heroic story of your survival, making certain that you are once again a trusted ally. Secondly, any mention of Morgana, the old hag," he added as they all laughed, "you will dismiss as mere fantasy or confusion. You will assure the prince and the giant Orestros, if he still lives, that you inspected the chamber moments before they entered, and there was no sign of the old woman. You must be convincing! You will depart when the sun rises! Go and prepare yourself! Morgana will assist you in making your story believable, and arrange a means to contact you after you have found the prince."

The wizard then pointed toward the shadows where the guard had been standing.

"Yes, My Lord, I will not fail you. You may rely on me completely," he said, smiling and then returning to the shadows where other creatures stirred.

The wizard then spoke quietly to Morgana before she took a step away from him, dropped to one knee, and kissed his hand. A flash of dark blue light illuminated the hall for an instant, and the wizard's semi-transparent image was once again transformed into the large black raven. Without hesitation, the raven flew into the air and dove into the pool of swirling dark green water.

Morgana waved her hand once across the surface of the pool and the swirling stopped.

"Akred!" she called out.

The guard readily came forward.

"Are you prepared?"

"Yes, My Lady."

"Go and stand over there, near the entrance to the hall," she said, throwing a green powder into the fire which made the flames grow very bright. She looked carefully around the hall.

"How will you contact me, My Lady?" he asked humbly.

Morgana turned toward him and as she did, her black eyes turned into fiery green balls.

"When you see these in the distance, you will know that I am there. Follow them, and you will find me. Now, go to the entrance and wait."

She watched Akred walk to the entrance and then turned to the creatures moving in the shadows. "Come now, friends, I have a small task for you." As she finished speaking, three large baboons appeared at her feet, growling and snarling, as their fangs dripped with foul-smelling saliva. They reached up and touched her black robes very submissively. Morgana leaned down to the largest of the three and whispered something unintelligible in its ear.

The baboon growled at the other two creatures beside him and, without warning, all three ran and jumped on Akred, standing unaware at the entrance. His blood splattered onto his yellow tunic when he tried to defend himself.

Morgana then stepped toward them and shouted, "Enough!" The baboons followed her command without hesitation and quickly returned to her side.

Akred lay sprawled on the ground, and Morgana pulled a dark cloth from her robes and wiped the blood from his eyes and a large gash on his cheek. "Are you all right?" she asked tenderly.

"No, I'm not all right. They were trying to kill me," he managed to say, checking the wounds on his side and leg.

"I'm sorry, dear boy, but we had to make your story to the prince and Orestros convincing." She removed the cork from a small green bottle and handed it to him. "Drink this, it will take away the pain and give you strength enough to get away, but you must hurry. Don't make a mistake; remember you are no longer Akred but rather the loyal guard named Bartholomew. Don't forget!"

"Hurry? Why? I need to rest," Akred said as he pulled the cork from the bottle and sipped the thick green liquid.

"In just a few minutes, those creatures will be coming after you. If I were you, I wouldn't let them catch you, because I won't be there to stop them, and they do have such nasty dispositions at times." She helped Akred to his feet. "Don't forget when you see my green eyes, simply follow them and you'll find me. Now, quickly, you know what you have to do." She smiled her wicked smile and she pushed him out the entrance.

Akred heard the baboons growling beside the green fire, as they began jumping into the air and running in small circles.

"Patience, little ones, we must give our friend a fair head start." She smiled again and walked over to the baboons, petting them and scratching behind their ears. "Run, Bartholomew," she called out. "Try to remember that all of this will only make your story more convincing, if you make it."

Akred quickly consumed the fluid in the bottle, grabbed his spear, and a small pack of supplies before running into the predawn light of the surrounding forest. He could hear Morgana laughing, when he tripped over a fallen log and then quickly sprang to his feet to run again.

When Morgana finally stopped laughing and playing with the baboons, she commanded two of them to begin their pursuit of Akred. The two growled and showed their long fangs before racing out the entrance. Several other baboons came to her side and, just as the others, growled and lightly touched her long black robes as if they possessed a secret power, which they craved and revered.

"I almost forgot about our other guests," she said and whistled slightly. From out of the shadows in another corner of the great hall, her two large black rats scurried to her feet and sat on their hind legs. The baboons growled harshly when the rats appeared. "Now, now, children, we must all get along. Come along now, and we'll show our other guests their new accommodations. We must all be pleasant."

Morgana smiled and walked across the dusty marble floor, picking up a bright orange cloak in the process. The rats and baboons sniffed it and squealed and growled, as she carried the cloak to a dark passageway at the far end of the hall. Pointing her finger to the walls while they descended a long spiral staircase, torches burst into bright green flames, lighting the stone steps in an eerie and smoggy glow.

At the bottom of the staircase, row after row of prison cells were illuminated. She opened the metal bars of the first cell and entered with the orange cloak still slung over her shoulder. She whispered to the rats and baboons that quickly formed a semi-circle around her feet. She unfurled the cloak and began shaking it into the air as she whispered a series of strange-sounding words. As the cloak seemed to magically waver in the air, from out of the cloak Princess Leda fell hard onto the stone floor and as Morgana continued to whisper the strange words, Axel also fell onto the hard stone. Both lay motionless.

"What have you done to us?" Axel finally managed to say, his face pale and his voice unsteady.

"You'll feel better in an hour or two," Morgana said almost humorously, as she leaned over and carefully observed them both before leading her creatures from the cell and locking the door with a green padlock that glowed for several moments after it snapped shut. "I'll send you some refreshment and food, when you're feeling a little better. Until then, enjoy my hospitality. I have
a feeling you'll be staying with me for a long, long while. But we can talk about that later. Come, children," she said

whimsically to the creatures. They all began to ascend the spiral staircase, following closely behind her as her long black robes swished against the stone steps.

Axel heard a hideous laughter coming from the stairs as she disappeared from sight. "Are you all right, Princess?" he asked but heard only a slight groan from Leda as she moved slightly.

"I think so," Princess Leda finally said, her body trembling. "But my arms and legs can barely move. I feel like I'm awakening from some kind of dream." She finally managed to roll over until she was facing Axel.

"More like a nightmare, I'm afraid," he said, still lying on his side. "Did you see the woman that brought us here?"

"Not very well, but I heard her voice," Leda responded.

"In her long black robes, she was very strange, almost beautiful, but something about her seemed terribly wrong. It's hard to explain," Axel said, struggling to move.

"That she's done this to us is strange enough," Leda added.

"She said we'd feel better in an hour or two, and that she would bring us food and drink," Axel reminded her.

"I wish I knew where we were. I've never seen any place like this anywhere in the Prism before," Leda said, looking around the cell and through the bars beside the locked door.

"She's obviously taken us some place outside the palace. She said we would be here for a very long while," Axel said, as he managed to prop his head onto his hand.

"Why? What could she possibly want with us?" Leda asked him.

Suddenly, they heard the heavy flapping of wings. They managed to sit up just enough to watch the great white owl, Hermes, pause slightly and then continue his difficult flight up the winding staircase.

As he entered the hall, illuminated by the green fire glow, Morgana also heard his massive wings flapping as he tried to gain height. "My bow!" she shouted. A flurry of activity filled the hall, as baboons ran in all directions trying to find her bow and arrows.

Hermes landed on a rafter for a few seconds. Then seeing a large hole in the ceiling, swooped down, nearly striking Morgana, causing her to fall to the ground to avoid his sharp talons. As he began to fly higher into the air, one of the larger baboons placed Morgana's bow and one arrow at her feet. She quickly picked up the bow and then dipped the arrow into her black caldron, bubbling with a thick green potion. She drew the bow as far as it allowed and then tracked Hermes's flight as he approached the opening in the roof. At last, she let the arrow fly and its tip glowed bright green as it raced through the air, passing through one of the great white owl's wings. Hermes continued to fly and desperately flap his long wings.

"Another arrow!" Morgana screamed as again the rats and baboons scurried, until one of them laid an arrow at her feet. She dipped it in the green potion and drew the bow back, but Hermes could no longer be seen.

Chapter Sixteen

Akred no longer cared that once again he would be using the name of Bartholomew. His only concern was to keep running toward the cluster of trees in the distance. Each time he paused and tried to rest, he could hear the growls of the baboons racing through the thick grass behind him. He momentarily took several deep breaths, still trying to see his pursuers, and then he ran toward the river.

He no longer felt the pain and deep cuts from the attack of the baboons, although running made him increasingly exhausted. The potion Morgana had given him was working, and he knew he would have already been caught, if she had not given it to him. He considered lying low in the grass to hide but in fear, he rose up and continued his long run.

Finally reaching the riverbank, he used his pack as a float and began paddling into the deep water. The currents drew him further downstream. As he turned back, he saw his shadowy pursuers standing on the riverbank behind him, screaming, yet unwilling to enter the deep water. He was relieved at the sight and kicked his legs more rapidly to overcome the power of the currents. Before long, he reached the far shore and pulled himself up beyond the sand and onto the soft grassy bank.

The sun had begun to rise, and he shielded his eyes from its bright light, the likes of which he had never seen. Placing his arm and hand above his eyebrow, he looked at the expanse of the tall green grass. It was Earth, he thought. For a moment, forgetting his past and the terrible deeds that he had done, he considered the possibility of changing his life. He imagined a life where he could help himself and others instead of hurting and killing and serving those interested only in their own lust for power.

Enjoying his thoughts, he slowly lay down and looked onto the deep blue skies of early dawn. When he began to drift into a relaxed sleep, he once again heard the growling of baboons not far away. Akred quickly came to his feet and, slinging the pack over his shoulder, ran along a broken path, which had recently been made by someone or something. It was the easiest way to go, and he was able to run at a much faster pace than if he had no path.

He considered that perhaps he was following Prince Ammon, though, at the same time, he thought that he might be following the paths of baboons. There was no time to ponder either. The sniffing and growling sounds grew louder as more creatures approached.

Before long, he came upon the remnants of an ancient stone wall. He paused for a moment, and then ran for a few hundred feet before he yelled out, "Prince Ammon! Are you there?" He stopped and listened for a reply but, other than the sound of the breeze passing through the tall grass, he heard nothing.

He continued to run along the crumbling wall for another hundred feet and paused to rest for a minute. He called out again, "Prince Ammon, are you there?"

Akred looked around in all directions and finally, looking up to the ridge above him, he saw Prince Ammon atop a large boulder, waving both hands high above his head. Akred began running again with renewed strength and, before long, he reached the boulder. Ammon greeted him with a fond embrace and took his pack. He led him through the fallen rocks and ruins to where Orestros stood next to a small fire, while Aleah and Lady Arianne were eating fish from small tin plates.

"Look, everyone! Look who I found! It's Bartholomew, alive and well," Ammon boasted, as he presented Bartholomew and began putting a portion of fish onto a plate.

"You'd better let me take a look at those wounds; it looks as if you ran into the baboons," Orestros said, standing and retrieving a small pouch of his medicine from his vest.

"It was more like they ran into me," Bartholomew answered as he revealed several gashes. "It wasn't easy, but I managed to escape. I'm certainly glad to see all of you. I was afraid the creatures," he paused, as he partially covered his mouth to conceal his teeth. He took a bite of the fish and then grabbed a tin cup of water and washed the food down, spilling most of the water on his tunic. He continued to talk with his mouth full. "Anyway, like I said, I was afraid the creatures had killed all of you."

Bartholomew then realized that everyone was watching his show of bad manners. He quickly searched through his pockets, produced a dirty handkerchief, and carefully wiped his mouth and yellow tunic. "You'll have to forgive me, it seems like I've been running for miles, with those things chasing me all the way. I guess I almost forgot how to behave around people."

"No need to apologize, Bartholomew. We're just glad you've found us." Ammon said, offering him more fish and water while everyone welcomed him back.

Orestros stepped forward and put medicine on his wounds and bandaged several gashes on his legs and arms. "How were you able to stay safe last night?" Orestros asked.

Bartholomew did not answer. He acted as if he had not heard the question. He looked nervously around trying desperately to think of an answer.

"Bartholomew?" the prince asked, lightly shaking the guard's dirty yellow tunic.

"I'm sorry. I can't help wondering where the creatures are. They were right behind me as I was coming out of the grass," he said, looking out at the wall he had followed. "They could be coming any moment! Maybe we should get moving," he said, with alarm, pretending to gather his things.

"I don't think they'll be bothering us up here as long as Orestros is with us," Ammon said reassuringly. "Relax, my friend. You're safe now." He smiled again as he patted the guard on his shoulder.

"It's just that I've never seen creatures like that. I guess I'm still a little shaken up," Bartholomew offered, looking to all of them for sympathy and understanding. He noticed Orestros observing him carefully. As he looked at Ammon, he found a friendly face and immediately moved a little closer, placing his plate in his lap, and eating fish and sipping water.

"I'm still curious," Orestros began again. "How did you manage to stay safe throughout the night?"

Bartholomew was clever and had thought through his answer since Orestros asked it the first time.

"Well," he said as if revealing a secret and speaking just above a whisper, "when I awoke yesterday, I was alone. I called out. I heard nothing except the sound of running water not far from me. As I followed the sound of the water, I began to hear strange noises coming from the tall grass. I called out for all of you but heard only growls and strange shrieks. I found this small pack and started running toward the water. Before I could reach it, one of them attacked me. I was able to beat it away with my spear.

When I finally got to the water's edge, I realized that I had nowhere to go, so I started swimming. The creatures lined the bank and screamed. Fortunately, they were unwilling to take more than a few steps into the water. Anyway, to make a long story short, I found some trees on the other side and stayed there safely. It wasn't until this morning that the creatures found me on the other side. That's when I finally found all of you."

"That's pretty much what happened to me," Ammon said. "We may have been closer than we know."

"You mean you were on the far side of the river last night too?" Bartholomew asked.

"I was there, but I didn't dare light a fire. Otherwise, we might have met up."

"Did you see anyone else?" Orestros asked, still watching the guard closely.

"Anyone else? No, I thought we were the only ones there. I'll tell you one thing: I didn't get much sleep," Bartholomew stated as he tried to make his story believable. In the back of his mind, he wondered what the giant might know. He could feel Orestros looking at him suspiciously. He knew he had better be careful.

"Why don't you get a little rest, while Orestros and I help Lady Arianne and Aleah get ready to travel?" Ammon suggested.

"Travel?" Bartholomew asked curiously, hoping they would reveal their plans quickly.

"No need to worry about that. You can rest here. You'll be safe, and we won't be far away," Orestros replied quickly.

"I just need a few minutes, and I'll be ready," the guard said as he took another mouthful of fish, drank the remaining water in his cup, and leaned back.

As Orestros and Ammon walked up the staircase out of earshot of Bartholomew, Orestros said, "Something's not right with Bartholomew. I'm concerned."

"What do you mean?" asked Ammon. "He was obviously attacked by the baboons. He was right about getting away by swimming across the river. We're lucky to have him."

"Did you notice that he hasn't asked about the other guard, his friend? And how he seemed to pause with his story, as if he hadn't heard me, when I questioned him on how he had remained safe?

"As if he were trying to think of an answer," Ammon added. "I just assumed he was shaken up from all that had happened. Is there something else that you're not telling me? Have you seen something?" He began to consider some of things he had seen. He wondered why he had not heard or seen Bartholomew during the night or this morning. "I did see strange green smoke coming up from the forest last night in front of the moon. I also thought I saw a dark figure on the cliffs that rose out of the forest."

"Lots of questions and very few answers from our friend, the guard," Orestros said curiously as he looked back at Bartholomew, who appeared to have already fallen asleep. "Two things I haven't mentioned that you should know. The first is that the other guard's throat was cut with a knife, and he showed no signs of being attacked by the baboons. Secondly, early this morning, as I searched for your tracks, I found those of Bartholomew and someone else. By the size and impressions of the tracks left in the sand, I believe a woman was with Bartholomew. Other small sets of perhaps baboon tracks were with theirs near the forest where you saw the green smoke."

Before Orestros could continue, he noticed Bartholomew watching them from underneath his cap. Orestros quickly slapped Ammon fondly on his back and laughed aloud before continuing to walk. "Say nothing more for now but be careful. We'll have an opportunity to talk later. For now, keep a close eye on him. We'll also tell Lady Arianne and Aleah to be careful of him."

Ammon walked with his friend, while all the possibilities of what he had just said began to swirl in his mind. He reached for his belt and took a firm hold of his dagger's hilt, otherwise looking over his shoulder at Bartholomew and remembering the dead guard. He then looked up to see Lady Arianne and Aleah on the ruins of the tower above him. The prince forced a smile when Aleah waved to him. His newfound worries filled his thoughts, as his hopes for a wonderful adventure on Earth seemed to be disappearing amidst treachery and perhaps even murder. He finally waved to Aleah in return, but he could not find a smile within himself.

Chapter Seventeen

King Hyperion arose early and walked restlessly through the empty palace corridors, as heavy concerns kept him from sleeping and consumed his waking hours with worry. Everything in his world was being threatened, along with everyone he loved. As the Prism sky grew lighter, he stood on the exposed platform where he remembered Ammon had flown a kite no more than a week earlier. The orange and turquoise skies rippled slightly as they changed from the dark emeralds and azure blues of night. As he peered over the edge, he could vaguely see the morning activities of people in the village below.

He motioned to one of his attendants, who quickly came to his side. "Send for the young sorcerer Xandros and have him present himself in the reception hall without delay. Also inform the other two," the king ordered in a voice dry and forlorn. His attendant quickly ran down the stone steps and disappeared.

The king gazed into the distance for some time, before he also passed through the arched doorway and entered the palace. He walked down the long corridor lined with large windows; his footsteps echoed on the dark polished stone. Silence abounded as the early morning Prism light crept through the open windows, illuminating the grand tapestries covering the gray walls.

❧ ❖ ❦

By the time the king arrived in the hall and took his seat, Xandros appeared and quickly stepped up to him, bowing with utmost respect.

"Your Majesty, I came as quickly as I could," he said, taking a seat beside the king.

"Xandros, I know that you have not yet aged much more than twenty years. This responsibility would be great for someone two or three times your age, but I must know what progress you have made," the king said dryly, without looking up.

"Sire, I believe you'll be pleased at my work and, with luck, we should be able to see what has become of the prince and his fellow travelers. We may possibly even be able to find Queen Thalia," Xandros said with a confident and sincere expression.

"When?" replied the king sternly.

"Everything is in place now, Sire, but I confess that I've not tested the power of the device. It could offer some degree of danger, but its benefits should far outweigh any such minor threat. Don't you agree, Sire?" he said, grooming his light beard and mustache confidently.

"I will not tolerate another disaster like the travel chamber. Have you determined how such an accident happened, before we embark on another perilous experiment?" the king asked, looking skeptically at the sorcerer.

Xandros stood and paced for a moment as he considered his answer, but before he could begin, the other two sorcerers entered the hall, bowed, and took their seats at the long table.

"Perhaps these two gentlemen are better equipped to answer your question, Sire, as I have relinquished those duties to them while maintaining my own focus on the preparations which you commanded of me."

Pelos, the older and grayer of the two sorcerers, stood, while Antare with his long, stark-white hair sat silently beside him, apparently absorbed in some deep thought.

"Your Majesty, if you are referring to the disaster of the travel chamber, I must report that we have no solid evidence but highly suspect that the old witch Morgana was somehow involved. We have searched for her since the disaster, and she is nowhere to be found either in the palace or the village below. Neither did she escape through the gates, so we must surmise that somehow—with help, perhaps—she managed to conceal herself in the chamber. With the various accounts of what each of us saw before the chamber failed and exploded, there is good cause to believe that she traveled to Earth with the others and may have sabotaged the chamber to prevent her own capture and return here." Antare sat down and looked at the king, awaiting a response.

"I believe I have created a means to answer that question and others of far greater importance, Sire, if you will allow me to show you," Xandros said.

"Precede my young sorcerer. I have waited long enough," the king replied impatiently.

Much to the surprise of Pelos and Antare, Xandros began pulling a long rope, causing the massive green drapes to part. He pulled a lighted torch from the wall, while walking confidently to the raised structure in the center of the room, where the chamber had once stood. Waving his torch through the air, he revealed a circular pool, sparkling with the blue fluid that had once filled the chamber.

Also surprised, the king quickly rose from his chair and walked to the edge of the pool, where he could see the tiny sapphire-like explosions from beneath the surface. As he and Pelos walked closer to the gleaming blue pool, Xandros extinguished the torch and began pulling yet another rope. As he continued to pull, a bright beam of radiating blue light began to shine from a large blue crystal embedded in the high ceiling above them. The light slowly descended, sparkling with blue and white twinkling lights shown only on the circular glowing pool below.

"Truly amazing, Xandros!" the king said, opening his eyes wide in wonder.

"But what can it do?" Antare finally said, breaking his silence as he crossed his arms and pursed his lips tightly, raising one of his heavy white eyebrows skeptically.

"Yes," Pelos added, "it's a marvelous show of light and reflections. Is this the extent of your so-called work in the forbidden areas of dark magic?" Pelos smiled and looked at Antare, who smiled back as they both then looked at the younger Xandros smugly.

"Fools!" Xandros exclaimed, pointing at Pelos and Antare, as his voice suddenly lowered, almost thundering through the great empty hall.

Pelos and Antare leaned back in surprise and fear at the power suddenly released in Xandros's voice, noticing the cold blue reflection issuing from his large piercing eyes as they turned to a bright red and orange of burning coals.

"Perhaps they are fools, Xandros," the king said. "I have faith in you and that is all that matters. Proceed with your demonstration." His voice was calm, as he marveled at the pool and the light descending from the blue crystal in the ceiling.

Xandros bowed to him and then his eyes had returned to their customary icy blue hue.

"Of course, Sire," Xandros said, sharply cutting his eyes toward Pelos and Antare, before instantly producing a wand from his long dark blue robes. At the tip of the wand, a small round glittering ball sparkled with a brightness only equaled by the blue crystal in the high ceiling. Outstretching his arm with the wand in hand over the shimmering pool, Xandros began to make slow circular motions and as he did, the sparkling blue fluid began to slowly swirl. The number of tiny sapphire explosions grew from ten to twenty, then from twenty to fifty, until the light from the pool illuminated the entire hall. All but Xandros shielded their eyes momentarily before their attention was drawn to Xandros whispering strange sounds that almost sounded like words but made no sense. As he continued, his eyes closed momentarily, then opened wide and gleamed as brightly as the sparkling pool.

A fine mist, similar to smoke, began to emerge from his mouth as Xandros continued to speak the strange-sounding words. The mist soon covered the gleaming fluid of the pool like fog, growing thicker with each passing moment. The swirling bright liquid was at last covered with the mist as Xandros became silent and replaced his wand inside of his robe.

Taking a sharp silver dagger from his belt, he raised both hands over the pool. Without hesitation, he sliced into the palm of his left hand. Blood immediately ran from the deep cut into the pool as a slight splashing noise came from the fluid. It quickly began to consume the mist until only the swirling fluid could be seen, along with the large red drops of blood mingling with the hundreds of tiny sapphire explosions. Xandros then closed his hand tightly and returned his silver dagger to its sheath. "Now, Sire," he said in a calm and confident voice, "look into the pool and tell me what you can see."

The king peered into the pool, as the swirling fluid gradually slowed to a stop and the tiny explosions ceased altogether. "I don't see anything," he finally said, staring into the water.

Xandros produced his wand once again and, waving it in slow circular motions, caused the fluid to move ever so slowly. As it began to move, its color changed from bright blue to dark purple. It continued to move slowly as the image of Ammon's face began to clearly emerge in the surface of the fluid. He appeared to be talking, but no sound came forth.

"Do you see him?" the king asked the other two sorcerers excitedly.

"We do, Your Majesty, but it is only an image as if from memory. It does not tell us what has become of him. Surely you must see that this is just some grand trickery," Antare suggested as he looked at the image suspiciously.

"What say you, Xandros?" the king asked, not looking up from the pool.

"Look further, Sire. We have only begun," Xandros stated confidently, as he made several quick circular motions with his wand and then raised it high above the pool. As he did so, the entire pool was filled with not just Ammon's face, but everything that surrounded him. In the pool's reflection, the prince continued to talk, but now it was clear that he was talking to Orestros while they walked side by side. In the distance, Lady Arianne and Aleah could be seen waving to them. The yellow tunic of the guard lying near a small campfire was also visible.

"It's a miracle," the king exclaimed, still watching the image of the travelers. "They're alive and well!"

"Today, gentlemen, we find ourselves in a time of great peril. The queen has been abducted. Armies under Deimos are uniting against us, and Prince Ammon, though apparently safe for now, may be in a more treacherous and unmerciful world than we first believed. We will use this new magic of our loyal and youthful Xandros. However, we will do so cautiously." As the king paused, he noticed the image in the pool beginning to fade. "Is this to be expected Xandros?" he asked.

"I'm afraid so, Sire. If you wish we can begin the process again tomorrow," Xandros said. He dipped his wounded hand into the purple fluid and pulled it back out.

"That is my wish. I saw nothing of the witch. We must know her fate, and more importantly, the fate of the queen," the king said. He noticed several drops of dark red blood dripping from Xandros's left hand. "How is your hand?" he asked with concern, looking into Xandros's eyes.

Xandros opened his hand and it appeared to be healed. "As you see, Sire, there is no danger to my magic. Tomorrow we will know the fate of our beloved Queen Thalia, and if the witch has survived. We shall find her and learn her plans. This was only our first use of this magic. I still have even greater hopes for its power."

Pelos and Antare grumbled. They returned to the table ahead of Xandros and the king, who were lingering behind momentarily to watch the pool turn from purple into the shimmering blue it had been. Xandros pulled the rope. As he did so, the blue crystal light shining from the ceiling once again went dark. The king left the pool and seated himself at the head of the table. Xandros pulled the other rope, closing the massive drapes, and returned to the table.

"This is a great achievement, young Xandros. You shall be richly rewarded, if this magic can be performed as you say it can. I want the pool ready for another viewing of the present conditions on Earth as soon as possible. If we acquire their knowledge, we can then plan our strategies in earnest. We must continue to monitor our travelers but of equal importance, we must ascertain the strength of Deimos and know how he plans to attack us."

"All will be ready, Sire," Xandros said with a slight bow, as he smiled at Pelos and Antare.

The king rose and walked briskly out the large oaken doors of the hall. Pelos and Antare followed a short distance behind him leaving Xandros alone at the table.

ৡ❖ৡ

Xandros sat there for several minutes staring into space, before he placed his left hand on the table. He noticed that the wound had reappeared and was beginning to bleed. He retrieved a white silk handkerchief from his pocket and wrapped it tightly around his hand. He then walked behind the drapes where the pool stood silently in the darkness. He dipped his wounded hand into the aqua-blue fluid and, withdrawing it, slowly unwrapped the handkerchief. Once again the wound appeared healed.

He looked into the pool and observed it changing colors again. He produced the wand from within his robe. As he held it above the pool, it immediately lighted the entire area in an icy blue glow. On the surface of the reflection he saw two dark eyes emerging and staring directly at him. The whites of the eyes were surrounded by dark circles, and he could almost see the image of a face.

"Who are you?" Xandros asked, questioning his own senses.

"I am your Master, Xandros. You will serve me henceforth, just as your father before you!" a deep, low voice replied, as the reflection of the eyes became larger and increasingly malevolent and sinister in appearance.

"I am my own master, and I serve King Hyperion of my own free will," the young Xandros replied sternly and courageously as he took one step back from the pool. The water began to bubble slightly as if coming to a boil. It turned black, and the dark eyes became clearer and clearer. Xandros took several steps back as he began to hear a dark and insidious laughter emerge from the bubbling water.

His heart began to race as he pulled the drapes apart and ran toward the large oaken doors. At the end of the long table, he stopped and, raising his right hand to his forehead in thought, turned and slowly walked back toward the pool.

"It must be my imagination," he whispered to himself. Again he heard the same menacing laughter. He shrank momentarily, as he rushed to his chair and placed his elbows on the table. He pressed his hands against the temples of his head. "What madness is this?" he said aloud, as the laughter slowly faded but lingered as loud as ever in his mind.

His first thought was to tell the king what had happened. He feared his plans to help the king would immediately be cancelled. As he considered his choices, his confidence began to return and he believed he could find a way to overcome whatever it was that he had seen and heard. It would be better to take a risk rather than reveal something that he really wasn't even sure had happened.

He decided to return to his tower far above the palace. He would try to find an answer or perhaps some protection from the dark eyes and insidious laughter. After all, he thought, he had powers of his own. He had simply been caught off guard. He firmly decided he would not make that mistake again.

As he started out the door, a guard appeared from the hallway to lock them. Xandros felt a sharp pain and noticed that the wound on his left hand once again had started to bleed.

Chapter Eighteen

Xandros reached the end of the corridor and looked up at the winding stone staircase leading to his sleeping chamber and laboratory. He knelt down to a small cask of fresh water and removed the cover, pulling a wooden cup from the wall and dipping it into the cask. After taking several long refreshing drinks, he replaced the cover and the cup on its hook before beginning the long ascent.

Before he had climbed far, he reached a small alcove in which there was a small wooden table. There, he lit three white candles to help him climb the steep stairs of the windowless tower. He had made this ascent hundreds of times before but each time, he had to remain vigilant, for any false step could send him plunging to certain death. Almost no one came to visit for that reason, and Xandros felt safe and secure from any unwelcome visitors.

When he finally reached the top, a much larger alcove opened up and revealed two heavy wooden doors with large black metal doorknockers and heavy black handles. He pulled one door open to a very large room with high vaulted ceilings illuminated by dozens of stark white and dark yellow candles. He blew out the small white candles he was carrying and placed the holder on a small table beside the door before closing it. He then pulled a large wooden beam across the doors, sealing and locking them in place.

A large fireplace with radiating orange embers glowed from one end of the room, and two large overstuffed green leather chairs were placed in front of it. Xandros walked to the other side of the room where the wall was covered with bookshelves from floor to ceiling, rising almost sixty feet toward the vaulted ceiling. Each shelf contained hundreds of hardbound and very old leather-covered books. A ladder that leaned against the wall and rose to the ceiling was connected at the top and bottom to small rolling balls, which allowed it to slide from one end to the other.

Xandros moved the ladder to a place toward the end of the wall, near a large arched door, and climbed nearly to the top before retrieving a large and very heavy volume. On the black leather cover were written the words Book of Secrets Volume VII. Placing it under his arm, he carefully climbed down.

As he walked to his chair, he heard a small knock on the arched door behind him, and it slowly opened with a dreadful squeaking sound of rusty hinges. A young boy of nearly fifteen slowly emerged from the opening. "Is it all right if I come out now?" he asked in a frail and gentle voice, just above a whisper.

"Of course, Isaac. I was wondering where you were," Xandros replied, as he walked toward the long ledge in front of the shuttered window. Isaac followed, trying to disguise his slight limp. "How did your experiment go?"

"It began well but another figure emerged, of which I'm quite uncertain."

Xandros then placed the volume in one of the chairs near the fire and, as Isaac watched closely, he tossed several logs onto the orange embers, making the logs immediately burst into flames. Beneath the large shuttered window, there was a long wooden table filled with colorful glasses and pewter plates, along with several large wooden bowls of brightly colored fruits and vegetables. In the middle of the table was a cutting board with a knife and a round loaf of dark yellow bread and a small round of white cheese, cut into small wedges.

At the back of the table, against the wall was a row of dark green wine bottles and long-stemmed cobalt blue glasses. Next to the cutting board was a large blue pitcher, which contained a dark purple fluid the color of Concord grape juice. Xandros cut a lime-green pear and a bright red apple and placed them on one of the pewter plates, before filling two of the glasses from the pitcher. He set them on the table between chairs beside the fire.

"I was concerned about the pool, Xandros," Isaac said, as he took his glass and drank from it.

Xandros was tired and worried but took a bite of the juicy pear and a sip from his glass, before opening the large volume and turning the pages intently. The pages were made of a thick and heavy parchment, and he turned them with more than a little effort. He then carefully observed the detailed drawings of men and women.

As he paused and read aloud the strange handwriting beneath a familiar drawing, it seemed to become almost real as the figure in the drawing began to move within the framed page. The longer he paused, the more real it became, until sounds came forth from the page.

Xandros paused a very long time on the drawing of a bearded old man, who finally looked directly at Xandros from the page and spoke, "If you have a question, go ahead and ask young apprentice," he stated rather gruffly.

"Yes, it's me, sir!" Xandros responded solemnly.

"I assume much has happened in the Prism since my death. We don't have much time, Xandros, so let us speak as quickly as we can. What is it, boy, why have you called me from the past?"

"Something happened today, and I'm not sure what to make of it," Xandros said, as he laid the heavy book on the table.

"You sound as if you're in trouble. I warned you about dabbling in the black arts. By the looks of you, you've done so, despite the warning I gave you when I was alive."

"It's true, teacher, but I did so in order to help the king. There's a dark force on the loose within the Prism. Someone is using black magic, and I'm the only one who knows enough to stop them, or at least give the king a fighting chance. I've used some of your books to show me the way to create the pool of visions."

"Someone else has appeared to you. Who is it? Have you seen him?" the old wizard asked, again looking at Xandros from the drawing.

"I saw his dark eyes in the pool and heard his laughter. He said he was my master and that I would serve him henceforth," Xandros said as he rose from his chair and began pacing.

"There is only one sorcerer capable of such magic, and I dare not speak his name. He is evil and ruthless, Xandros, and he will not hesitate to destroy you or anyone else that stands in his way, even your apprentice, young Isaac. If he has revealed himself in your vision pool, it is because he is confident and ready for you," the old wizard said, as his image began to move around the room within the page of the book.

"What can I do? I believe he has taken the queen prisoner and formed an alliance with Morgana on the Earth's surface. I don't even know his name."

"To speak his name is to call him forth, so you must be careful what you say and when. Place a sheet of parchment on the table, and I will reveal it to you," the old man said, as within the drawing his image picked up a long feathered pen.

Xandros went to a shelf across the room and returned with a blank sheet of yellowed parchment. He placed it on the table beside the book. He watched as the image of the old wizard began to write. Distinct letters formed on the parchment before Xandros, until a name was clearly present:

MORPHEUS

As Xandros looked fearfully at the name, the old wizard began to speak again. "Remember never speak the name unless you are prepared for him. He will try to deceive you and offer you great power, perhaps even riches, but you must not be fooled."

"How can I prepare? He has already appeared in the pool."

"Look into your oldest books; you'll find answers there, but don't underestimate him and don't delay. He's already aware of you and will undoubtedly be back when you least expect it."

"Thank you, sir," Xandros said as he sat in his chair again and reluctantly closed the book.

"Was it really him?" Isaac asked as he looked into the fire and then carefully at the book itself.

"In a way, Isaac. It is everything that he was, and everything he felt. In that sense, he really did appear. But remember he has been dead these many years," Xandros gently waved his hand through the air, as if demonstrating the vast passage of time and circumstance. "I'll see you in the laboratory. I have some work to do before I retire," Xandros concluded as he looked into the ebbing flames.

He finished eating the fruit on his plate and drank the juice before getting up and unlocking the arched door at the end of the shelves. The room was as large as the alcove, but it contained several long tables, each with various experiments and strange contraptions sitting on them. In the very center of the room were three very large books on individual pedestals.

Dozens of faded yellow candles slightly illuminated the large room in a warm glow. Stepping forward, Xandros waved his wand in the direction of two large torches, and they immediately burst into bright blue flames. The room was immediately covered in an icy blue aura.

Isaac followed close behind, awaiting any order Xandros
might give. A massive stone fireplace covered an entire wall
as it rose more than fifty feet to the stone ceiling. Midway
up the large stones was a very large, round stained glass
window with a bright red dragon head, looking fiercely
down at everything and everyone below it.

Scattered throughout the room were perfectly carved,
life-size wooden statues of men and women. Still others,
standing at attention or ready to strike, were soldiers clothed
in armor, some with axes and swords in their hands, all so
realistically carved that even Isaac sometimes had to assure
himself that they had not come to life. Beside the soldiers
were wild beasts, including fierce wolves with glass eyes that
reflected the blue light of the torches.

Xandros walked to the fireplace and added several logs to
the embers. He looked carefully around the room and
inspected the life-like statues, as he remembered what the
wizard's book had said about the evil wizard, Morpheus. He
walked to a metal spiral staircase in the middle of the room
and took several steps up, until he could clearly see
everything below in his laboratory. What he could not see,
however, was the black raven perched at the very top of the
staircase, watching his every move intently. He sat down on
a step and thought. After a long while, he finally descended
the steps and retired to a dark corner of the room. His
left hand was still throbbing, but the bleeding had stopped;
only the open wound remained.

"Isaac," he called out, and from the far side of the room
near the fire, Isaac emerged, rubbing his eyes from sleep and
pulling his black hair away from his face.

"Yes, sorcerer," Isaac replied.

"Mix a potion as I have instructed you for pain and then
retrieve a needle and thread."

"Are you injured?" Isaac asked with concern.

"Only slightly, but I'll need your help to close this wound," Xandros replied as he showed Isaac his hand.

Isaac tucked his shoulder-length hair behind his ears, examined the wound, and carefully observed Xandros's face as he grimaced from the pain. Then from a shelf beneath the middle table, he produced an empty glass container, added a small amount of black paste to a small portion of water, and set the container on a metal holder over a brightly burning candle. After the black paste dissolved in the hot water, Isaac poured the contents into a cup and handed it to Xandros. He consumed the potion and quickly became sleepy, as the pain in his hand began to diminish. Isaac sewed the wound shut, then returned to his bed beside the fire.

His hand still aching from the stitching, Xandros sipped more of the potion, then removing his wand from a pocket. He removed his outer blue robe, placed it on a hook, and lay down on his large overstuffed bed. With a wave of his wand, the torches and candles slowly became dim, and he closed his eyes. Thoughts and memories reeled through his mind, until he finally drifted into a restless sleep. Isaac awakened with a start, as if from a nightmare, but couldn't remember what the nightmare had been about and quickly returned to sleep.

Xandros had fallen into a deep, dream-filled sleep, and tried to awaken but was unable to open his eyes or move his arms and legs. He thrashed about in the bed but was helpless, as he heard the insidious laughter of Morpheus coming closer and closer. From the foot of his bed, Xandros saw an image, in his dream, of Morpheus, standing in his black robes and staring at him as he slept. Again Xandros tried to awaken but remained in his bed unable to move. The face of Morpheus became stern and sullen as his low voice resonated through the dream world of Xandros.

"There's no need to be frightened, young Xandros. I've not come here to harm you but rather to help you," Morpheus said with assurance, as a threatening fog seemed to surround his image.

"This is merely a dream, a nightmare!" Xandros exclaimed, still struggling unsuccessfully to reach for his wand.

"I've merely come to offer an invitation to accompany me to the castle of Master Deimos, under my protection. Are you interested? I assure you there is much to see: his battle plans, his strengths and weaknesses, even Queen Thalia, whom you have sworn allegiance to, if I'm not mistaken." Morpheus was then silent, as he awaited a response, continuing to stare at Xandros through the dark fog gathering around him.

"Why would you do such a thing, and how?" Xandros asked, momentarily resting from his struggle.

"We are sorcerers, Xandros, not merely ordinary. These ordinary men are not to be trusted, whether they use the names of King Hyperion or Deimos or the very lovely Queen Thalia. You will eventually acquire the power to travel as I have offered this night, but by that time it may be too late to offer your king any assistance. I am simply offering to help a brother sorcerer. Perhaps one day you can offer me some help when I am in need," Morpheus finished and smiled broadly.

He extended his arms over Xandros, releasing a black electrical light from his fingertips, which covered the restrained body of Xandros. As the black current pulsed through his body, Xandros felt his invisible restraints being removed until he could
move freely again. He sat up and then rose from his bed until he stood facing Morpheus. "You see, you are able to

move freely. Have you decided to accept my invitation?" Morpheus asked with confident sincerity.

"Even if I do, I don't understand how you can perform this magic," Xandros said, looking at his hand, where the wound remained stitched and painful.

"Look," Morpheus said as he pointed to Xandros's bed. He immediately looked at his bed and saw himself lying on the covers still sleeping. Xandros then raised his hand in front of his face and looked at his own arm and hand. The image he saw was not solid but transparent. He looked through it, as he turned around in his laboratory.

"What is this?" he asked in wonder.

"It is your ghost image, Xandros. In this form, you can travel with me nearly anywhere we wish to go but since it is my magic, you must do one thing before we depart." Morpheus placed his hand on Xandros's shoulder. "Shall we begin our journey?"

"What is it I must do to travel with you?" Xandros asked suspiciously.

"Merely repeat and whisper these words to yourself." Morpheus drew closer to Xandros and whispered in his ear. "When you have completed saying these words exactly as I have taught you, you must end the spell with the repetition of my name, spoken aloud twice, for all to hear."

"I'm not familiar with the language you whispered to me, Morpheus, what does it mean?" Xandros asked, remembering what the old wizard in the Book of Secrets had warned.

"They are merely words from an ancient tongue which existed on Earth long before the Prism was ever created. The words mean nothing in themselves, but they create the power and the magic which can transform us and allow us to travel beyond the constraints of time, space, and visibility. Your childish attitude however, makes me wonder if perhaps I have chosen a sorcerer unworthy of my help," Morpheus said as he glared at Xandros impatiently. "If you are afraid of such power, simply say so now, and I'll be gone. You decide! Perhaps King Hyperion's other wizards, Pelos or Antare, would be equal to this power."

Upon hearing the mention of his rivals' names, Xandros began to whisper the words of the ancient language as Morpheus had taught him but hesitated as he came to the moment when he was supposed to repeat the name of Morpheus aloud, again remembering the warning of the old wizard.

Morpheus sensed his hesitation and loudly exclaimed, "Do it now, Xandros! Do it now, you fool, or live in darkness forever!"

The dark fog surrounding Morpheus became even darker and expanded like the dark clouds of a thunderstorm. As broken shafts of menacing black electricity began to break through the ominous fog, Morpheus's eyes peered and gleamed like lanterns through the darkness at Xandros.

At last, Xandros spoke the dreaded name aloud, though his voice slightly quivered, "MORPHEUS, MORPHEUS!"

Chapter Nineteen

The ghostly image of Xandros was immediately consumed in the dark fog, and he could feel pulses of energy surging through his nearly transparent body. Squinting through the bellowing black and gray fog, he could still see his own body lying on the bed. A strange and piercing high-pitched tone began to surround him, as he could see Morpheus dimly, with his black eyes and sinister grin. Beneath the irritating sound, he heard Morpheus say something.

"What's happening?" Xandros shouted above the loud volume of the piercing noise.

"Follow me!" Morpheus commanded, as he walked across the laboratory, directly through tables, until he reached the door, where he then turned to watch Xandros.

Xandros hesitated and walked around tables and chairs as he tried to follow Morpheus. His actions elicited a deep and sinister laugh from Morpheus.

"Follow me; it's time to visit your vision pool," Morpheus said, as he walked directly through the door, unimpeded by its solid three inches of oak and hundred pounds of weight.

Xandros followed, but when he came to the heavy door, he hesitated and extended his right arm through it first to determine whether or not he could pass through as Morpheus had. His arm tingled as it passed through the heavy wood, then he slowly followed with the rest of his body until he stood on the other side. He caught up with Morpheus, after passing through the double doors and into the alcove at the top of the spiral staircase. Xandros fully expected Morpheus to begin a slow descent of the dangerous stone steps. He was frightened, when Morpheus simply stepped over the edge and began falling feet first toward the bottom.

Xandros stood at the edge and looked into the darkness of the pit, then quickly but carefully began descending the steps. Unable to see but feeling his way along the wall, he was surprised when an eerie torch illuminated each single step in front of him but turned dark when he stepped onto the next one. He knew it must be the magic of Morpheus, and he was truly impressed while still being more than a little frightened.

ೞ❖ஐ

When he reached the bottom, he could barely see the transparent image of Morpheus who walked through the heavy oak doors to the reception hall without being seen by two Royal Guards standing at attention. With greater confidence, Xandros followed, pausing for a moment and waving his hand in the face of one guard, who appeared to see nothing but moved his hand as if swatting at a fly. Xandros then stepped through the heavy oak doors and again felt the same tingling sensation throughout his body. "Amazing," he whispered to himself and as he did, the guards looked at one another.

"Did you say something?" one guard asked.

"I didn't say anything, but I heard a voice," the other guard replied.

"This place gives me the creeps," the first guard concluded.

Xandros quickly crossed the hall, past the long table, and went through the long green drapes, where he found Morpheus inspecting his vision pool.

"All in all, this is not bad work for someone of your age. You learned your lessons well, especially those from the forbidden books of old," Morpheus said, as he looked at the ceiling. "And that is your source of power. Where did you come by it?"

"I created it," Xandros replied confidently.

Morpheus looked at Xandros and smiled, "Of course you did. To enter the pool and travel to my chamber in the palace of Deimos, you'll need to transform yourself. I assume you can perform this simple magic." As Morpheus finished speaking, he transformed himself into a large black raven. He then perched on the side of the pool, staring at Xandros.

Xandros smiled and, pulling the long rope, opened and revealed the shining blue crystal from the ceiling. As its light sparkled and began to illuminate the pool, he huddled in his robe close to the ground. In a flash of bright blue light, a long, glowing blue serpent appeared with the bright red head of a small dragon.

The raven looked surprised and turned its head from side to side in amazement and curiosity. As the gleaming blue light fully illuminated the pool, the raven flew briefly into the air and dove into the glowing blue water. The blue serpent with the red dragon head slithered into the pool behind him.

Xandros in serpent form slithered from the pool and found himself in a large room, where Morpheus stood before him. He raised his fierce-looking dragon head and viewed the room around him, recognizing it as a laboratory not unlike his own but darker and less welcoming. Dark figures, apparently made of stone stood throughout the room. These, however, were very different from the wooden carvings in his laboratory. They appeared even more lifelike, as if they had been frozen in the actual moment of death or perhaps fear. They seemed to somehow call out to him in a whisper that he could hear in his deepest and innermost soul; more than just call out, they seemed to cry out not only for help but also for release.

As he closed his eyes in disbelief for an instant, the figures seemed to move a bit closer and they seemed to increase in number. Where once only a few figures stood in the shadows, a moment later it appeared that there were two or three more. All still remained covered in cobwebs which made him question his senses. He slithered around a portion of the room to better inspect them but found no movement. Still other figures, those of animals, which he had never seen except in drawings, looked as if they were frozen in time. The fury in their eyes was so lifelike that he cringed, as he turned to face one after another.

He summoned his powers once again and with a flash of almost blinding light, he transformed himself into human form, where he stood facing the outlined form of Morpheus.

"You're cleverer than I had ever thought, young Xandros, and less perhaps." Morpheus waved for him to follow, as they walked through several doors and large halls, all the while passing heavily armed soldiers who were unaware of their presence. Some he noticed were stone statues, but others were very real and breathing. In the shadows of the Prism night, it was difficult to tell the difference between them, and his heart raced as he approached each one.

After passing into a beautiful courtyard, filled with neatly trimmed small trees and bright red flowers, Morpheus pointed to a balcony several stories above them. Xandros placed his hand above his eyes to see better through the light of many torches. There on the balcony above, he saw Queen Thalia, looking to the snow-capped mountains.

"Do you know the lady?" Morpheus asked.

"I do, Morpheus. It is Queen Thalia!" Xandros exclaimed.

"As you can see, she is in good health and well taken care of, largely due to my influence over Master Deimos."

"So you say, and so it appears," Xandros replied skeptically, knowing the power of illusion and its part in magic.

"Yet you still doubt me? If I were you, I suppose I would do the same. What can I show you to reveal that I am your friend and not your enemy?" Morpheus asked, an almost pleasant expression crossing his otherwise sinister face.

"A friend would allow me to wander the castle freely, rather than guide me to sights and visions that may well be contrived and created for my benefit," Xandros stated quite frankly and without hesitation.

"You do have a suspicious nature! Can you find your way back to my laboratory from here?" Morpheus asked simply.

"I'm sure I can but should I get lost, I'm certain you will find me," Xandros replied casually.

Morpheus smiled and began to walk away, then returned and, as if whispering a secret, said, "If you're looking for Deimos's planning room, you'll find it behind the third set of large doors to the right in the corridor beyond that staircase." Morpheus pointed to a set of shadowy stone stairs and then walked to a stone table in the middle of the courtyard.

On top of the table was a large, sand-filled hourglass. "One other thing, young Xandros, even my magic won't maintain you for much more than an hour, at which point you'll need to return to the pool. Beyond the passage of that time, you'll become visible to everyone and everything. If you're late and get captured, say nothing of me! I may be able to help you if such a thing does occur but don't rely on it. Deimos is clever and does not tolerate even the possibility of betrayal." Morpheus then turned the hourglass over, and the fine grains of sand began to fall from the top chamber to the bottom chamber.

Xandros watched as the sorcerer's outline and transparent image disappeared through a doorway on the other side of the courtyard. He could still see the image of Queen Thalia, leaning on the ledge of her balcony. He noticed the figure of another young woman join her and observed the queen place her arm affectionately around the younger woman. He tried to calculate which way he must travel through the castle to get to them and then quickly stepped to the staircase where Morpheus had indicated he would find Deimos's planning room.

❧ ❖ ❧

As he reached the top of the staircase, he found two heavily armed soldiers. They were nothing like the guards of King Hyperion, as their armor was dark with tarnish and their faces cruel and unforgiving. Their swords were well-used, still stained with remnants of blood.

Xandros did not hesitate as he passed by them but was nervous enough that he looked back in fear that perhaps they had detected his movement. He remembered that the palace guards had heard his voice as he whispered to himself, and he was especially careful to remain silent as he continued looking back at them. Before he could look for the doors in the passageway ahead of him, he nearly ran into two more soldiers. He stood frozen in place, not more than a few inches from the grizzled face of one of them, smelling the soldier's foul breath.

Xandros ever so carefully stepped away from the soldier and into a shadow on the far gray stone wall. As he looked down the long passageway, he saw pairs of soldiers at each set of double doors. Cautiously he moved from one shadow to the next toward the third set of double doors that Morpheus had said would open to Deimos's planning room.

As he moved through the corridor, he began to wonder what might lay behind the other well-guarded doors. Along the walls were ghastly shaped figures of men, black, as if frozen in time. Cobwebs stretched from the arms to the feet and from the tips of the noses to the frozen chins of each pathetic creature. They were terribly similar to the figures he had seen in Morpheus's laboratory.

Fear and questions overcame him, but he knew he must continue to find the answers that might save his king and the Prism world to which he had pledged his loyalty. He crouched down in a long shadow as he considered. Perhaps Morpheus had directed him only to something he wanted him to see and not the real plans of Deimos. Even worse, perhaps the third door was a trap. He decided that he would have to look into each room and as he started to move back to the first set of doors, one of the soldiers sniffed and spoke to the other soldier in a gruff and violent voice.

"Do you smell something? Something sweet, almost like a woman." As he continued to sniff the air, the other guard did the same, and they began to look around suspiciously. Then they both turned and called out to the guards further down the passageway.

Xandros seized the opportunity to rush through the first set of doors. As he entered the large room, he noticed a round table with chairs around it in disarray. A large candelabrum hung over the table, where documents with long lists lay scattered. Xandros quickly began sifting through the documents, looking for battle plans but found only lists of supplies. He concluded that the supply lists were those needed to maintain a large army for a long period of time.

Another set of documents listed lands and supplies confiscated from farms and merchants. Beside the names of the farmers and merchants, written in red ink, was either the word *executed* or *imprisoned*. Xandros was amazed at the number of names and the riches and supplies that had been taken from each of them.

In the very back of the room on a single shelf was a glass case containing a scroll neatly tied. Xandros tried to open the case, without success. As he tried again to pry its lid open, he dropped it and it shattered into pieces. He quickly grabbed the scroll and stuffed it into his shirt. Without warning, as he walked back to the table and continued to look at the lists, the double doors to the room swung open and the two soldiers appeared with their swords drawn.

"Who's in here? Step forward and show yourself!" one of them shouted, as the other slowly waved his sword throughout the room.

Xandros fell back into a corner and felt a strange tingling sensation as he realized his body was passing into the stone wall. He continued to move into the wall, until the strange sensation covered his entire body. As he tried to move through the wall, it seemed that the dense stone was consuming him. Each attempt to move became increasingly difficult, and the tingling became almost more than he could bear. Convinced that he would soon be trapped in the stone, he summoned all of his energy and struggled until he felt his arm become free on the other side. At long last he collapsed on the floor of the next room. He was thankful that he had not become a permanent prisoner in the stone wall.

ℒ❖ℓ

The second room was very similar in size to the first one. He sat on the floor trying to gather his strength and estimate how much time he had left in the hourglass. His best guess was that nearly a quarter of an hour had passed since he left Morpheus in the courtyard, meaning that he had already used at least one-fourth of his remaining time, and perhaps more. His arms and legs were sluggish to respond as he finally stood.

Looking around, he was amazed at the sight revealed by the candlelight from a chandelier. Large open chests filled the room. Each chest was overflowing with countless jewels, gold coins, silver cups, gleaming white pearls, rings with brightly colored precious gems, all of such beauty that he had never even imagined that such things and so many could exist.

He dipped his hand into a chest of golden rings with dozens of different gems and pulled out an aqua-blue topaz, the size of a thumbnail. As he placed it on his finger, it gleamed almost magically. He pointed towards a dark corner of the room and a beam of blue light illuminated the corner completely.

Beyond the closed doors, in the passageway, he could hear a great commotion and the voices of more soldiers shouting. He moved as quickly as he could to a space beside the double doors and braced himself just as the doors swung open. Three armored soldiers entered with their swords drawn and began searching each corner and hiding place among the chests.

Seizing the opportunity as they searched, Xandros ran into the passageway and cautiously walked through the third set of doors. Soldiers at the entrance showed no sign of noticing him, as he carefully looked around for any possible trap. The room was empty, save for a detailed map that covered the floor. The map showed mountains and rivers, along with the castle of Deimos and near the far other side, the palace of King Hyperion.

Chapter Twenty

Miniature soldiers on horses and on foot were painstakingly crafted, along with long, painted red arrows denoting the pathways to be taken by Deimos's armies as they engaged the king's soldiers. Xandros realized that it was, in fact, the Prism world in miniature, complete with nearly every detail. In the mountains rising from the floor with almost perfect realism, a cave emerged above the king's palace; Xandros had never seen it or heard about. Apparently, it was being constructed to hide a large tunnel. A very large number of miniature soldiers were placed in the tunnel along with a red arrow leading to King Hyperion's palace gates.

Xandros walked around the map several times, trying to memorize the exact locations of the soldiers and the red arrows showing their planned pathways to the palace. As he started toward the doors, he estimated that another quarter of an hour had passed, perhaps a little longer.

He passed through the heavy oaken doors easily but paused and hid among shadows trying to get past the soldiers at the doors and others running back and forth through the passageway. He realized that somehow they were aware that an intruder had entered the first room and even perhaps the second and third.

As he ran down the staircase and entered the courtyard, he found that the hourglass contained less than ten minutes of time. He looked up to the balcony where he had seen Queen Thalia, but she was no longer there. He considered running back to Morpheus's laboratory and escaping through the pool but instead dashed through an open doorway and ascended two steep staircases which he guessed would lead him to the queen.

Soldiers continued to prowl through each passageway, and Xandros was forced to stop repeatedly as he made his way toward the queen. At last coming to a part of the castle, which seemed like the right location, he walked through a set of doors to find a balcony. The queen was nowhere to be seen. Feeling his heart racing from running and knowing that within minutes he would be visible, he finally called out.

"Queen Thalia? Are you here?"

"Who is it?" a woman answered from behind a linen curtain.

"My Lady, it is I, Xandros," he said excitedly.

She stepped into the open room and looked around curiously, unable to see anyone. Xandros moved very close to her and startled her when he spoke, "There's no time to explain right now, but King Hyperion will now know that you are here and safe. We'll be returning for you as soon as we possibly can. Tell Deimos nothing of this visit and, no matter what he says, do not trust him or let him know that you are suspicious. He is gathering a massive army against the king."

"I don't understand ..." Queen Thalia replied, still looking through Xandros as his image slowly became visible. "I can almost see you now. Can't you take me with you?" she pleaded.

"I'm sorry, Your Majesty, I cannot, but have faith. I will find a way to return. For now, I must flee or be captured myself."

"Go then, and be safe," Queen Thalia replied. "One more thing before you leave..."

"Yes?" Xandros responded on his way to the door.

"What news of Prince Ammon and Orestros? Did he survive?"

"He did, My Lady, and is now safely on Earth with the prince."

"Thank you," Queen Thalia said and smiled vaguely, as Xandros saw a deep sadness in her eyes.

He passed through the door and ran down the torch-lit corridor, again staying in the shadows whenever possible, and then leapt down the stairs two and three at a time. Forced to crouch down and hide as two solders climbed the stairs, he looked out of the window toward the hills and mountains after they passed. Campfires dotted them as far as he could see, and dozens of armed soldiers on horseback rode through the gates and departed without pause.

As he arrived in the courtyard, he noticed the last few grains of sand pass through the hourglass, just as his image slowly became more visible. Gruff voices shouted at him from the staircase as he ran through a doorway and into the passageway leading to Morpheus.

After dodging and hiding from several guards, he arrived at the laboratory. He could no longer walk through the door, and the door was locked. He knocked firmly and awaited an answer, as he heard more soldiers coming in his direction. He knocked again with even greater urgency and at last the door opened, and Morpheus pulled him in and bolted the door shut behind him.

"You young fool. You'll get us both killed. Go quickly over there. Beside the pool is a small closet. Hide there until it is safe," Morpheus said desperately, as they heard a firm pounding on the door.

Xandros ran to the closet and noticed that he was completely visible. He closed the closet door behind himself, leaving a small crack from which to see.

Morpheus unbolted the door and Deimos, along with two very large soldiers, wearing polished silver armor and red capes, burst into the laboratory.

"Search the place!" Deimos shouted as he pushed Morpheus aside. The soldiers immediately drew their swords and began to search, recklessly overturning chairs and tables.

"Lord Deimos," Morpheus said calmly and humbly, "I don't understand. What is the meaning of all this?"

"Someone has disturbed the secret rooms, a man to be exact! This man, a stranger, was seen not more than a few minutes ago in the passageway outside your door."

"I assure you, Lord Deimos, you'll not find him here, but with your permission, I'll assist you in his apprehension." Morpheus bowed and looked up at Deimos, observing the rage in his face.

The soldiers returned to Deimos and bowed. "No one here, My Lord, but the place is a honeycomb of closets and secrets rooms, for all we know," one of the soldiers said, glaring at Morpheus.

Before the soldier could say more, Morpheus interrupted. "My Lord, if I may make a suggestion? If a spy has indeed entered the secret rooms, then reason dictates that he may also make an attempt to contact Queen Thalia, perhaps even free her.
If King Hyperion sent this man, she might very well try to hide him. Would not our time be better spent searching her rooms instead?"

"Perhaps!" Deimos snapped in response. "You, Morpheus, come with us, and we'll seal this door. If we cannot find him with the queen, we will return here and destroy the place, if need be." Just before he reached the door, he turned to face Morpheus. "Or this could merely be a clever diversion." Deimos then drew his sword and marched to the closet beside the pool. Prepared to strike, he raised his sword and swung open the closet door but saw only a large serpent coiled in the corner beside a broom.

"Have you taken to keeping snakes in your laboratory, Morpheus?"

"He's only a pet, Lord Deimos, an experiment which may be used to our benefit in time," Morpheus replied with a smile.

"A snake? How could that benefit me?" Deimos asked with sudden interest, after pausing for a moment and stepping away from the large serpent.

"A well-placed poisonous serpent, which will do my bidding and can travel through places that an assassin cannot, could be of great benefit, My Lord," Morpheus offered with his usual sinister grin.

"You're a devil, Morpheus!" Deimos replied, laughing, before he slammed the closet door, marched across the laboratory, and exited with Morpheus at his side and the two soldiers following closely behind them. As they passed two other soldiers in the passageway, Deimos shouted at them, "No one or no thing is to enter or exit the chambers of Morpheus, is that understood?"

"Yes, Lord Deimos!" they both replied, as Deimos continued to walk determinedly down the passage.

❧ ❖ ☙

Xandros heard the door slam and in a burst of gleaming blue light returned from a coiled serpent to human form. He quickly looked around the laboratory and then returned to the closet, opening a secret panel cleverly concealed in the woodwork. He withdrew a long velvet covered object and laid it on one of the tables. As he carefully uncovered it, he was amazed to discover King Hyperion's sword. He carefully examined it to be certain that it was actually the treasured sword, which he knew was vital to the fulfillment of the ancient prophecy.

Then, without further delay, he slowly lowered the sword into the glowing pool of aqua-blue water. Another flash of gleaming blue light covered the room, as he transformed himself into the blue-scaled serpent with the red dragon head and slithered into the pool, quickly disappearing beneath the sparkling surface.

Chapter Twenty-One

As Xandros began to awaken in his bed, he had no recollection of leaving the pool in the reception hall, passing through the green drapes, or climbing the steep steps to his tower laboratory. He began to think that the entire experience had been nothing more than a dream. As he lay there staring at the vaulted ceiling of his workshop, remembering all that he thought had happened, his bed began to shake violently. Pieces of stone fell from the ceiling and crashed onto his tables, one nearly missing his head as he tried to hold onto the bedpost. As the shaking continued, Isaac appeared at his bedside with a terrified expression on his face. "It's an earthquake within the Earth, My Lord! We need to take cover!"

Xandros was still dazed as he tried to sit up in bed. "King Hyperion! Find him quickly, Isaac!" Xandros shouted in a panicked voice, as if speaking from a strange dream or delirium.

As Isaac ran to his side to assist him, a large stone fell from the ceiling, striking Xandros in the head and opening a large gash. As the room continued to shake, Isaac stumbled to a small table, grabbed a towel, and dipped it into a bowl of fresh water, just before the table and water crashed to the floor.

Isaac, too, fell hard. He crawled across the floor still clutching the wet towel until he reached Xandros and collapsed on the floor beside his bed. Isaac wiped the blood from Xandros's forehead and held the towel in place as he looked around, desperately trying to think of what else he could do, as the shaking and rumbling continued. Reaching onto the bed for a pillow or blanket to cushion Xandros's wounded head, he caused King Hyperion's jewel-encrusted sword to fall onto the floor. Isaac quickly hid it beneath the mattress and then positioned himself to shield Xandros's head from the debris that continued to fall from the ceiling.

As suddenly as it had begun, the shaking stopped and far below, the rumbling finally faded away. A deafening silence followed, broken only by the occasional crash of a glass container as it rolled from a countertop or a stray loosened stone, as it finally broke loose and fell from the ceiling.

Isaac waited until he felt sure that nothing else would fall, and then dragged the body of Xandros back to his bed. He carefully laid the sword beside him, covered him with a blanket, and ran toward the door. As he reached the alcove just above the staircase, he heard the distinct sound of footsteps coming up from the tower.

"Help!" he shouted, as he heard the footsteps ascending the staircase.

The voice of an older man, along with several others, shouted in response. "We're coming! Stay where you are!" the voice of the older man replied, as Isaac saw torches lighting the tower stairs.

Within a few minutes, two Royal Guards wearing yellow tunics arrived at the top and, with swords drawn, proceeded to carefully inspect the alcove before opening both doors and searching the first chamber. The Royal Guards then opened the door to Xandros's workshop, looked around the room, and stood beside his bed. "He's here, Sire!" one guard shouted, while the other guards in the alcove escorted King Hyperion to Xandros's bedside.

The king immediately noticed the large gash on his sorcerer's forehead. "Send for a physician!" the king shouted, and two other guards in the alcove immediately left. "Bring the apprentice here at once," he then commanded.

The guards quickly ushered Isaac over to the king and forced him on his knees.

"Did I tell you to treat him roughly?" the king asked, as he helped Isaac to his feet. "I'm sorry. Please, can you tell me what happened?" the king asked sincerely, as he affectionately helped Isaac to straighten his clothes and brush dust from his blue shirt.

"I was asleep when the quake began, Your Majesty. I tried to warn and shelter my master, but a stone fell from the ceiling and struck him before I could arouse him to seek shelter. Since then I have tried to protect him and treat his wound," Isaac said, as he carefully wiped blood from Xandros's head wound.

The king knelt beside Isaac and tenderly tried to arouse Xandros, but he remained motionless and unresponsive. "Has your master been here all this evening?" the king asked with concern and attention.

"Indeed, Sire, though he has been restless in sleep, as if in a nightmare. I was concerned and looked in on him more than once."

"And you found him in a restless sleep? Only that?" the king asked curiously.

"Until the quake began, Sire. It seemed as though he were about to awaken, when the stone struck him from the ceiling. I found something important, and I believe he was trying to hand it to me. He called out your name, Sire," Isaac said cautiously, as if unsure whether or not to reveal his master's belonging.

"Show it to me at once!" the king demanded.

Isaac reached beneath the mattress, retrieved the red velvet-covered sword, and presented it to the king, solemnly with both arms outstretched.

Taking the sword with his one hand and laying it on the bed, the king slowly unwrapped the red velvet cover, revealing the sparkling bejeweled sword in the orange torchlight of the room.

"How?" the king asked aloud in astonishment.

Antare and Pelos stepped forward from the shadows. "Xandros has once again violated our laws, Sire," Antare said with his usual conviction and condemnation.

Pelos, who was standing at an open window, looking out onto the night sky of the Prism, spoke with a dark and ominous voice. "Sire, Antare, you should look at this. I believe the ancient prophecy has finally begun!"

King Hyperion looked at the dark orange and deep emerald green of the Prism sky and noticed a long black crack, which he guessed to be hundreds of miles long, running across the sky. From out of the crack, he could see large boulders falling more than a thousand feet and crashing onto the ground.

"What's the meaning of this? How could this be happening?" King Hyperion said, as he gasped at the sight.

Antare placed his hand on the king's shoulder. "For generations, even before my great grandfather, it was said, told to my grandfather, told to my father, and to me that the prophecy would be fulfilled one day. It said that this very thing would happen."

"We've all heard the old rumors of prophecy, Antare, but I never thought we would live to see it," the king added, shaking his head in disbelief. "There's more to the prophecy than what you've said. If we are to survive, we must know what else will happen. I want all of the old books searched and everyone's recollections of what their fathers and grandfathers have told them until an answer is found.

"We also know that Prince Ammon's birth was foretold and that somehow he is destined to be a part of this. Perhaps the answer lies with him. Since Xandros is our only way to reach him, I command you, Pelos, and you, Antare, to assist the physician in every way to revive him. The lives of all within the Prism may depend on his revival."

The king returned to Xandros and tried to arouse him without success. The physician arrived. He gently pulled Xandros's eyelids open for a moment, then leaned back and shook his head, while he observed Xandros inhaling and exhaling. The physician rubbed his chin thoughtfully, placed his ear against Xandros's chest, and listened. He leaned back again with a curious expression on his face, as he opened Xandros's shirt, revealing the neatly rolled scroll hidden there. The physician handed the scroll to the king and continued to examine the wound on Xandros's head before applying a clean white bandage.

King Hyperion carefully unrolled the scroll, as he walked to the window where Pelos and Antare stood, still watching and wondering at the massive crack in the Prism sky. The king showed the opened scroll to his two sorcerers, but all three of the men looked puzzled.

"It's written in an ancient dialect of some sort," Pelos finally observed.

"Definitely not a language that I'm familiar with," Antare added.

"Do you mean to tell me that neither of you can even translate an ancient dialect? What is it that you *can* do?" the king demanded harshly.

"Sire, Xandros has always insisted that he was a master of such dialects, so we naturally allowed him to advance his studies," Pelos said humbly, as Antare nodded in agreement, then added, "We can translate the scroll, Sire. It may take a little time."

The king shrieked.

"Perhaps as little as a few days," Pelos replied, as he looked doubtfully at Antare.

"Certainly no more than a week," Antare added, as they both nodded to one another in agreement.

"My only true sorcerer lies gravely wounded after having somehow retrieved my sword, along with a scroll that may contain answers to a prophecy, which threatens our very existence, and all the two of you have to say is this! Both of you get out of my sight before I throw you in the dungeon!" The king then raised his left hand as if to strike them, as they scurried out of the room.

Isaac shyly approached the king. "Sire, if I may take a look at the scroll, I may be of some help," he said, slowly extending his hand.

"You're only a child. This is a matter for men of great learning," the king said, as he patted Isaac on his shoulder.

"Perhaps so, Sire, but I have studied with my master for more than two years and have learned much," Isaac persisted, still shyly offering his hand.

The king looked at him curiously for a moment, and then with a stern and serious expression he passed the scroll to him.

Isaac held the scroll closer to a candle. He began to study the scroll with great care and slowly sounded out words with difficulty. He followed the script from line to line and said them aloud, trying to pronounce them and, as he did, Xandros began to stir in his bed.

The physician tried to hold him down, but Xandros pushed him away and stumbled to the table where King Hyperion and Isaac were studying the scroll.

"Master Xandros!" Isaac exclaimed excitedly, as he helped Xandros to sit on a stool at the table. Xandros studied the scroll for a moment and immediately began reading his translation out loud in an undistengable language.

"המלכה המלכה כאשר. המלך ארמון מאיים, פזיז חמדנות לנופף רע כאשר" ותירגל עשויה כעת הנבחר המלך כאשר. הרצפה מנסרה שמיים, דבר ועוד

שניתן החזרת, עתיקים לבית מחוץ. חותמות כל החזיק קסומה חרב לפי
הנסיך ידי על רק ושלום צדק של סלע גביש חרב עם הנסיך לאחזר."

The king looked at Xandros in amazement. "Can you tell us the meaning of these words?" the king asked.

"My mind is still spinning, My Lord, and my memory of this language is vague."

Still the king was impressed, as well as surprised, that Xandros was able to read what was written and thought that after recovering, he would be able to translate the strange writing.

"Is there anything we can do for you, Xandros? Can you tell me what has happened and what I need to do now?" the king asked. He placed his hand affectionately on Xandros's shoulder, as he laid his sword on the table.

"Plans must be made in haste, Sire. Deimos is mounting a far greater attack against you and the palace than we had feared." He looked sternly at the king as blood soaked through the bandage on his head. When he collapsed, Isaac and the king helped him to his bed.

Muttering, sometimes in ancient languages, Xandros revealed the plans he had seen in Deimos's secret map room. He told the king all that had happened throughout the night on his trip with Morpheus, what he had seen in Deimos's castle, and his brief meeting with Queen Thalia. He explained the retrieval of the sword of fire and light, and especially the retrieval of the sacred scroll containing the prophecy. When he had told King Hyperion everything, he turned his head sideways on the pillow and closed his eyes.

"Sire, if he does not rest, I fear he will die," the physician said. "Within his brain, there is a swelling from the blow. If the swelling does not stop or grows larger, he will perish. Any activity will most certainly cause the swelling to increase. I suggest that we give him potions that will force sleep upon him and perhaps save his life." The physician looked humbly and sincerely to the king for a response.

The king turned to his two Royal Guards. "Assemble my advisors and all generals of the armies in the reception hall at once. Make sure Pelos and Antare are also present. Send word throughout the kingdom to all leaders, majors, and advocates to join us, as well, without delay."

The Royal Guards left immediately on their mission as two more took their positions beside the king. He then turned to Isaac. "Until your master Xandros is able, I appoint you, Isaac, to act in his place!"

"Sire, that is not possible! I'm just an apprentice," Isaac pleaded.

"Are you refusing a direct order from your king?" he asked sternly and without hesitation.

"No, Sire. I pray my master is revived quickly. I will assist you in any way possible until that time," Isaac replied submissively.

"Be in the reception hall in an hour! I expect you to be prepared!" the king stated soberly and exited the chamber. His Royal Guards followed closely behind.

178

Chapter Twenty-Two

Some months had passed in the foothills on Earth. The prince, Aleah, and Lady Arianne held one another, as the ground beneath them rumbled and shook, finally forcing them to their knees. In the tall pine trees high on the mountainside, Hermes, the stark white owl, took to the air and circled above, watching the Earth shutter and the ground move in waves. The giant Orestros, still higher on the mountain and deep in the pine forest, stood on a large outcropping of boulders but lost his balance and fell to the ground.

Finally able to stand again, Orestros retrieved the long tubes of cut bamboo that he had been carrying. He looked out onto the expansive valley below. Small groups of wild horses intermingled with hundreds of buffalo, and still more groups of wild antelope grazed in the long open grasslands.

In a small stone fortress on the slope below him, he could see the Ammon, Aleah, and Lady Arianne waving to him, as if to reassure him that they were safe. Midway across the river, Orestros could see a heavy fog engulfing the far bank but not the trees of the forest that had been so clearly visible earlier.

Above the cliffs, a strange and stormy cloud formation rumbled with flashes of lightning illuminating the dark clouds tinged green throughout them. He had watched it for several days, and it had not moved but increased in size while becoming a darker green, along with the strange lightning. Even from a distance, Orestros saw vultures flying in and out of the dark green-and-gray cloudbanks.

He made his way down the steep slope toward the small stone structure where the prince, Aleah, and Arianne stood brushing the dust from their clothes.

"Are you ready, Prince Ammon?" Orestros asked, as he stepped inside the structure and retrieved a large backpack.

"It'll be dark in an hour or so. Are you sure you don't want to wait until dawn?" Ammon asked cautiously.

"Better to travel as far as we can as the sun sets, and get closer to where the clouds are emerging under the cover of darkness," Orestros replied confidently.

Aleah walked away, while Lady Arianne looked with concern toward the storm clouds in the distance. Bartholomew stepped into the open from the cover of the fortress with a small pack, his dagger and spear, along with his yellow tunic, cut into a trimmer heavy shirt.

Grumbling as he started down the long slope toward the high grasses off in the distance, Orestros turned to Ammon and whispered to him. "I still think there's something wrong about him."

"Perhaps," Ammon replied, as he turned from Orestros and walked over to Aleah.

"I would rather Bartholomew were not going with you, Prince Ammon. I have a bad feeling about this," Aleah whispered.

"All will be well, Aleah. We are just going to explore what's causing the strange storms. We'll return in a day or two, perhaps with good news and supplies that you know we need."

He then affectionately brushed a loose lock of hair from her forehead and gently raised her chin, so that she could look into his eyes. "If you and Orestros leave, I'm sure you won't be coming back," Aleah said softly, turning her head again toward the ground.

"There's really no need to worry. We'll be back soon. Orestros and I have collected wood for a bonfire and placed it on the hill above. If you are in trouble, you merely need to light the fire and we'll race back to you." The prince kissed her lightly on the cheek, then turned and started down the steep slope to join Orestros and Bartholomew.

"Prince Ammon!" Aleah shouted as she ran towards him, almost stumbling on the incline before she caught up with him. "Don't trust Bartholomew!" she pleaded in a desperate whisper.

"I'll be careful!" he whispered and once again kissed her cheek, then disappeared down the long slope and into the tall green grass.

ஒ❖ஒ

Within an hour, the evening's first stars began to appear. A crescent moon slowly rose above the mountaintops, where long shadows stretched across the open fields and pastures. Ammon and Bartholomew emerged from the tall grass and looked uneasily across the water.

Orestros joined them and peered into the fog but could see nothing. "This is strange, Prince Ammon. I don't understand what's causing this, and it seems as though the temperature is much colder over there."

"Did you prepare the raft?" the prince asked, as Bartholomew finally joined them.

"Over here. I covered it in grass and willow branches." With Ammon's help, Orestros dragged a raft made from the broken crates that had carried supplies in the travel chamber. As they pulled it into the water, Bartholomew looked at it skeptically. Orestros had notched the bamboo stalks, filled them with fresh water from the river, and tied ropes to each end. He slung two of the tubes over his shoulder and tossed one to Ammon, who handed it to Bartholomew. Orestros then tossed another bamboo tube to Ammon who quickly tied a rope to each end as Orestros had done.

"What's this for?" Bartholomew asked, as he examined the tube and pulled the notched cap off, spilling the water on him.

"You might get thirsty," Orestros said with a grin.

Ammon tried to hold back his laughter as he finished his knot on the rope and slung the tube over his shoulder. He then noticed that Bartholomew didn't understand, and tied the rope for him and refilled the bamboo tube from the water before handing it to him.

"I'm not a very good swimmer. Do you really think we can all fit on that wreck?" Bartholomew asked, as he tossed the bamboo tube onto the raft carelessly and began shaking the boards and pulling at the ropes that held them together.

"You've made it across before. This time we have a raft; it'll be easier, and you won't get nearly as wet," Ammon replied, as Orestros loaded their packs onto the makeshift craft.

"We're going across, Bartholomew. Stay here, if you wish," Orestros said with a smile, as he picked up a plank of wood and climbed onto the front of the raft. Bartholomew looked at the raft and clamored onboard just behind Orestros. Ammon gave the raft a push from the riverbank and jumped on, quickly picking up a plank of wood and, like Orestros, paddling the raft with massive strokes.

When they reached the edge of the fog, Orestros and Ammon paddled just enough to keep their position without being carried downstream by the river currents. Orestros turned back to look at Ammon, who nodded in approval, before they both began paddling into the heavy fog. Bartholomew held onto the sides of the raft and trembled noticeably.

When the fog had completely surrounded them, it was so dense that Ammon could barely make out Orestros's heavy blue coat. The temperature was much colder, and Ammon could see his breath as he breathed into the fog. They paddled steadily, as Bartholomew looked around with dread and excitement, almost as if he expected someone or something to attack them at any moment. Even the sky and the sun were covered, as the river water beneath them turned to a dark, almost black color.

"My father used to say that black water is a warning," Ammon said. He could feel the cold penetrating his coat, and his hands became stiff, making each stroke of the paddle harder and harder to accomplish. At last, the raft bumped into something very heavy, and Ammon could see Orestros stand up for a moment and then leap from the raft. A sudden heavy pull brought the raft partially out of the water, and Ammon and Bartholomew stepped quickly onto the riverbank. "Quickly, away from the river!" Orestros commanded just above a whisper.

Ammon took several steps and tried to see the trees where he had spent his first night but could see nothing more than a few feet in front of himself. As he followed Orestros, he expected to find tall grass like on the other side of the river, but he found that it was wet, flattened against the ground with small ice crystals embedded between the blades.

Orestros tapped Bartholomew on the shoulder firmly, signaled him to follow, and made his way to stand beside the prince before whispering to the two of them. "From now on, say as little as possible and never speak above a whisper. We don't know who or what to expect, but something has definitely changed since we were last here. Just follow me and don't fall behind. If nothing else, we know there are baboons, and probably large groups of them."

Bartholomew said nothing when he saw the two dim green lights appear not far away in the heavy fog, though the prince thought he saw something odd in the dense fog. When he looked again, it had disappeared.

Orestros started out in front. Although the sun, like a large orange ball, appeared on the horizon, the heavy gray fog, like eerie darkness, soon settled in all around them. They began to tire from the long afternoon and evening of travel. Orestros paused and raised his head, trying to see something.

At the same moment, Ammon felt something fly quite close to his head. Both he and Orestros swatted at the air, though they could see almost nothing. Orestros knelt down and opened his backpack. He withdrew a stick with linen wrapped around one end and, striking a flint, ignited it. He then raised the lighted torch into the air.

Ammon quickly ran to his side. "Did you feel that? What was it?" he whispered.

"I don't know, but it wasn't an insect. Much bigger I think," Orestros whispered in return, as he waved the torch slowly around them and looked into the illuminated fog.

Ammon looked around several times with concern, before tugging on the sleeve of his friend's heavy blue coat. "I don't see Bartholomew. He was behind me just a minute or two ago," he whispered, as Orestros turned the dim torchlight behind them, still engulfed in the dense fog.

"There's no telling. We'll give him a few minutes to catch up and then go on," Orestros again whispered, as he patted the prince on the shoulder. As he lowered the torch, they both felt something fly close to their heads and, in another moment, Ammon felt something hit his forehead. He reached up to feel a slight stream of blood and the pain of a cut. Just as he began to tell Orestros, the air was instantly filled with small winged creatures, striking them both over and over again.

As they fell to the ground, Orestros covered Ammon with his huge body, as more creatures attacked. Orestros swatted several of them and grabbed the torch, swinging fire at them until they disappeared once again into the pitch-black darkness.

Orestros he sat up and held one of the fallen creatures into the light of the torch, "Are you hurt?"

"I'll be fine. Mostly just a few small cuts and a little scared. I think they might have killed me if you hadn't covered me," Ammon replied, as he tried to regain his composure, wiping blood from his forehead and smarting as he touched the wound.

"I've never seen bats behave like this. These ugly, little creatures are much bigger than those I've seen in the caverns of the Prism," Orestros said. He turned the bat over, and they both stared at its large ears, which stood up from a grotesque face with a strange nose that looked as if it had been pushed up to rest directly between its eyes. Opening its mouth, he revealed two razor-sharp, yellowed fangs, still dripping with fresh blood. He then extended its slick black sculpted wings, which stretched nearly three feet from end to end.

As Orestros laid the creature down, it suddenly blinked its beady black eyes several times and leapt into the air, flying directly at Orestros and striking him on the forehead. Without hesitation, it made a loud screeching sound before disappearing once again into the utter blackness of the night.

Blood immediately trickled from the wound and into Orestros's right eye. Ammon pulled a cloth from his backpack and held it on the deep gash. "Are you all right?" he asked.

Orestros wiped the blood from his eyelid and blinked widely several times to clear his vision. Pulling the bamboo tube from over his shoulder, he opened one end and poured water into the palm of his hand, splashing water into his eye while continuing to blink until his vision became clear again.

"I'll be fine. We need to move quickly. Maybe we can find some shelter in the trees up ahead," Orestros pulled Ammon to his feet, while holding onto his coat, and ran into the fog. They could hear more bats screeching through the air around them.

After running blindly for nearly a hundred yards, they stopped under a large tree and leaned against its massive trunk while trying to catch their breath. The bats continued to shriek all around them. Ammon pointed to the branches above, and as he tapped Orestros on the shoulder, they looked up but could barely see the branches. Each branch seemed to be moving.

Orestros slowly and carefully took a small pouch from his heavy blue coat and silently removed its cap. He squirted thick oil onto the trunk of the tree. Then he gathered a small pile of dried grass and placed at the base, covering it in oil, as well. From another pocket, he opened a tin container and emptied it into a small opening in the tree bark. The prince gathered more dried grass, as every few seconds another bat swooped down and struck them. He and Orestros stayed very still, despite the bites and screeching. Orestros carefully replaced the cap and returned the pouch and tin container to his coat, then pulled a flint from his pocket.

"When I set fire to the grass, grab hold of my sleeve and keep up with me. The air is going to be thick with bats, and we need to get away from the tree as quickly as we can, before the black powder explodes. Are you ready?" Orestros whispered, as he placed his huge hand on Ammon's shoulder and gripped it firmly as if to help brace him for what they were about to do. Ammon nodded in agreement.

"On three," Orestros whispered, pointing in the direction they were to run. The prince again nodded in agreement, as Orestros tightened his backpack. "One, two ... three!" he said aloud, as he struck the flint twice, sending two large sparks into the dried grass and oil.

They immediately leapt to their feet and ran as the base of the tree burst into flames. A few seconds later, a small explosion rumbled through the darkness, with bats swooping out in all directions.

Orestros pulled Ammon to the ground and covered him, until the bats disappeared. As they both sat up, they could see the large tree slowly being engulfed in flames. The bats on fire streamed through the darkness before they fell back into the fog.

As soon as they caught their breath, Orestros and Ammon began walking again. The further they traveled from the river, the thinner the fog became. Orestros once again lit the torch. With its yellow light, they could see that they were entering the low foothills, remembering they had seen this from far on the other side of the river. Steep white marbled cliffs rose up on either side of the trees, and large boulders, partially covered in a dark moss, frequently blocked their way.

❧ ❖ ☙

Orestros discovered a small cave among the rocks, and they entered it to rest. Inside, he quickly made a small fire and unwrapped two large dried pieces of fish. He handed one to Ammon. They drank fresh water from the bamboo tubes and talked about all that had happened since they left that afternoon.

"Do you think the bats got Bartholomew?" Ammon asked. He stared into the small fire and warmed his hands.

"Something—instinct, I suppose—tells me that he either turned back or has found some shelter. He disappeared before they first attacked," Orestros said confidently.

"Not much more than a mile. In an hour or so, it'll be near midnight. We'll wait until then. Leave our packs here and make our way there quietly in the cover of the night. I want to climb on the rocks above to see if what I suspect is true," Orestros said, all the while staring out of the cave and into the darkness.

"You think someone is really there?" Ammon asked with a concerned expression covering his face.

"Someone or something. We'll know in a few hours." He leaned back and rested his head on his backpack. "Better get some rest, Prince Ammon. It's going to be a long night."

"I've got a bad feeling about this," Ammon said, as he closed his eyes. He tried to rest, but his mind was reeling with thoughts and fears and memories. With his eyes closed, he pictured Aleah and when he had first met her in the courtyard. He was with his father and Lady Arianne. He remembered flying his kite from the platform of the castle. He adjusted his rough pack under his head, while remembering how soft his bed and pillow in the palace had been.

As he continued to reminisce, he could almost smell the scent of lilacs that his mother had placed on his sheets and pillowcases before she was mysteriously taken away. He tried to remember her face and her expressions but try as he did, he could only see a vague image of her. He tried to remember his father, the king, but it was much the same as with his mother.

So much had happened since arriving on Earth's surface; it all seemed a lifetime ago. As he wandered through his memories, he at last heard the voice of Orestros and realized that he had fallen into a light sleep.

Chapter Twenty-Three

"Prince Ammon," Orestros said, as he reached over and gently tapped his shoulder to awaken him. "It's near midnight and time to go. Get ready."

The prince sat up and splashed a small amount of water onto his face, then quickly strapped his pack on. Orestros was standing at the cave's entrance looking out. The heavy fog was gone, but a light mist covered the ground. Orestros covered the glowing embers of the fire with dirt and started out into the night, as Ammon followed quickly behind. He could see the glimmer of the crescent moon in the sky high overhead.

After about a half a mile, Orestros began climbing up a steep incline, where a cliff jutted out of the grass and rocks. Several times, he had to reach down to pull the prince onto the next higher ledge. The higher they climbed toward the edge of the cliff above them, the thinner the mist became. They sat in the clear moonlight on a ledge far above the forest below.

As they settled themselves on the ledge, Hermes circled them once and then landed on the outstretched arm of Orestros. The two of them seemed to communicate for several minutes and then, as suddenly as he had arrived, Hermes took to the air again and swooped down toward the clearing. Every few minutes, a large dark black cloud passed overhead, obscuring the light of the moon, casting giant shadows on them.

They peered into the night toward a strange green light in the middle of a large clearing below and slightly ahead of them. Orestros pulled a small brass telescope from inside his coat and focused on the clearing. After looking through it for several minutes, he handed it to Ammon. He could see dark-hooded figures walking around a dark green firelight but even in the low light, he could see a large black pot with smoke rising from it. The fire and the hooded figures were surrounded by tall gray walls, made from the same stone as the cliffs. Not far from the green fire, a large pool of water stood and a large closed gate opened into the expansive hall.

"Do you think they're friendly? Perhaps they can help us," Ammon whispered, as they continued to watch the activity below.

"Not likely. Look carefully, Prince Ammon. Watch the air as the moonlight shines through the clouds," Orestros whispered.

Ammon watched as a dark cloud passed over. At first, he saw nothing more than the hooded figures. As the moonlight fell across the clearing, he saw what Orestros meant. Hundreds of bats swarmed in chaotic circles above the hall and landed in large dark door openings and corners.

"What do you think they're up to? The men in the black hoods seem to be busy doing something," Ammon asked, handing his friend the brass telescope.

"They're too small to be like any men I've ever seen," Orestros said, as he looked at them carefully again.

"The legends talk about dwarfs. Do you think maybe they survived all these centuries here, while we were in the Prism?" Ammon mused, remembering strange drawings he had seen in the big book his father gave him.

"It's not likely, but we'll have to get closer to find out." Orestros placed the brass telescope in his coat. He helped the prince to his feet and started to climb down from the steep ledge.

❧ ❖ ☙

They followed a newly worn footpath through the forest until they came within sight of the green fire and the large gates, which opened to the enclosed hall. Orestros tugged at the prince's arm, signaling for him to be quiet by placing his finger to his lips. He led him away from the trail to the cover of the bushes further in the trees. The prince could see the bats swirling in the green light of the fire, as Orestros pointed to several of the hooded figures walking on top of the tall gray walls.

As they remained quite still and watched the activity through the metal gates, several figures suddenly began opening them.

From the darkness of the forest, a dozen of the hooded figures with shadowy, indistinguishable faces carried brightly lit green torches and walked in a steady procession in front of the tall figure of a woman. She was dressed in a long, flowing black robe and a black skullcap, which completely covered her head and hair, as it came to a sharp point in the middle of her forehead. Her eyes darted from one direction to the next and seemed to glimmer and reflect the bright green torch lights surrounding her. She carried a long staff with the brightest burning ball of green light. Walking directly behind her was Bartholomew.

As the bright green lights flooded the trees and bushes surrounding the walls, Orestros and Ammon had to quickly cover themselves in the bushes, while still watching the spectacle before them. They watched Bartholomew to see if he had been injured or was perhaps captive, but he showed no sign of injury or fear.

"All stop!" the woman commanded in a deep voice, causing the hooded figures to immediately halt and turn to face her, while Bartholomew cringed in fear only a few feet away from her. She then turned toward the forest where Ammon and Orestros were hiding and raised her torch, moving it slowly, as it became brighter and brighter.

The prince could feel his medallion trembling and growing warmer as his heart raced. She looked out into the bushes and trees. She spoke with a kind and concerned voice, and her face was beautiful when she smiled. They watched her from the cover of the bushes, but her smile seems to contain something else. The prince considered it for a moment.

"Prince? Orestros? Is it you? We've been so worried!" she waved her torch and look for any movement. Prince Ammon and Orestros remained silent and motionless.

"They could not have come this far, Mistress. Even if they survived your pets," Bartholomew offered.

"Perhaps!" she said. Morgana's voice reverted to a deep and sinister tone. She continued to watch the bushes and forest suspiciously. "Double the patrols tonight and allow no one else in or out of the walls! Send as many as can be spared to find them. I want the prince's head on a stick when I rise tomorrow evening."

"Yes, Mistress, as you command," Bartholomew responded. Half a dozen of the hooded figures scurried down the path toward the river, as still others began combing through the trees and bushes, brandishing sharply curved knives, which gleamed in the light of the crescent moon.

As Morgana led the procession through the gates, the forest once again became dark enough for Orestros and Ammon to move further back into the trees. The strange green glow from the fire inside the gates still shone all along the high stone walls, and a light mist still covered the forest floor.

When they had quietly moved to a safer distance, they heard Hermes call from a tree branch not far away. The prince looked up into the tree next to them. He could see Hermes's golden eyes blink, as he watched them carefully. When Orestros extended his arm, Hermes swooped down from the tree and landed on it with ease. The prince watched them, as once again they seemed to be communicating. "What do we do now?" he asked.

"Return to the cave and wait until things settle down, and her guards stop searching. Then we'll return," Orestros said confidently. He watched Hermes take off into the night and disappear. The prince moved cautiously from tree to tree until he reached the cave opening where they had left their packs.

"Who is she? Where did she come from? Maybe she really does want to help," Orestros said, as he gathered sticks and small pieces of wood from around the mouth of the cave. "She was beautiful in a strange sort of way," he concluded, as he looked up at Ammon, tying a heavy cover over the entrance.

"Do you remember the old witch from my father's palace?" he asked.

"Her name was Morgana, but surely the tall woman in the black robes couldn't be related!" Orestros said, turning his head and looking at him curiously.

"Appearances can be deceiving, Orestros. Remember, I thought Bartholomew was a loyal guard but, as you saw, he's a traitor and probably has been for a long time."

Orestros entered the cave and pulled the cover closed behind him. After lighting a fire, he returned outside to see if any light from the fire could be seen, then slapped Prince Ammon on the shoulder as was his custom.

Laughing they went back into the cave. "Let's eat something while we can. We've another long night ahead of us."

ॐ ❖ ॐ

A few hours later, they made their way to Morgana's hall. Each time they tried to get closer to the gates or gaps in the walls, the hooded figures appeared nearby. And each time they were nearly discovered. The prince, at last, found a safe place in the forest where they could watch but not be seen. They waited for the sun to rise, while watching the activity inside the hall throughout the night.

Morgana and the hooded figures gathered around the fire, before the moon slowly fell behind the mountains. They repeated strange words over and over until it became a chant. At the height of their chanting, large bolts of green lightning burst from her fire into the billowing dark storm clouds, until they were all that could be seen above them. Even as the sun rose onto the dark and foggy earth below, the black storm clouds nearly blocked all of its light.

"If she continues to create these storms and clouds, what will happen?" Orestros asked the prince, as he peered from the trees at the lightning and heard the thunder rumble for miles around them.

"I don't know, Orestros, but complete darkness seems to be when her powers are strongest."

"How do we stop her? It must be near the middle of the morning, and it still seems like night is about to return," Orestros said. He raised his head to see what was happening within the gates. As they looked carefully, they saw neither Morgana nor the hooded figures. Then Orestros slowly walked through the fog toward the gates, after signaling for the prince to stay covered.

When he saw no movement around the embers of the green fire, he tried to pull the gates open. They would not budge.

From the darkest corners and doorways, he heard the screeches of bats and sounds of something else rustling in the pitch-black darkness. Pulling his long knife from its sheath, he tried to pry the latches open, but even with his knife he could not move the latches. He looked for a way to climb over the gates but saw that the tops were lined with razor knives and jagged pieces of rusted metal wire, which would not give him any place to hold onto.

As he stepped back to look for some mechanism or secret opening, a bolt of lightning erupted from the storm clouds and missed him by inches. The explosion of the lightning as it struck the gates it knocked Orestros to the ground and left him dazed for a minute. He rubbed his eyes, blinded from the brightness of the flash of light.

Ammon abandoned all caution and ran to his side, trying his best to help Orestros to his feet and away from the gates. Strange noises from the dark shadows grew louder, as Orestros leapt onto the gates shaking them in hopes that the lightning had weakened them, but it had not.

Chapter Twenty-Four

As Orestros and the prince looked through the metal bars, they observed a long blue serpent with a strange red head slither from the pool of water inside the courtyard of the hall. It slid across the courtyard, hissed at the dark corners and then, coming quite close to the gate, it extended its body upward, raising its head into the air to look the prince directly in his eyes. In a blue flash of light, which caused them to cover their eyes, the serpent transformed itself into the shadowy image of a man dressed in a long blue robe.

"Who are you?" Ammon asked, as Orestros pulled him back from the gates.

The shadowy image withdrew a wand from his robe, which immediately ignited with an intensely bright blue flame. He then took the wand and slowly followed the outline of the metal bars separating the two gates. As he finished, the gates slowly swung open, and the man spoke, though his voice was strange, echoing, as if he were calling out of a long tunnel. "Take the prisoner from below—there is only one—then leave this place and quickly. It is time to travel back to the Prism."

The man then turned directly to Prince Ammon. "From the heights of the mountains to the north, you will find in their depths a treasure which value was foretold. Remember these words of the prophecy from the ancient dialect of the scroll:

"When the evil tide of reckless greed,
threatens the palace of the king.

When the queen is queen no more,
and the Prism sky falls to its floor.
When the chosen king can no longer wield,
the sword which holds all seals.
Faraway from his ancient home,
will return a prince by his crystal stone.
The sword of justice and of peace
can only be recovered by one prince.

"Mark my words, Prince Ammon, any brave hesitation now will lead only to loss." With another flash of blinding blue light, the shadowy image of the man was gone. The serpent stood with its head raised in his place.

Prince Ammon and Orestros walked quickly through the gates and followed the serpent, as it stopped at the opening of a dark staircase. It looked at them and hissed, "Take the prisoner and leave this place." It then slithered back to the pool and, quickly winding its body over the edge, disappeared beneath the water's murky surface.

"I think I recognized the man that opened the gates," Ammon said, as he looked to Orestros, and then started down the steps.

Orestros stopped him abruptly. "What do you mean? This could well be one of Morgana's tricks to lure us into the darkness below." Orestros would not release the prince, as he struggled.

"Trust me, old friend, it wasn't a man at all. It was my father's sorcerer, Xandros. I don't know how he did it, but he's told us what to do. Orestros, you have to trust me!" Prince Ammon continued to struggle, and Orestros finally released him and followed him down the steep winding stairs.

Ammon pulled a torch from the wall, and Orestros lit it with his flint, illuminating the remaining steps and a long line of locked prison cells. "Is anyone here?" the prince called out, while he ran from one cell door to the next. "Is anyone here?" he called out again.

As they listened, they heard a faint voice not far from where they stood. "I'm here."

At the cell, Ammon waved the torch in front of the metal bars, and he and Orestros saw the huddled, dirty body of a young man lying on a stone floor, loosely covered with damp straw. In the corner an old wooden bucket stood beside a broken clay pitcher.

Ammon pulled at the door to the cell but could not open it. Orestros initially tried without success, until he braced himself firmly, using other metal bars for balance, and, with great effort and Ammon's help, they broke the door open.

Ammon then shone the torch into the cell, forcing the huddled figure to cover his eyes. "Who are you?" he asked, finally revealing his face to the light.

"Axel!" Ammon called out excitedly, as he knelt beside him.

Axel replied weakly, his voice dry and strained. He then pushed Ammon away. "No more of your tricks, Morgana! Let me die in peace!"

"This is no trick, Axel. We were told we could find you here, but you've got to understand we must escape from this place quickly. There's no time to explain."

"It's really you, Prince Ammon!" Axel managed, as his eyes adjusted to the light of the torch.

"It's me, all right. Are you ready to get out of here?"

"I don't think I can walk, but I'll try! Give me a few steps in the open, and I'll bloody well run!"

"That's the way. Let's move!" The prince placed Axel's arm around his own shoulder and helped him to his feet. Orestros held Axel's other arm, as they began to climb the spiral staircase toward the dim light above.

As they reached the opening to the gray marble courtyard, Orestros extinguished the torch, noticing the fog and darkness had become more overwhelming in the time they had spent in the dungeon. The three men rushed toward the entrance, just as the gates began to slowly close. Orestros let go of Axel's arm and ran forward, wedging himself between the closing metal gates.

Prince Ammon struggled to help Axel toward the gates, as he heard the screeches of bats and other frightening sounds rumble and stir from the dark corners of the courtyard. There was no longer any sign of morning light, and vague images of the hooded figures began to arise from the dark shadows.

The prince helped Axel through the gates, and Orestros managed to get through, before the gates snapped shut behind him. They ran haphazardly along the trail, until Orestros pulled them into the ferns and bushes of the forest and held them down. They looked back and saw the hooded figures once again moving along the tops of the walls and within the hall. Though it couldn't have been much more than noon, the sky was so dark that it seemed to be late evening. As they began to move again toward the cave where the prince had covered the entrance, Bartholomew suddenly appeared in front of them.

"I thought I would never find you!" he exclaimed, as the bushes rustled behind him. "I've found a safe place for us and help from a beautiful queen. Let me help you to her castle," he said, as he approached the prince and offered his hand in friendship. As he drew closer, he realized that Axel stood beside him. "What's this?" he asked as he quickly pulled a dagger from his belt.

"Traitor!" Axel shouted, as Bartholomew leapt forward. The prince stepped aside, but Bartholomew managed to stab his dagger deep into his left shoulder.

When Bartholomew raised his dagger to strike again, Axel knocked him to the ground and choked him with his bare hands until Bartholomew lost consciousness. His bloody dagger fell onto the mist-covered forest floor. Axel searched for the dagger until he found it and put it in his belt.

Orestros quickly ran to the prince's side and pressed his giant hand on the bleeding wound.

"Move away, old friend. It's not well with me," Ammon uttered, his eyes rolling back in his head as it dropped onto his shoulder. Bright red blood dripped onto his left shoulder.

Axel immediately supported Ammon's head and neck and pressed on the wound to help stop the bleeding.

"Axel, help me exchange the prince's clothes with Bartholomew's!" Orestros commanded, as he began to strip the yellow tunic from Bartholomew.

"We've got to stop the bleeding!" Axel said, as strange green lights appeared from the forest trail behind them, and the sound of heavy steps drew closer.

Orestros finished changing the prince's blue cloak with the silver cross onto Bartholomew.

"There's no time, Axel, follow me!" Orestros quickly lifted Ammon in his arms and ran into the forest toward the cave. Axel followed behind as the bright green procession illuminated the forest around them.

Arriving at the cave, Orestros helped Axel through the cover and gently laid Ammon on the ground. As he attended to his wound, they could hear Morgana's voice and her entourage marching along the path, amidst thunder and rain, which increased with the cold and fog. Her procession stopped abruptly and the rain was the only sound in the forest, until her soft and delicate voice broke the silence.

"Are you there, my friends? You can trust me. I want only to help you!" She listened for a response, and when none was forthcoming, her voice returned to a low and angry tone, "Move on! We'll find them in time!" she commanded.

When Ammon turned his head from side to side in pain and began to cry out, Axel carefully covered his mouth to conceal the sound and whispered ever so lightly to him, "Stay quiet for a few moments, and we'll be safe!"

The prince seemed to awaken for a moment and nodded in understanding before closing his eyes and silently grimacing in pain. After the procession had passed, Orestros peeked through the cover of the cave. He realized that it couldn't be much more than midday, but it looked like the sun was about to set. The black clouds seemed closer than ever, and the thunder rumbled and shook the earth beneath them The fog was once again so thick that it was difficult to see more than two or three feet in any direction. The temperature had dropped so that as he breathed out of the covering, he could see his breath form into a frozen vapor.

When he was certain that Morgana and her creatures were safely away, he gathered more kindling and logs for a fire. From his backpack, he applied a green moss to the prince's wound and from the water in the bamboo tubes, mixed herbs and small portions of a white liquid into a cup, which he gave to the prince and Axel. As the small fire illuminated the cave and warmed the chilly air, a feeling of safety and comfort inspired all of them.

As they rested, Axel told the prince what had happened since their arrival and the collapsing of the travel chamber. He explained how Morgana had captured him and Leda inside the orange cloak. Axel then told them what he understood about his capture by Morgana and his imprisonment with Princess Leda. Sadness overcame him as he spoke of her. Orestros and the prince noticed the lonely and distant look in his eyes.

The thunder and rain became so loud at times that he often had to stop speaking or repeat what he had said. Orestros covered them with blankets. "We searched all the cells in Morgana's dungeon but didn't find any trace of her," the prince said, as he noticed Axel looking sadly into the flickering flames.

"Two days ago, Morgana took her away. She said something about adding Leda to her collection." Orestros spoke with alarm and concern, as he turned his attention to the prince. "Can you travel, Prince Ammon?"

"I think so. If not, go on without me."

"What's going on?" Axel asked with surprise, watching the prince and Orestros load their packs.

"Morgana is going for Aleah and Lady Arianne. There's no time to spare. Can you keep up?" Ammon asked Axel directly, as he paused at the entrance to the cave.

"Don't worry about me. Whatever was in the potion has nearly revived me. I can keep up," Axel said. He put on Bartholomew's yellow tunic, picked up the wicked dagger the guard had used to stab the prince, and followed them out of the cave.

Bats swooped through the fog at times but did not attack after they saw Bartholomew's yellow tunic. Orestros, swatted at them almost continuously as he ran past the stand of trees, still smoldering from the fire he had ignited the day before.

Chapter Twenty-Five

Thunder and lightning strikes continued all around them, and even Orestros was forced to rest when he finally reached the riverbank. Within a few minutes, the prince and Axel arrived out of breath to find Orestros uncovering the raft and pushing it into the water's edge. The fog was somewhat lighter as they boarded the raft, and then Orestros gave it a final push into the water.

When they reached the middle of the river, they could see that Aleah and Arianne had lit the distress bonfire on the far mountainside. As hard as they paddled, something about the water had changed. It had become even darker and seemed thick and heavy.

Ammon started to speak, when Orestros turned and looked at him and Axel. "We've got to paddle harder. Morgana is probably already there!" Orestros tossed a paddle to Ammon. He began to paddle with renewed strength. Axel continued to paddle relentlessly.

Nearly a half of an hour later, Axel felt the raft lurch to a stop. Orestros leapt past him and pulled the raft onto the river's bank. In the mist of all the urgency to make it a shore, no one had seen the Prince Ammon slip silently off the edge of the raft into the freezing dark water. The wound in his shoulder continued to bleed slowly, leaving a light red trace of blood in the water.

Axel and Orestros looked back for the prince, seeing only the bloody water trail off where he had gone under. Orestros dove underwater for him. Axel looked about but saw only a series of bubbles rising from the swirling currents. He finally noticed Orestros's head emerge from the rippling water, then take a deep breath before submerging again. Axel then sprang from the edge of the riverbank into the cold black water.

A moment later, Axel crawled up on the riverbank and sat down, carefully and attentively watching the river as the currents swirled in the rain. He heard Orestros's distinctive voice from nearly a hundred feet downstream. A few seconds later, he saw Orestros's soaked form emerge from the fog, carrying the limp body of the prince over his shoulder. He laid him down and pushed with his massive hands onto his back. Water gushed from Ammon's mouth with each push. Orestros then turned him over and pushed on his stomach, while Axel turned his head from side to side, as another gush of water came forth. Orestros continued to turn the prince from his back to his stomach, as he and Axel worked furiously to save him.

Ammon's skin color was paler than either Axel or Orestros had ever seen on a living person, and he had a green tinge around his mouth and nose. Axel tried to find a heartbeat through the pulse in Ammon's wrist, but there was none. Orestros placed his ear against Ammon's chest but heard nothing.

They looked dumbfounded and at a loss for words, yet they continued their efforts to save Prince Ammon. Finally they realized he was dead. Slowly standing and looking down at him as if all had been lost, the medallion began to slowly shine a bright blue.

Axel, reaching down quickly, opened Ammon's shirt, revealing the medallion. As he did, there was an explosion of blinding light that sent Axel back into Orestros's arms. Slowly Ammon came to his senses and tried to sit up. The two men immediately pulled the prince upright and slapped him on the back to help him get air, until finally he began to breathe normally.

"Are you all right, Prince Ammon?" asked Orestros.

"I feel very tired and cold," he managed to say, as he sat shivering uncontrollably and coughing. Orestros went to the water's edge and pulled the makeshift raft onto land, then leaned it against a willow tree to shelter Ammon from the storm.

Axel, still weak somewhat from his ordeal with Morgana and her hooded baboons, held Ammon to try to warm him.

Orestros then carried him to the covered lean-to, cleaned his wound, and applied more dark green moss and tree bark. The green tint to his skin was becoming more obvious.

"Do you have the dagger that Bartholomew stabbed him with?" Orestros asked Axel.

He quickly pulled the dagger from his belt. It had a wicked and jagged blade with a strange green discoloration on its edges.

"This is Morgana's poison. The prince isn't going to be able to travel for awhile, at least until the medicine begins to work," Orestros concluded.

"What about the potion you gave us earlier? Would it help him if he drinks more?" Axel whispered.

Prince Ammon raised himself onto one elbow and spoke clearly. "You have no choice but to leave me here and go help Aleah, Leda, and Arianne before it's too late." Coughing uncontrollably, the prince lay down again.

Orestros began mixing some potion into a metal cup and added water from the bamboo tube. He then helped Ammon to sit up and drink the bitter-tasting potion.

"I'll meet you there as soon as I'm able to travel," Ammon said, trying to hide his pain with a reassuring smile.

Orestros covered him with the warm, dry blankets and then turned to Axel. "Are you going to be able to keep up?" he said, as he hoisted his backpack onto his back.

"It's hard for anyone to keep up with you, my friend. I'll try not to be far behind. There's a chance Princess Leda may be with Morgana. I have to help her if I can," Axel responded with determination, turning toward the prince. "If you're not there in a few hours, I'll come back for you."

"I'll see you both in a little while. Now, get going," he said, forcing another smile.

∾❖∾

Orestros and Axel left the shelter and made their way back through the tall grassland toward the ruins. As they reached the crumbling wall, they could clearly see the distress bonfire burning. Among the ruins they could also see dozens of Morgana's hooded figures. On the tower, Morgana herself stood with a large bow and a quiver of green, glowing arrows.

Orestros quickly concealed himself behind the wall. Axel, still wearing Bartholomew's tunic, lowered his head to conceal his face as he jogged closer. Morgana turned to face them. She pulled an arrow from her quiver, placed it in the bow, and drew it back. She carefully watched Axel, who waved at her before she lowered the bow.

The clouds overhead seemed to draw closer and closer to the ground with each passing moment. The wind whipped the fog and mist all around them. Sleet formed without warning and stung their faces as they continued to move closer to the ruins.

Axel had run to a large broken block of stone just beyond the walls of the fortress ruins. He hesitated, as if to rest. Orestros quickly made his way up the incline behind the stone wall to where Axel waited. He covered his mouth from view; as he shouted to be heard above the driving sleet and wind. "What are we going to do when we get there? We don't have anything to match that bow and those poisoned arrows."

"When we get there, find something to shield yourself with," Orestros said. "Use the pack, if you can't find anything else. I will take care of the rest."

Without hesitation, they ran toward the ruins. Upon their arrival, Morgana and her hooded creatures were gone. There was no sign of Aleah or Arianne. The bonfire was nothing more than a heap of ashes, smoldering in the freezing wind.

❧ ❖ ❦

Beside the riverbank, the prince left the shelter of the raft and began making his way through the tall grass toward the ruins. Thunder rumbled, as the bright flashes of lightning illuminated the dark clouds. The wind and sleet made it difficult for him to see. He covered his head with a blanket, peering out only long enough to make sure that he was on the path that Orestros and Axel had taken.

In the distance behind him, he hadn't notice the green torch lights. Nor did he notice Morgana drawing her bow back with the green glowing arrow tip. The prince caught the flash of the arrow as it left the bow and dropped down into the tall grass. It had zipped silently above him, barely missing his head. Crawling further off the trail, he heard Morgana's voice. "I must be seeing things. I could have sworn I seen one of them fools from the Prism."

She then pointed her torch toward the river. "Move along now. There's much to be done. Hopefully that idiot Bartholomew has enough sense to follow us!"

The prince lay close to the ground, while watching them pass and, for a moment, he thought he saw Aleah and Lady Arianne in chains stumbling along behind Morgana. As he looked up again, they were gone. He began following Morgana's procession in the cover of the tall grass. He watched them arrive at the river and discover the shelter of the raft against the willow tree. Morgana used her torch to set the shelter on fire, and then walked to the riverbank. She began to speak strange words, as she touched her glowing green torch to the surface of the water, turning it to ice so that she and her hooded creatures could walk across.

As they approached the middle, the prince drew closer. He could see Bartholomew, waving his arms and still wearing his dark blue cloak with the silver cross in its middle. He was shouting but in the wind, it was impossible to understand him. Morgana drew her bow as soon as she saw the prince's coat, and within seconds released two gleaming green arrows, striking Bartholomew in his chest.

From across the frozen river, Ammon could hear Morgana shouting. "Bring the body of Prince Ammon to me. Before dawn, I will send his head to his father, King Hyperion!"

Ammon managed to smile, as he started to follow Morgana across the frozen river. He then felt Orestros and Axel grab hold of his arms. "There's no time for her now, Prince Ammon. Remember what Xandros warned!" Orestros said with authority. By the time he had finished speaking, Morgana has disappeared out of sight and the river once again flowed freely.

Chapter Twenty-Six

The three took shelter in the same ruins from which Morgana had taken Aleah and Arianne. The prince tried to rest, despite his worries about the long trip to the summit. Orestros prepared suitable clothing and packed food for the journey into the snowy heights, as well as the extended trek through the caverns that he hoped would lead them back to the Prism. He tried to remember what Xandros, the sorcerer, had told the prince of the prophecy. He spoke the words aloud; the prince added the parts that Orestros had forgotten. Axel carefully wrote them down. When they had finished, Axel took the parchment and read the prophecy aloud.

> "When the evil tide of reckless greed,
> threatens the palace of the king.
> When the queen is queen no more,
> and the Prism sky falls to its floor.
> When the chosen king can no longer wield,
> the magic sword which holds all seals.
> Far away from his ancient home,
> returns a prince by the crystal stone
> The sword of justice and peace
> can only be recovered by this prince.

"Prince Ammon, you must be the chosen one," Axel said with excitement in his voice as he looked at him.

As the prince began to repeat the prophecy, they were surprised that he remembered it word for word, and the sound of his voice had changed, as if Xandros had found a way to magically speak through him. They watched the prince in amazement as they also noticed his medallion slightly glow blue in its middle as he quoted the prophecy.

As Ammon finished, the medallion ceased to glow and he himself appeared to be coming out of a trance.

"Are you all right?" Axel finally said, after a short but strange silence that followed the prince's words. The sound of the wind and rumbling thunder from outside, which had seemed to be quiet as he spoke, returned.

"I'm better. We need to be on our way. Is everything prepared?" Ammon asked Orestros.

"Everything is prepared but remember once we get through the trees, there'll be no protection from the wind. We'll have to tie ourselves together with ropes so we don't get separated or lost," Orestros answered. He wrapped a long scarf around his long black stocking cap, leaving an opening only large enough to see through. The prince did the same and Orestros, who had already prepared suitable clothing and a red scarf from blankets, assisted Axel.

They tied a rope nearly fifteen feet long between each of them and left the shelter. They were immediately slapped by the freezing wind and sleet. As they left the shelter of the trees, the wind and sleet grew more intense, just as Orestros had warned. Using the strong walking staffs that he had gathered from the forest, they forced them into frozen snow, crusted over with a sheet of ice, as they made their way up the mountain. Orestros tried to make footholds for Axel and Ammon, as he led the way up the steep frozen incline.

After an hour, the wind still continued its ferocity, but the sleet had turned to blowing snow making it difficult to see the fifteen feet that separated each of them. If Axel, who was following behind Orestros, hesitated too long or slowed down, he immediately felt the rope tugging him forward again.

๑๛❖๑๛

Another hour of difficult travel finally brought them to an outcropping of boulders, which partially sheltered them from the raging wind. Orestros insisted that they drink from one of the bamboo tubes. The water tasted bitter; Ammon and Axel knew that it contained more of his potion. Ammon pushed it away at first, but Orestros insisted that he drink it, and he even drank a smaller portion himself. The wind whistled and howled through the boulders, making any conversation almost   impossible, unless they shouted loudly.

After a short rest, Orestros pulled the scarf away from his mouth and in his booming deep voice, shouted, "Another mile and we'll need to start looking for the entrance to the cave. It's the steepest part of the climb. Check your rope and make sure the knots are secure. Are you both ready?"

Ammon and Axel nodded as Orestros covered his face and stepped back into the open, taking one firm step after another. Each step became increasingly difficult, and gaining a firm foothold in the deepening snow was a challenge. Ammon and Axel relied on Orestros's steady pulling of the rope, though neither of them could see the rope itself as it disappeared into the blowing white powder.

Axel fell into the knee-deep snow repeatedly and had to struggle to stand and regain his footing. Loud claps of thunder shook them every few minutes, sometimes knocking them off of their feet. Despite the wrappings around their hands and feet, they had become quite numb in the freezing temperatures. He slipped on the frozen snow, pulling the rope tight that connected him to Orestros. He tried to catch himself but was out of breath in the high altitude and lay on his side gasping for air and holding onto the rope. The prince quickly joined him and helped him to his feet, just before the rope jerked and pulled Axel another two steps up the mountain.

For another long stretch, they helped one another around massive boulders and up steep cliffs, and at times had to stop to catch their breath in the high altitude. The prince and Axel leaned against the side of a boulder, blocking the wind, and were relieved when Orestros joined them. As he pulled his scarf away from his mouth, he still needed to shout, but the boulder blocked the wind enough for them to hear him more clearly than before.

"Up ahead, maybe thirty or forty feet, there's something that looks like an opening. It's hard to see clearly, but we can take cover there. The summit is not much more than a hundred feet above us. We can rest in the opening. Come on; it's not much further." Orestros covered his face again and started upwards without waiting for them to respond.

The opening was not very large and Orestros had to slowly negotiate his large frame through it. The prince and Axel easily slipped through and, after taking only a few steps, were relieved to find that they were completely out of the wind. The three slowly uncovered their faces and looked around the opening, which expanded some fifty feet above them. Not far in front of them, a ledge revealed a dark chasm. They all stepped to the edge, and Orestros tossed a large stone into its depths, as they listened for it to hit bottom. Only silence followed except for the wind whistling through the small opening to the outside.

"Look!" the prince exclaimed, as bright colors of blue and ivory momentarily illuminated the smooth stone walls from a pool of water far, far below them. As they gazed into the sparkling darkness below, they heard the distinct sound of a splash as it echoed up through the abyss.

Orestros set his pack beside the wall near the opening where light still filtered in from the outside, and opened it. The prince and Axel laid their packs down and removed some of the layers of clothes in which they had been so tightly bound. Orestros constructed a torch and ignited it, then stood as the light slowly revealed the walls of the space leading to the ledge.

After looking at the ceiling above and the stone walls surrounding them, Orestros returned to the ledge and found a chiseled square stone, covered with dirt and a light layer of snow which had blown in through the opening. He quickly wiped away the snow and dirt and held the torch closer.

Above the words, there was a deep impression, a simple line, which seemed to draw one's attention to the words below it. As the torch illuminated the chiseled words, Ammon and Axel stepped closer. The blue stone in the center of the prince's medallion began to glow.

"I've never seen words like that," Axel said, as he touched the deep groove etched into the square stone.

"It's the prophecy that the Xandros image told us about in Morgana's castle," Ammon said without hesitation.

"Can you read this?" Orestros asked, watching the prince carefully studying the chiseled words.

"I don't need to. I already know," the prince replied confidently.

"Then what do we do from here? What does it say?" Axel placed a hand on the prince's shoulder with pride and renewed hope.

"Don't you see? We are the prophecy! Hundreds and hundreds of years ago, they left this for us to find. There's a path that leads to the Prism. All we need to do is to find it and follow it home, the same way they did when they left Earth's surface so long ago."

Prince Ammon was excited. He stood up straight and began to carefully search the walls surrounding the ledge. Axel and Orestros did the same, carefully pressing and rubbing their hands against the stone and trying to find a seam or opening, any hint of a concealed passageway.

After the three men had searched every inch of the exposed walls and found nothing, Ammon and Axel sat down and drank water from their bamboo tubes. The prince was lost in thought, and Axel in frustration finally got up and began tapping the walls, hoping to find a difference in sound which might indicate a hidden opening. The prince continued to look at the walls and ceiling, but neither of them found anything but solid stone.

Orestros, at last, tied a rope to an outcropping of rock and slowly lowered himself over the ledge, then swung himself in large arcs, hoping to find another ledge or opening which might lead below but found nothing beyond the sheer, flat walls which didn't even offer a single foothold. He pulled himself back to the top and joined the prince and Axel.

"I don't see any way down. It may have been destroyed in an earthquake or who knows what. Anything could have happened in such a long time. We may have to go back outside and try to find another way," he said, as they listened to the howling, relentless storm only a few feet away.

"It's water at the bottom. What if we jump?" Axel suggested as a final plan.

Orestros then tossed another large stone over the ledge. They listened as the prince softly and slowly counted aloud, "One, two, three, four, five, six, seven, eight, nine," and finally heard the distant echo of a splash. The prince ran to the edge and watched the blue and ivory colors arise from the distant pool once again. He then took the torch from Orestros and carefully looked at the words chiseled into the square stone.

"None of us could survive that drop, even if the water were deep, which it probably isn't," Orestros concluded.

"The answer's got to be here. Maybe it's in the words!" The prince ran to his pack and pulled the parchment on which they had written the words of the prophecy. "Maybe we can figure it out based on what Xandros told us. He must have known what the words meant exactly." He then followed what he had written, word for word. "The number of the words is the same," he said, as Orestros and Axel joined him. He pointed to a line toward the end of the penciled writing and then to its counterpoint chiseled in the square stone, "Far away from the ancient home returns a prince by his crystal stone. That's got to be it!" the prince exclaimed.

"What?" Axel responded.

"My father gave it to me when I was a little boy, and I've always thought of it as a treasure. It's been passed from father to son for centuries. Somehow it lights to show the way."

Prince Ammon quickly took the medallion from around his neck and slowly moved it through the air, while looking through the clear blue gem in its center, but nothing happened.

Orestros unexpectedly pulled the knife from his belt and leaned over the square stone. He then carefully used the knife to remove the dirt from the chiseled line above the words.

"Try placing the medallion here. See if it fits, anyway," Orestros said, immediately evoking a smile from Ammon.

He looked at the chiseled groove and as he moved the medallion closer to the square stone, they both began to slightly glow. As he touched the bottom tip of the medallion to the line on the stone, it turned a soft shimmering blue, and the medallion glowed brightly as it easily went into the stone. He waited for a moment, but nothing happen. He then slowly turned the medallion in the impression and, as he did, a small, white twinkling started from its center. "Put the fire of the torch out!" he whispered excitedly.

As Orestros extinguished the torch flame, the twinkling blue stone within the medallion began to spin. Beneath their feet they sensed massive stones moving, making slow rolling and grinding sounds. They stepped away from the square stone, when a large rectangular door began to open on the floor directly in front of the shimmering square stone.

As they moved closer, a brilliant white beam of light shone directly into the opened doorway, revealing stone steps descending into the darkness. Thick and very old cobwebs hung heavily from the corners of the stone walls and at times even obscured the dark pathway completely.

"No one has been down there in a very long time," Axel said in astonishment.

"Several centuries, I would guess," the prince added, as he started packing his backpack.

"Do you think it's safe?" Orestros and Axel asked in unison.

"Safe? Does it matter? It's the path that we've chosen, perhaps the path chosen for us. The prophecy seems to be leading us down there whether we choose it or not. If the king and the palace are in danger, then I have no choice but to leave at once. Would you rather stay here and wonder, or start down the steps to find out if something written centuries ago was meant to foretell what's happening to the three of us?"

Chapter Twenty-Seven

After stuffing his heavy clothes into his pack and closing it, Prince Ammon began carefully coiling the long climbing ropes into a circle on the stone floor in front of him. Orestros and Axel didn't answer his question with words but rather followed his example and filled their packs before assisting him with the ropes.

The prince cleared away the cobwebs from the top of the first descending steps and removed his medallion from the square stone. As he did so, the heavy slab of stone, which had concealed the doorway, ever so slowly began to close. The grinding sound of massive stones echoed throughout the steeply descending stairs, and all three of the travelers braced themselves against the smooth stone walls until the rumbling ended. With the closure of the stone slab, the darkness of the passageway was so complete that he could not see his own hand in front of his face.

He hung the medallion once again around his neck as he started down the steps. Axel and Orestros followed closely behind him.

"I can't help feeling that we've entered a crypt," the prince said in the darkness, his voice echoing down the long path.

"Crypt?" Orestros said, fumbling through his pockets to find his flint so he could light the torch.

"You know, one of those stone chambers is where they bury very important figures, figures like kings. My grandfather is buried in one," the prince replied just above a whisper, hoping not to create an echo, but even his low whisper repeating itself clearly several times below them.

Orestros dropped his flint in the pitch black darkness and was on his knees feeling the cold steps with his hands, trying to recover it, when a soft blue light slowly began to light the passage around them. The prince quickly realized that the light was coming from his medallion and removed it from his neck. He held it high enough for all to see its glow clearly.

The prince led the way down a very long section of the steep staircase, with Axel and Orestros walking side by side and clearing cobwebs and large pieces of broken stone from the steps, which twice almost completely blocked their way.

❧ ❖ ❧

After nearly an hour, the staircase opened into a moderately large chamber, which contained two benches and a circular table, masterfully chiseled from the same stone as the walls that surrounded them. On one of the side walls of the chamber, a small golden faucet extended from the stone. It was molded to resemble the head of a beautiful fish. Despite its hanging cobwebs and the heavy dust, as the prince shone the blue light of the medallion onto the faucet, it began to slowly flow with clear water. When the eyes of the fish began glowing brightly, they shone a beam of light from them. One beam hit the wall above the circular table making a dim light fill the room; the other passed directly through the middle of the room to a doorway leading down more steep steps. The water silently flowed at a steady rate into the small sink, which somehow drained continuously so that the water remained at a constant level.

They all laid their packs on the dusty table and cleared more cobwebs from around the table and sink, before opening their packs and unwrapping packets of fish and bread. They sat down on the ornately chiseled benches beside the table. Axel took his metal cup to the faucet and filled it halfway, then carefully taking a small sip of the water. "You won't believe this, but this is fresh and clean." The prince and Orestros tasted the water and agreed.

They were all tired after the long day's travel and, though they didn't want to say it aloud, they wanted to lay out their blankets and sleep after eating. It seemed to them that the chamber and the ancient faucet, which still supplied fresh water, was an invitation to renew their strength with a good meal, fresh water, and a restful night's sleep.

After they shared the contents of their food packages, they discussed what had happened since they'd left the ruins that morning. Eventually they spoke sadly about what might have become of Aleah, Leda, and Lady Arianne. Axel tried to assure them that Morgana had some other mysterious plan for them and wouldn't harm them, but he wasn't sure if he believed it himself. Despite the mystery of the prophecy, they couldn't deny what they had seen and done and if nothing else was certain, they believed that the king and the Prism were in danger.

Orestros and Axel didn't say it aloud, but they believed that Prince Ammon was somehow the most important part of the puzzle. Before despair could overcome them from the long and dangerous day's travel, Orestros realized how much the other two men had struggled—and managed—to keep up with him throughout the day. He understood that the potion of leaves and tree bark mixed with herbs had given them a greater power of endurance, but their courage and commitment was the real power that sustained them. This was on his mind as he poured water into their cups before refilling the bamboo water tube.

"I think we should rest here for the night and regain our strength for what promises to be an even longer day tomorrow," the prince said, noticing Orestros and Axel smiling in relief that he wasn't suggesting that they start again toward the bottom of the long steep staircase.

All three men then opened their packs and prepared pallets on the stone floor with extra blankets to cushion them. As Orestros and Axel lay down, the prince, carrying the medallion, started through the open doorway to go down the steps.

"Where are you going, friend?" Axel asked, as he and Orestros sat partially up and leaned on their elbows.

"I'm just going to scout ahead a short way. I'll be back in a little while. Go on and get some sleep while you can," the prince smiled slightly. It was a smile of confident reassurance, so they both lay down and closed their eyes, as he disappeared through the doorway and down the stone staircase.

❧ ❖ ❧

After Ammon had meandered down the steps for nearly an hour, the temperature began to change from that of a slight chill to one that was warm and comfortable, almost causing him to perspire. He could smell a slight trace of smoke in the air, and as he returned the medallion to the inside of his shirt, he saw an orange light dimly rising from the darkness further below. It gave just enough light for him to see the outline of the steps falling steeply in front of him, and he continued on with a renewed sense of excitement and increasing curiosity.

With the passing of another forty or fifty steps, he began to notice that the dim orange light was growing a little brighter as the slight smell of smoke became stronger and the temperature a little warmer than before. He stopped and sat on the step, peering down the long steep staircase but saw only more steps disappearing into the glimmer of the orange light.

Small droplets of sweat had begun to form on his forehead and, despite the extraordinary strength he had gained since putting the medallion into the stone, he was beginning to tire. He took a long drink from the bamboo tube and considered turning back to retrieve Orestros and Axel.

෨ ❖ ෭

A sudden burst of orange light from the darkness below brought him to his feet again, and he began to step quickly downward to see what caused it. The prince finally reached the last step and in front of him, an immense room opened with a ceiling that extended on one side to about a thousand feet into the air. Looking up, he saw a small light and, as he walked further to better see how high it was, he stepped into a shallow pool of water disturbing the surface of it, causing it to burst into glimmering shades of blue and ivory. He thought that he had reached the very pool into which Orestros had thrown rocks when he stood on the ledge high above.

He turned to look around the rest of the great cavernous room and noticed other pools, not of smooth water, but of orange molten lava, which bubbled and spat small spheres of orange and white hot rock into the air. Though he had seen similar things deep in the caverns of the Prism, nothing could compare with what he was seeing before him now. The room extended so far in the other direction that it faded in the distance but was still illuminated.

He pulled out the small brass telescope that Orestros had given him and peered toward the far end of the cavern. Slowly scanning the orange lighted areas in the distance, he could see what he thought were figures standing in several long rows. They were dressed in an ancient fashion, which he had seen pictures of many years before. It was so far away that he didn't trust his own vision and, returning to the colored pool, he splashed its water into his face and rubbed his tired eyes, as he tried to understand and remember where he had seen such figures before.

He took a long drink from the water in his bamboo tube, replaced its cap, and then looked again. The vision through the telescope was dim and waved from the rising heat escaping from the orange molten pools of lava, but he was almost certain of what he had seen there. He tried to estimate the distance and finally guessed it to be about ten or twelve miles away. He had never seen a subterranean cavern with such depth and width; in fact, he had never imagined that such an enormous place could exist beyond the Prism. He took another drink of water, replaced the telescope in his coat, and though he stumbled once and hit the stone floor hard, he found the stairs and climbed them as quickly as he could.

❧ ❖ ☙

He ran steadily up the stairs for an hour without pause, before he finally stumbled into the dimly lit room where Axel and Orestros were sleeping. He gasped deeply to catch his breath and threw water from the sink into his face to cool himself down. The sound of his heavy breathing and the splashing sound of water awakened them the two men.

"Prince Ammon, are you all right? What's happened?" Axel asked, concerned.

"Quickly now! Come and see for yourselves!" the prince shouted.

"What is it?" Orestros asked, as he and Axel tightly rolled their blankets and gathered the supplies into their packs.

"What did you see?" Axel asked.

The prince did not respond but finished packing his own supplies, splashed more water onto his face, and drank from his cupped hands. He rushed back through the doorway and began descending the staircase.

Orestros and Axel looked at one another amid their controlled confusion, pulled their packs onto their backs, and followed the prince without further questions. He seemed more excited than they had ever seen him, but they couldn't distinguish anything more than excited wonderment. They couldn't detect fear, but he seemed concerned somehow. He had definitely sparked their curiosity, and they were more than a little anxious to see what he had found in the darkness below.

When they arrived at the bottom of the staircase, they too were amazed at the immense size of the huge, vaulted room. The prince handed Axel the telescope, as Orestros wandered aimlessly, staring into the far distance and then looking up at the vast, high ceiling.

Arriving at the pool, Orestros knelt beside it and touched it with his fingers. The water immediately rippled into the blue and ivory hues that he had seen before from the ledge far above them. Axel joined Orestros and also touched the water. Once again it burst into vibrant ripples.

Axel climbed a few feet onto a boulder and peered through the telescope. At first, he observed the massive size of the orange-lighted cavern, but as he looked at the very distant border of the cavern, his saw the slightly illuminated figures standing tall in perfect formation. As he continued to observe, he estimated that even in the obscurity of the darkness, there must be several hundreds or even several thousands of them. He tried to look more closely, but the wavering heat and steam rising from the molten lava pools obscured his vision. There was no doubt that they were men, and there seemed to be many of them. Whose men they were, he couldn't distinguish.

"Where did they come from, Prince Ammon? How long have they been here?" Axel asked.

"When we get a little closer, we should be able to understand more. Let's get moving!" the prince replied, urging Axel to hand the telescope to Orestros. He carefully viewed the distant figures and then returned the telescope to Ammon.

"How far do you think it is?" Axel asked.

As the prince began a brisk pace along the remnants of a once well-worn road, made from precisely cut pieces of stone, he said,

"Not much more than five or six miles. We could be there by mid-morning if we can keep up with them!"

"Are you sure it's morning?" Axel asked.

"I'm pretty sure," the prince answered, as he peered through the telescope toward the farthest end of the cavern again.

The road was covered with a thin layer of black ash and, looking back, they could see their footprints in the orange light emitted by the lava pools. As they continued walking, they came across random pools of water. Some were bubbling and boiling, while releasing a steady fog of hot steam; others were formed from small running streams, created from small and sometimes long waterfalls from the dark walls overhead. The sound of the waterfalls and the slow-moving streams echoed throughout the cavern mysteriously. At times it seemed as if a strange, natural kind of music, similar to the sound of wind chimes, intermingled with the sound of water and drifted through the air all around them.

After they had walked about two miles, the prince heard a strange growl from the boulders and rocks above them. As he turned quickly, he saw a glimpse of something black move but couldn't distinguish what it was. The ceiling of the cavern above the road narrowed slightly.

Still curious, Axel took the telescope and climbed to a higher position on the rocks. He peered into the distance, once again looking for the tall figures he had seen before. He scanned the orange-lighted areas, until he was able to focus on the images of several tall men trapped in the shadows. He had come close enough that he could begin to see their facial features. They were stern-looking and remained quite still. He returned to the road and soon caught up with the prince and Orestros.

"Are they still there?" Ammon asked.

"Yes, "Axel answered as he handed him the telescope. "They are definitely men, soldiers I think, but I can't see much more than that through the heat and steam."

"Could they be your father's soldiers?" Axel asked the prince, as all three continued to walk.

"I don't know," he replied. "I've never heard my father or his generals mention such a secret place."

"It's not your father's army, Prince Ammon!" Orestros said confidently.

"Could it be Deimos's?" Axel suggested.

"They seem to be waiting for someone or something," the prince said, remembering the stern looks that appeared on the distant faces.

Chapter Twenty-Eight

When they had come to within a mile of the figures, the prince signaled them to follow him into a small shallow cave, about fifty feet from the road. Orestros passed the water tubes around, opened the top of his pack, and unwrapped a large piece of fish. He broke it into pieces for all of them to share.

As the prince cautiously watched the rocks and ledges above them, Axel and Orestros looked to the road ahead, where they could finally see the end of the cavern looming in the distance. The sound of the waterfalls could barely be heard behind them, and the temperature had become quite warm. The pools of orange lava were larger at this end of the cavern, and their light caused a bright glow on the ceiling overhead.

The tall figures were covered by the shadows of large boulders. Although the prince tried to see them through the telescope, he could not. "It's probably best that I go ahead and find a safe place for us to observe these men, before we become exposed," the prince offered, noticing Axel's apparent disappointment.

"Let me go first," Axel insisted. "I'm smaller and less likely to be seen."

"I should go," the prince said firmly. "If I'm discovered or captured, both of you can find another way to get through. I'll lead them on a chase away from you. Maybe you can find a way to come back for me."

"He's right, you know," Orestros agreed.

The prince looked seriously at Axel and Orestros, but they knew in the end, he was right. He then pointed to a V-shaped opening among two massive boulders at the side of the road and very near where they had seen the tall figures through the lens of the telescope. "Keep your eyes on that spot. If it's safe, I'll signal you by waving both arms in the air just once. If you see this, gather the supplies and continue along the road until you reach me. If something has gone wrong, I'll wave my arms several times. If you see that, go back and wait for me at the stairs. If I haven't arrived within the passage of a day, go back up the stairs that enter this cavern." Prince Ammon was more serious than they had ever seen him, and they nodded that they understood his instructions.

"What will we do then?" Axel asked.

"When there's a break in the storm, go back to the ruins and wait for help. If need be, hide until help arrives."

They finished eating their fish, and then the prince firmly slapped them both on their backs before leaving.

❧ ❖ ❧

Prince Ammon began moving in and among the large rocks beside the road. He concealed himself well and before long, Orestros and Axel could no longer see him at all. They watched the place that he had indicated for at least an hour without any sign of him.

"How much longer should we wait?" Axel finally asked.

"Until we're sure, one way or another," Orestros replied, momentarily glaring at Axel before immediately returning his gaze to the boulders for a sign of the prince.

"I didn't mean to suggest that we leave. I guess I'm just worried," Axel said as he repositioned himself and continued looking to the distance.

"It's all right. I'm worried too," Orestros replied and patted him gently on the shoulder.

Another half an hour passed in silence as they watched. Axel began to consider what they should do next, and then Orestros tapped him and pointed to the rocks. They could see the prince standing between the boulders. They waited until he waved his arms. They waited again, hoping he would not wave to them again, and he did not. They eagerly placed their packs on their backs and started toward him. Within a half an hour, they were standing beside him.

From the height of the boulders, they could see a vast army standing in perfect assembly before them. Horses and cavalry, row after row, seemed to be awaiting commands, although all remained motionless. The only movements among them were in the tattered flags, which swirled above the various regimens. As they looked more closely, they could see cobwebs, fluttering in the warm movement of air.

The prince was the first to speak. "The flag that seems to lead them looks very similar to my grandfather's flag. We must ask them to whom their allegiance lies."

"I thought you might want to ask them that," Orestros replied and smiled proudly.

The prince and Axel shared a puzzled look, as they began their way down to the front of the armies standing before them. There was still no movement, and Orestros handed the prince a torch, as he stepped closer to the perfectly aligned soldiers. Neither Axel nor the prince had seen soldiers with such perfect armor or aligned in such perfect rows. The prince took the torch and began to walk in front of them. He waved it to better see their faces, and as he did, he finally realized something extraordinary about them.

"Can you see, Prince Ammon?' Axel asked.

"It's amazing! How could this have happened? Were they once real?" he asked, as he touched the face of one of the soldiers with his fingertips. "They're all made of stone!" he observed in astonishment.

"There are hundreds of them!" Axel remarked in continued disbelief.

Prince Ammon took the torch and jogged through the rows, periodically observing their faces. "Each face is different!" he exclaimed. When he reached the circle, he was almost dizzy. A circle of stone guards stood there, with their hands holding one another's and their feet spread apart so that it was impossible to pass between them. He walked around their circle and peered through their arms into the center. Turning, he looked up to see Orestros standing beside him as Axel quickly joined them. "Can you see it?" Prince Ammon asked his friends.

They peered through the arms of the guards and noticed a young squire of polished black marble, not dressed in armor but rather the very sturdy clothes of someone who might serve a knight. In his arms lay a sword, the likes of which they had never seen before. On the edge of the sword a piercing white light gleamed and sparkled. From its center and tip, open flames burned against the shiny metal of armor, which lit up the seals of all the kings of the past on the side of the sword. The seals were precisely burnt into its body, each shone in a different color. The squire's stone hands were tightly clasped around the sword, though to reach through the armored guard's hands on the outside of the circle proved impossible.

The prince paced around the guards and, as he did, he stumbled upon a square stone, much like the one that they had found on the ledge. He quickly brushed the ash and dirt from its surface and, holding the torch closer, carefully looked at the polished black stone. As the first square stone, it had a line chiseled into it, but no ancient language. Orestros used his knife to clear the dirt and debris from the chiseled line.

The prince took the medallion from around his neck and easily placed it into the open groove. The stone turned to a shimmering dark blue as the medallion began to glow brightly, and the clear blue middle began to spin and send a brilliant white light onto the polished black stone squire. At first, it looked as if the light was burning a hole through it, then a soft white light began to spread above the ring of stone guards around it and over the body of the soldiers.

As the light continued to spread and turn into a thick white mist, the prince could no longer see the top of the cavern. Then silently the mist settled over the soldiers, covering everything. Hundreds of the stone soldiers turned around to face the princ and the circle of guards which protected the squire and the magnificent sword he held. After they had turned, all in unison, they returned to their frozen position, their faces set and without emotion.

The prince, Orestros, and Axel were startled by the sudden movement of the stone statues and slowly stepped closer to them to study at their facial features and eyes. Nothing had changed and the statues continued to look straight ahead emotionlessly.

"Maybe we should just walk past all of this and make our way to the Prism," Axel suggested.

"It's the sword of the prophecy, Axel. I was meant to take it with us, and perhaps the army will follow. This must be the way to save the king and those within the Prism! We know that Deimos already has an army and may be attacking the palace while we waste time debating," Ammon said with certainty.

He continued to study the medallion. Looking at the shimmering dark blue stone and remembering the previous experience when he turned the medallion in the stone; it had opened the hidden door. He slowly turned the medallion. As he did, the stone statues that formed a circle around the squire and sword, suddenly released their hands from one another, and stood straight up, and then stepped aside to create an opening for the prince.

The squire in the middle stepped forward and, kneeling, presented the sword to Prince Ammon. His skin still looked like the polished black marbled stone, but it had somehow changed and seemed to be transparent, while his eyes looked like white shiny marbles. "You are the prince we have waited for. I have held this sword for many years," the squire said, then bowing and offering the sword to Prince Ammon, laying it on his outstretched arms.

He slowly and carefully took hold of the jewel-encrusted hilt with one hand. He felt a charge of energy and power surge through his hand and then slowly course throughout his entire body, as he had felt when he turned the medallion in the shimmering stone, but a hundred times more intense.

He slowly raised the sword and pointed it toward the vaulted ceiling of the cavern. As the sword reached its zenith, its sharp bright edge sparkled, and the seals gleamed an almost blinding white and blue light from its tip. Fire erupted from the tip of the sword in a steady stream all the way to the top of the cavern ceiling, illuminating the entire army around him.

A glowing white mist encircled Prince Ammon's feet, as he stood with his sword raised into the air. The mist then moved outward, consuming the army and their horses in a glowing light. From the frozen marble of the statues, each well-armed man in his silvery armor came to life, and a subdued commotion arose from their ranks.

All around Prince Ammon, Orestros, and Axel, the entire army at once dropped to one knee and spoke clearly in unison, "Hail Prince! We have awaited your command for these many centuries!" The volume of the hundreds of voices filled the entire cavern for miles, from one end to the other. The horses, just a few minutes before concealed in solid stone, clamored and became restless to run.

Two captains, dressed in highly polished silver armor, approached the prince and bowed with dignity and grace, then placed their hands on their swords and waited for him to speak. Another soldier in even more regal armor then presented himself before Prince Ammon. "I am General Zarrus. We await your instructions, My Prince."

As the mist engulfed even the prince, he seemed to age. He became somehow taller, and his features more sculpted and dignified. The squire and two other guards appeared beside him, carrying beautiful armor, ornately gilded, and in gold on the chest plate was the emblem of King Hyperion, though different, he noticed, for it also contained the emblems of his grandfather and great grandfather.

"How far to the Prism, General Zarrus?" the prince asked.

"We are on its border, Prince Ammon. We will be through the concealed wall within minutes of your command and begin the evacuation."

The prince repeated curiously, "The Prism sky will fall, evil will abound, and all will perish."

"We exist to assist you in leading the people back to the Earth's surface," Zarrus explained.

"General Zarrus much has happened and many deceptions have taken place. It's true that I am the prince of the prophecy, but the knowledge of my role has been concealed from me and those I trust. It's also true that evil abounds in the Prism, and I believe the palace of my father will soon be attacked. The rest is still a mystery to me."

"You are the chosen one, My Prince. We live to serve you." Zarrus said and bowed.

"Line a path to the Prism's entrance and gather your generals there," Prince Ammon said with an authority, which surprised no one. "Bring horses for me, Axel, and Orestros. I will direct our movements after we have assessed the enemy's strength and location." The prince's voice had changed as he spoke to the general and his captains; it now contained an undeniable element of confidence.

Within a few minutes, three black steeds in shiny armor were brought before them. The squire assisted Prince Ammon and Axel into their armor and then presented the reins of a tall black steed to the prince. When he mounted the steed, a roar came forth from the army of over five hundred. He raised his sword and another roar came forth, echoing throughout the cavern. A clear path opened through the ranks, with shining armor and swords drawn as the prince held his black high-stepping steed back, then slowly began an ascent toward an opening at the very end of the cavern.

Chapter Twenty-Nine

The prince reached a large clearing, just beyond the opening from which he could see the Prism's light, and paused as three generals approached on stallions similar to his own. General Zarrus was seated in the middle of the three and urged his horse forward so he could speak with the prince.

"The palace is under siege, My Prince. Nearly half of your father's army has already fallen, and the first of three gates has been taken. Without intervention, the palace will fall within the next two to three hours. I'm sorry to say that the invaders are taking no prisoners; executions are taking place across the battlefield. Soldiers and citizens are being slaughtered, as we speak. What are your orders?" The general immediately bowed his head and then looked directly to the prince, engaging his eyes.

Prince Ammon urged his horse further into the opening beyond the cavern and observed the merciless slaughter below as the general rode closely beside him; a group of twenty heavily armed and mounted soldiers followed directly behind them. The prince stood in the stirrups for a moment and gazed at the horrific sight.

"Where is Master Deimos?" he shouted above the clamor, as hundreds of his soldiers poured out of the cavern behind him. They found themselves high on the mountainside above the palace.

"There!" his general shouted above the marching soldiers and horses, pointing to a far hillside where the prince immediately noticed Deimos and a figure dressed in black robes, watching the horrible spectacle below them.

Prince Ammon shouted as he again stood up and looked about. Orestros left his horse and ran on foot to stand at the prince's side.

"Yes, My Prince," Orestros said, as he looked angrily on the bloody fields far below.

"Take twenty archers on foot and twenty swordsmen on horseback to capture Deimos! Spare his life, for only he can tell us where he has hidden the queen! Also spare the man dressed in black robes beside him; he is no doubt a wizard and has much information. Let any of his soldiers who stand in your way perish, and anyone who wishes to surrender let them be shown mercy."

The prince then spurred his horse to gain a better vantage point, as the general shouted orders and forty men followed Orestros down the mountainside and into the forest, making a quick and steady pace toward Deimos.

From the edge of a cliff overlooking the palace, the prince paused as he watched Deimos's armies slowly entering the first gate into the village. General Zarrus handed a small silver telescope to the prince, who looked carefully at the gate and the progress the invaders were making, as they slammed a massive metal-tipped wooden battering ram into the palace gates.

From a tower window within the palace, the prince noticed a bright blue flame, so bright that his entire army could see it gleaming like a beacon. Holding a staff, like a torch, through the telescope, he could see Xandros looking directly at him. Beside Xandros he could see his father, the king, pacing back and forth, worried and concerned. He waved to Xandros and his father, then handed the silver telescope back to General Zarrus and dismounted his fierce black steed.

The general joined him. With Axel at his side, Prince Ammon used his dagger to draw his plans in the dirt. When he finished, the general signaled for two captains to join them. They studied the drawing in the dirt, saluted, and ran to their horses. At a full gallop, they joined the army still emerging from the cavern. Within minutes, armored soldiers on horseback and on foot began taking positions on the slope above the palace.

Deimos's armies continued their vigorous attack and showed no sign that they were aware of the army arriving above them. With the prince in the lead and Axel and General Zarrus directly behind him, Deimos raised his sword and spurred his horse to a slow and steady trot down the slope. At the moment his sword rose into the air, heavy drums began pounding a steady beat which resounded throughout the valley below.

In the open fields, which lay in front of the palace walls, Deimos's soldiers looked at the prince's approaching army in shock. Though some tried to run toward the forest, most simply laid their weapons down and fell to their knees. Those that had already passed through the first palace gate stopped their advance and dropped the battering ram. They looked to their commanders for help and instructions, only to see those on horseback charging out of the palace toward the forest, while others ran after them, trying desperately to escape.

❧ ❖ ☙

Within the hour, King Hyperion stood before the open gates of the inner palace and greeted the young Prince Ammon and Axel with great joy and relief. All the villagers shouted, "Hail to Prince Ammon and King Hyperion," as they rode through the streets, reassuring the people that all was well.

Returning to the palace, at last they arrived on the platform far above the reception hall where Ammon once had once flown his kite. From that great height, they could see Orestros and his soldiers returning on horseback, leading a group of prisoners. Xandros stood beside Ammon and Axel, although his face remained stern and filled with worry. They could no longer see any sign of Deimos, and they continued to relate to one another all that had happened, both on Earth and within the Prism.

King Hyperion pointed to the Prism sky, where they could clearly see several long cracks in the wavering distant orange and blue sky. Large boulders continued to fall through, even as they spoke. Within the passage of an hour, Orestros had joined them and appeared exhausted from his long chase.

"What is the news of Deimos?" the prince asked his old friend.

"Deimos and his wizard have escaped for now and managed to block the way behind them. They appeared to be returning to his castle. Strangely enough, it seemed that he was prepared and had planned his escape well," Orestros said, still considering the escape and what he had seen.

"No doubt Morpheus had much to do with his escape," Xandros added.

"Is there anything we can do?" the king asked Xandros.

"I believe he'll find some rather harsh surprises upon his return," Xandros said with a slight grin.

"The army is prepared to begin the evacuation of everyone in the Prism back to Earth," the prince told his father.

"That will take some time to organize. Deimos has inflicted terrible hardship on our people. Many of them have died. We need time to gather ourselves together, and time to mourn," the king said, looking out onto the fields where bodies were scattered. He then looked down at the houses that still smoldered, leaving trails of black smoke in the orange and turquoise Prism sky.

"Morgana is well on the way to making Earth a dreadful place," the prince added, his voice sounding worried and his brow furrowed.

"We must resolve the problems here," the king said, with concern as he pointed to the boulders falling from the massive cracks in the Prism sky.

Axel began to pace slowly back and forth across the platform and finally, unable to keep his silence any longer, he spoke out. "If Morgana spoils the Earth, then all of our efforts here will be in vain. What about Princess Leda, Lady Arianne, and Aleah? If nothing else, let me return and try to free them!" he demanded impatiently.

"He's right, Father, but he can't go alone. Let a few of us go with him," the prince said in a serious tone, as he placed his hand on Axel's shoulder.

"You've just returned. Let's take some time to think about this. I refuse to act in haste. We've just survived a terrible disaster and need time to consider before making such a desperate decision," the king said and began walking toward the steps of the platform.

"Wait!" Orestros called out, as he stepped to the edge of the platform and peered into the sky.

Everyone's attention immediately followed Orestros. In the distance, a small flying image came closer and closer until Hermes's long, expansive wings could be seen clearly gliding through the Prism sky. Within a minute, he circled once, hovered briefly, and then landed on the outstretched arm of Orestros. He stroked the great white owl several times and then removed a small square leather pouch, which was tied to his leg. He carefully unfolded it and read the message and then handed it to the king. He read it carefully and then handed it to Prince Ammon.

"What does it say?" Axel finally asked, no longer able to stand the suspense.

"It's from the queen," the king replied. "She is alive! She and a young friend named Rosalyn have been transported somehow to Morgana's castle on Earth, where they are being held in a dungeon along with Princess Leda, Lady Arianne, and Aleah. She says that something terrible is happening and that the sun has not shone in over two days."

"It's Morgana's plan to blot the sun out completely and turn Earth into complete and perpetual darkness," the prince responded.

"We have to go back, Sire. If Morgana succeeds, there will be nothing left on Earth for us to escape to," Axel said solemnly.

"He's right, Father. Morgana already had begun when we left. The longer she is left alone with her black magic, the worse it'll become. Every plant and animal on the surface will perish, leaving only her own wretched creatures," the prince said with an urgency and wisdom that the king had never seen in him before.

"Leave enough of your army to help me finish Deimos and begin the evacuation. Then make haste back to Earth, stop Morgana, and free her prisoners." As the king finished speaking, a great rumble shook the platform and the entire palace. From the widening cracks in the sky, massive boulders fell with thundering blows as they struck the countryside below. Panicked cries rose from the village, as aftershocks shook the ground and houses crumbled at random.

"The people of the Prism are depending on all of you, and we will not be far behind you," the king said, embracing Ammon and Axel. The king then whispered something to Orestros, who bowed and followed the prince and Axel down the staircase, as yet more rumbling sounded throughout the land.

❧ ❖ ☙

The king watched Ammon and Axel mount their horses and ride through the shattered gates of the palace and into the chaos of the village, as people tried to find cover. Within the passage of two hours, he could see them disappear into the cavern on the mountainside above the palace. They no longer looked like the boys he had once known but now, clothed in shining armor and directing their horses with skill, they were mature in stature and, most of all, character.

Once again the platform shook as the ground quaked far below, and attendants had to help King Hyperion back to his feet. He looked up at large boulders falling from the sky and then turned to Xandros, whose eyes gleamed blue.

"There is much to be done, Sire. I have an idea to slow or delay the collapsing sky, but I'll need your orders to get the help I need. Shall we begin?" Xandros asked, extending his arm to assist the king down the platform steps.

On the mountainside above the palace, Orestros quickly scribbled a note and placed it in the pouch before attaching it to the leg of Hermes. The great owl extended his massive wings and flew into the cavern; his large yellow eyes open wide as he glided silently through the darkness toward Earth.

The End